THE
STRIKE

THE
STRIKE

a novel

Anand Mahadevan

We acknowledge the support of the Canada Council for the Arts for our publishing program.
We also acknowledge support from the Ontario Arts Council.

 Canada Council   Conseil des Arts
for the Arts   du Canada

ONTARIO ARTS COUNCIL
CONSEIL DES ARTS DE L'ONTARIO

Edited by MG Vassanji

Cover designed by David Drummond

Library and Archives Canada Cataloguing in Publication

Mahadevan, Anand, 1979-
    The Strike : a novel / Anand Mahadevan.

ISBN 1-894770-30-7

    I. Title.

PS8626.A376S87 2006   C813'.6   C2006-903031-6

Printed in Canada by Coach House Printing

TSAR Publications
P. O. Box 6996, Station A
Toronto, Ontario M5W 1X7
Canada

www.tsarbooks.com

To

Finn and Toral

A novel is an impression, not an argument.
THOMAS HARDY,
Tess of the D'Ubervilles

Now our aim is not to get to the bottom of things,
but to stay afloat.
MARGARET TRAWICK,
Notes on Love in a Tamil Family

New Delhi ⭕

⚬ Gwalior

⭕ Benaras

⭕ Bhopal

⚬ Itarsi

⭕ Nagpur

⭕ Bombay

⚬ Warangal

Vijaywada ⭕

Ennore ⚬
Madras ⭕

INDIA
in
1987

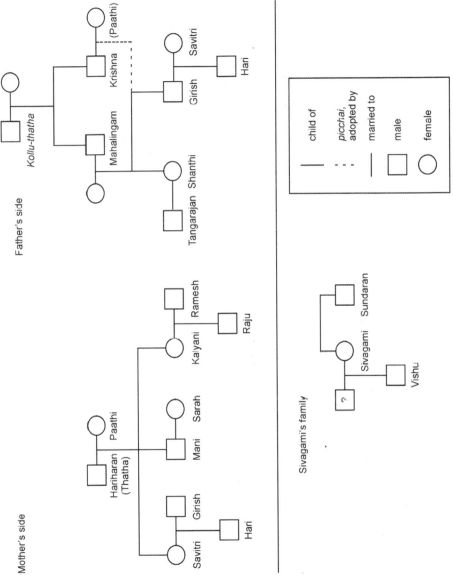

Father's side

Kollu-thatha

Krishna (Paathi)

Mahalingam

Girish — Savitri

Hari

Tangarajan — Shanthi

Mother's side

Hariharan (Thatha) — Paathi

Ramesh — Kalyani

Raju

Mani — Sarah

Savitri — Girish

Hari

Sivagami's family

Sivagami — Sundaran

Vishu

?

child of
picchai, adopted by
married to
male
female

Prologue
1982
Acai (desire)

HARI'S ORIGINAL PLAN was only to pee on the tracks. But once the rivulet of yellow disappeared into the gravel bed, he pulled down his pants and sat on a rail. The railway yard in Nagpur station appeared deserted. Hari liked the feel of the cold smooth iron rail against his skin. As his body warmed a section of the track, Hari inched forward so he could yet again feel the cold of metal. It was in this half-naked state that the idea of climbing into the steam engine presented itself to his mind.

Hari stood up, carefully buttoned up his shorts, and walked over the tracks of the sprawling goods yard north of the station to the engine on the deserted siding. The engine was painted pitch black. A band of orange ran along its side, above the large wheels. Someone had painted rays of red, white, and yellow radiating from the lamp that was set in the centre of the engine face. The rays reminded Hari of the sun though the lamp was unlit. In his imagination, the steam, hissing from valves under the boiler, formed billowy clouds for his lamp-sun. The chill of the January night lingered in the morning. The gravel pricked the soles of his feet through the thin plimsolls, and he walked slowly, navigating the gullies and raised track beds.

Cinema scenes played out in his mind as he noted the switches alongside the track. In the Hindi films that played on the television, as soon as someone tried to cross the tracks where they branched, the mechanical switch would trap his foot and a train would roar down to crush him. Hari walked around these mechanical switches. There were many tracks and it took him time to navigate his way to the steam engine.

As he drew closer, he felt the warmth radiating from the hissing and breathing engine, the noise of machinery reassuring. Hari measured himself against the wheels; his head almost reached the crankshaft. Tiptoed on the gravel, he stretched his right hand far above his head to reach the top of a wheel, his fingers brushing against the grime-covered lip of metal.

The engine driver, his dark blue clothes covered in soot, had observed the little boy's approach in the mirror. He stood at the door, above the steps, watching the child, who looked about seven years old.

"What are you doing?" the driver said. "Don't stand so close to the engine."

Hari jerked his arm off the engine and wiped his palm on his shorts.

"Look now, you've dirtied your clothes," the driver said.

His teeth were stained brown and red from chewing tobacco and betel nut. Hari brushed his shorts with his clean hand.

"Don't rub it in. It'll only be harder to remove. Just leave it."

Hari looked at the grease and dirt stain. "My mother will be very mad."

The driver nodded. "What"s your name?'

"Hari."

The driver squatted at the doorway. "What's a young chokra like you doing in a railway yard this early in the morning? Have you run away from home?"

Hari shook his head. "My parents are over there," he said, pointing to the bungalow beyond the tracks.

"That's the house of the deputy superintendent," the driver said. "Are you related to Iyer Sahib?"

"My aunt will marry his son," Hari said. "The engagement ceremony is today."

"Oh, that is good news indeed. So what are you doing here on such an auspicious occasion? You should be in the house eating sweets."

Hari knelt to pick up a piece of gravel. "I was bored. Give me a ride on this engine."

The engine driver laughed. "Where to, little Sahib—Delhi or Calcutta?"

"Madras."

"Madras? No, child, this engine has never crossed the Godavari River. It's old, like me; we just hobble from one end of the yard to the other."

"My father says all engines should be diesel or electric. Steam engines are history."

"It is fate," the driver shrugged. "They want faster engines, longer trains. But Béta, these new engines, they don't even have names."

"Engines have names?"

"Of course, like you. This one is called *Raat ki Rani*—Queen of the Night. Once we hauled the night mail…" The driver gestured to the goods yard where he and his old engines were now confined.

"*Raat ki Rani*, my grandfather has flowers of that name. They smell nice. Will you give me a ride?"

"It's not allowed, but if you don't tell anyone, I'll let you in."

A voice called out to them from the bungalow. "Hari!"

Hari's father and Tangarajan stumbled over the uneven ground as they ran towards the boy.

"Do you have any idea how worried we were, looking for you?" Girish, his father, said.

"But Appa, I just came to—"

"I don't want to hear another word," Girish cut him off. "I'll skin you if you keep running away like this. Dragging Tangarajan out of his own betrothal ceremony…"

"It's okay," the young man said. He patted Hari on his head. "Besides, I could use the fresh air."

The engine driver said, "Sahib, the boy says you are getting married."

Tangarajan laughed. "I'm settling down."

"Yes, bachelor fun days are over," the driver replied, grinning. "But it is good to marry and raise a proper family."

"Come on, let's go back," Hari's father said.

"But Appa, the driver promised a ride in the engine."

The driver raised an eyebrow at Hari. "I also told you not to say a word to anyone."

Tangarajan laughed.

The driver continued, "Listen to your father, your clothes will get dirty. Maybe you can come up some other day, when you are not all dressed up."

Fat easy tears collected in Hari's eyes. "But you said today…"

Girish spoke up, "Stop making a fuss, Hari."

Tangarajan knelt to be close to the little boy. "You like train engines, don't you? Maybe you'll grow up to be an engineer one day just like your dad."

"No, a train driver."

Tangarajan laughed. "All right, a train driver. Then we'd better go home and ask my father if he'll let you ride his railway engines."

"Yes, that's right," the driver said from his high perch. "You get permission from Iyer Sahib and I'll give you a ride through the yard."

Hari wiped his eyes with his shirt. He reached past his father's outstretched hand and took Tangarajan's arm for the walk back.

I
Parakkam (habits)

ONE

"25...24...23...," MOHAN COUNTED the numbers out loud.

Hari was playing hide-and-seek with the other colony kids in Nagpur. Mohan, his best friend, was "it." As they always hid together, Mohan knew where to seek Hari. So Hari decided to break the rules of the game and hide in Mukherjee-aunty's house.

"18...17...16..."

Mrs Mukherjee was a stocky and soft-spoken Bengali woman, whose home was always open to the colony kids. Hari, eleven years old that winter, had a crush on her daughter Anamika. But Anamika was out hiding in the maidan or among the bougainvillea-covered hedges as Hari wriggled past the holy basil and the curry leaf shrubs beside her house to get to the kitchen door in the back. He could hear Mohan counting,

"10...9...8..."

Hari smelled the pungent aroma of hot mustard oil from Mrs Mukherjee's kitchen. The door to the kitchen was open and Hari watched Anamika's mother lift a fish fillet from the wok, the oil still bubbling on its crispy brown crust. Mrs Mukherjee smiled and beckoned him in. On the counter beside her lay another fish: its grey and white scales shone in the light and Hari felt himself watched by the round black eye. Hari stared at it, fascinated, and stepped in to stroke the fish skin.

"...3...2...1."

The game outside forgotten, he watched as she showed him how to gut the fish, sliding a sharp thin knife along the base of the skin to pull free the flesh. Hari touched the creamy wet fish, small white bones spread throughout like the stubble on his father's face. Mrs Mukherjee raised the wok off the stove and brought it close to him so he could slip the fish inside.

As the evening darkened the kitchen, he listened to the sound of the fish bubbling in the oil. "I am not allowed to eat fish," he said.

Mrs Mukherjee looked at him. "Do you know why?" she asked.

Hari nodded. "Because I am a Brahmin." He pulled at his shirt to show her the sacred thread running over his left shoulder.

"You have the janoy," she said. "When did you have your ceremony?"

"1982, when I was seven," Hari said. "Before you moved to this colony. Why do you call it a janoy? It's called a poonal."

"Just different names for the same thing. Bengali Brahmins call it janoy. You are Tamil and so you call it poonal."

"Aunty, are you a Brahmin?"

She nodded.

"But you eat fish?" Hari meant it as a question but it sounded like an accusation in the kitchen.

"Yes we do, and there is nothing wrong with eating fish. Some people even call them the fruits of the sea, and you eat fruits from the trees, don't you?"

Hari shrugged. "I only like mango. But aunty, if fish are the fruits of the sea, then why won't my mother let us eat them? She says that Brahmins must be pure vegetarians."

Mrs Mukherjee sighed. "It's the way we are brought up, Hari. In your family, eating fish is not proper. In our family, eating fish is a way of life."

"She gives me little pills, like jellybeans," Hari said. "Cod liver oil. It smells nasty if you cut them open. Not at all like this smell when you cook it."

Mukherjee-aunty laughed. She laid a plate on the kitchen table and slid the fish, now crispy and caramel-coloured, onto it. Hari pulled out a chair and sat down, and stared at the gleaming layer of spiced oil coating the fish, its heady aroma of mustard seducing him.

"Will you tell my mother if I tried a little bit?" Hari asked.

She looked at him uncertainly. Then with a little smile, she laid a spoon beside the plate. "Careful of the bones," she said.

Hari cut out a small piece with the spoon and slid it into his mouth. The flavour of the seasonings and oil was delicious. When he tried to bite the fish, however, the bones crunched and the flesh resisted in a strange and novel sensation. Small bones, and there were hundreds in this fish, scratched against his palate; the sharp bones poked him in the spaces between his teeth, others tickled his throat on the way down.

"Spit them out," she said.

The novelty of the first bite aside, Hari ate ravenously, and the pile of thin white bones grew on the plate. Mukherjee Aunty turned off the stove and sat next to him at the table.

"Did you hear the story of how Lord Vishnu once turned himself into a fish to save the world?"

Hari shook his head. His mouth was full and his lips smooth with oil.

"Long time ago, the ancient law giver and king Manu ruled the world. When he grew old, he renounced his kingdom and decided to live as an ascetic on the banks of the Ganges."

"Is that the same Manu who wrote the *Manusmriti*?" Hari asked. He reached into his mouth to pull out a thin needle bone.

"Yes, that's him. How did you know that?"

"We're learning it in school."

"Good. Well, one day when Manu dipped his kamandalu into the river next to his hermitage to collect water for his prayers, a small minnow became trapped in his water pot. Not wishing to harm such a little creature, he put the fish into a larger vessel to give it space to live. The next morning, however, the fish had grown as large as the pot. Manu was surprised; but he realized the fish was growing and so he released the fish into a small pond behind his hermitage."

"Really, fishes grow that fast?"

"Keep listening. The next morning, when Manu was trying to pray, he heard this loud splashing from the pond. He went to see and the fish had grown beyond the pond. Now the fish asked Manu for a bigger home, so he carried the fish to the largest lake in the region. Tired from his trip, Manu decided to rest at the lakeside for the night. The following morning, the enormous fish towered over him, having grown bigger than the lake overnight."

"That's just weird."

"Manu thought so too. So he decided that his only recourse was to take the fish to the ocean. So they travelled down the Ganges to the ocean and Manu pointed to the endless waters, finally pleased that the fish couldn't outgrow its new home. The fish, thankful for the king's help, asked him to stay the night by the ocean and promised to bring him good tidings the next morning. The next morning, the fish had grown so large that Manu could not even see the waters in which the fish lay. The boundless growth of the fish and its gigantic size suddenly made Manu realize that he was dealing with Lord Vishnu himself and he prostrated himself in front of the fish, asking forgiveness for not having recognized the divine."

"Really, so it was an avatar of Vishnu? Just like Rama and Krishna?"

"Yes, the first incarnation of Vishnu. The fish praised the heroic efforts of the king to find it shelter and warned the sage that the world had lapsed into wickedness and was about to end. It asked the wise king to build a boat and bring all that was good in the world within. When the waters of the oceans rose to cover the earth and drown the wicked at the end of the first great age, the matsya avatar—the fish form of Vishnu—led Manu and his boat through the turbulent oceans, protecting all that was good in the world until the waters receded. The sage-king then led the animals and humans back onto the land to repopulate it and began the second of the four great ages. The fish swam out into the ocean and disappeared."

"That's like Noah's story in the Bible."

"Maybe, but this is our story and much older than the Bible," Mrs Mukherjee said. "Look at you, you must have been hungry. Do you want to eat some more?"

But before Hari could answer, the doorbell rang. Mukherjee Aunty went to answer it. She returned quiet and subdued into the kitchen. Hari's mother, a withering look on her face, followed her.

"How could you do this?"

Mrs Mukherjee preempted Hari. "Savitri, it's my fault."

As his mother shot a look of rage at Mukherjee Aunty, Hari saw Mohan and Anamika cowering in the living room. He found it strange that Anamika should be afraid in her own house.

Emboldened by this thought, Hari spoke up, "Don't blame her, Amma. I wanted to try some, so I asked her."

"Keep your mouth shut," Savitri said. "How could you, Lata? He's just a boy. He'll ask for anything. That doesn't mean that we say yes every time. You know better."

"Savitri, there is nothing wrong in it. He just tried a little fish. It's good for him."

"It's completely against our culture," Savitri replied, her hand slicing through air in a gesture of finality. "You know that we are very strict about such things in our family. Imagine what my mother-in-law would say if she found out."

"Come, Savitri," Mrs Mukherjee smiled. "Who are you fooling? Don't you give him cod-liver oil?"

"That's completely different," Savitri said.

Mrs Mukherjee leaned forward. "How?"

"Eggs," Hari spoke up. "What about the eggs you make me eat for breakfast?"

"You keep out of this," Mukherjee Aunty turned to him. "In fact go out and wait in the living room. You shouldn't listen to adults talking."

Hari slid out of his chair and walked past the two women. Savitri hit him on the head as he passed her.

"Turning into a real rascal this one," she said.

"Savitri! Don't hit the boy!"

"He's my son. I can hit him if I want to."

"But this is my house," Lata said. "And we don't hit children in our house."

"No, all you do is feed them fish and corrupt their culture."

Mrs Mukherjee bristled at this. She pulled herself straight. "I think you should leave now, Savitri."

Hari listened from the living room, Mohan and Anamika beside him.

"I'm sorry, yaar," Mohan said. "It's my fault."

Hari turned to him. "Why?"

"The game was over," Anamika said. "We all began looking for you."

"Then I saw you in here, the door was open," Mohan said.

Anamika snickered. "He told your mother what you were doing."

Hari put his hand on Mohan's shoulders to comfort him. This was not his fault. Anamika drew closer.

"So, do you like fish?" she asked.

Hari looked at her, the oval face with the large black eyes peering at him, and nodded. She laughed, and the two pigtails that rose from the sides of her hair bobbed above that happy face. In that moment, Hari forgot all but the face of the girl in front of him.

His mother came storming out of the kitchen. "Chalo, Hari, let's go home."

Hari hung his head low and followed her out of Anamika's house.

"How could you do this?"

"What? But Mukherjee Aunty is also a Brahmin," Hari told her. He had to trot to keep up with her busy strides as she barrelled down the street to their house.

"A Bengali Brahmin. Fish-eating Brahmin. Why must you always test my patience like this? Do you even know the hell that old beggar-hag of my mother-in-law is going to raise if she finds out? Do you even realize how you stink of macchi? There is no hiding your shame."

She led him around their house to the back. There, in the tottam where Manjulabai, their day servant, washed the clothes and dishes by the foot-high municipal tap, she stripped Hari of his clothes. The tottam was scarcely five feet square, about six inches deep, and surrounded by a raised brick border where Manjulabai usually sat on her haunches to work.

"Open your mouth," Savitri commanded.

Hari obeyed, naked and shivering in the evening cold. She deftly stuck a finger deep inside his throat. Hari gagged and pushed her away. The response was quick. She slapped him hard across his bloated stomach with the saliva-coated hand.

"You have to learn that there are consequences to your actions. Do you know how long I have been looking for you...and here you are with a tummy filled with animal flesh. Don't you dare complain! Now open your mouth."

Hari's mouth ran with salty saliva. His vision blurred as tears gathered, and his stomach contracted viciously each time she rammed her fingers down his throat. Finally, Hari coaxed the fish back up. The rising bones scratched his insides and the acrid bile burned his throat and ruined the pleasant taste that lingered in his mouth. As he bent over, regurgitating mouthfuls of the fish, his mother went into the bathroom, fetched a plastic bucket of water, and poured the cold water over him. Then she left to bring him some clean clothes.

He watched, shivering and wet, the clumps of shapeless vomit float down into the water and collect at the edge of the enclosure, stubbornly refusing to go through the rusted grill into the municipal drains. He sat naked on the brick ledge of the tottam, feeling both angry and sad.

What business did his mother have, barging into someone else's home like that and dragging him away? Hari felt ashamed of her, the way she yelled and screamed at Mrs Mukherjee. After this escapade, he was sure that he would never again be invited into Anamika's house. If he had not hidden in her house, this would have never happened. That was Mohan's fault. He had to break the rules because Mohan knew where he hid.

Now his mother knew that he had eaten meat. Nothing was secret from her. She would tell his father and he would be mad at him too. At this thought, Hari moaned.

The kitchen door creaked and Hari looked at the silhouette of his paathi, his father's mother.

"Hari, Kanna, is that you?" she said, squinting in the dark. "What are you doing in the tottam?"

His shame was complete. Hari said, "Nothing, just go away."

His grandmother stumbled out of the house, in her traditional nine-yard sari with its fold that looped between her feet and was tucked behind her back. She ran out to him, the cloth getting in her way.

"What's wrong, Kanna? Where are your clothes?" Fumbling with her glasses, she ran towards him through the semi-darkness of the back garden lit by a single 40-watt bulb.

Hari balled himself, hiding his nakedness as he watched his grandmother rushing towards him. As she lifted her mud-streaked foot into the tottam, Hari raised his arm in a gesture to stop her. But he was too late. In the smooth concrete enclosure laid for Manjulabai to do the dishes and clothes, her foot landed in the slimy pool of his vomit. Hari stood up and leaned forward, forgetting his naked state, but she slipped, skidding past him, and her body fell away from him. The ledge of the washing area arrested her movement and her head hit hard against the concrete floor. Hari winced as he heard the crack, like a coconut shell being smashed. Her glasses flew to the side and rested, quite broken, next to the drain amid the puddle of vomit and water.

He watched the underside of his paathi's sepia sari darken as water soaked through the cloth. Her wrinkled skin appeared soft and blemish-free in the dim light. A single rivulet of red ran from under her grey hair to the festering pool of vomit on the grill.

The creaking of the back door restored motion and Hari turned in horror as his mother came out bearing new clothes and a towel to wipe him dry. He watched her as she approached. The look of annoyance on her face turned to horror and she dropped his clothes and ran to the body, screaming for Girish.

"I didn't do it!" Hari cried out.

TWO

IT WAS LATE by the time Hari heard the tinkling of Kabir's rickshaw bell. He had been waiting all afternoon in the verandah for this sign of life. On any other day, he would be in the rickshaw returning to the colony with Anamika and Mohan, but his grandmother's death had led to a reprieve from school.

"How are you doing?" Kabir asked, voicing a genuine concern.

Hari shrugged and waited for his friends to come out.

"So what happened?" Mohan asked.

"We had to go to the hospital," Hari said. "To the morgue."

Anamika wrinkled her nose; she looked towards her house down the street as if wanting to escape.

"They had to perform the last rites," Kabir explained to Anamika.

Hari nodded. "They put her into the furnace and my father lit the flame. That was it. She came out as a heap of ash."

Even Mohan looked shocked at this statement.

"She's in there, you know," Hari pointed towards his house. "Inside two silver urns in the living room. My father is going to take the ashes to Benaras so we can spread them in the Ganga."

"Very holy," Kabir nodded.

"Are you going with them?" Mohan asked.

Hari nodded.

"You're going to miss more school." Resentment tinged Mohan's voice.

"They won't arrest you, will they?" Anamika asked.

"Why?"

She looked at Mohan, who now stared at the ground.

Hari came close to her, blocking her view of Mohan. "What did he say?"

"He said that your grandma died because you ate fish," Anamika said.

Hari screamed and lunged for Mohan. But Mohan was already running, his satchel swinging on his shoulder. Hari set off in pursuit.

"Stop, you bastard!"

"I'm sorry, I didn't mean it!"

Kabir sprinted behind the two boys and reached them just as Hari caught the strap of Mohan's satchel. He pulled Hari off before his punch could land. Mohan dropped to the ground. They were in the small maidan off the colony where the kids played cricket. Unable to hit Mohan, Hari swung wildly at Kabir as he cried. Kabir drew him close to muffle his sobs, to restrict his punches. In the dank dark embrace of the rickshaw driver, Hari smelled the sweat and felt the warmth of the sinewy body that drove him and his friends to and from school. He crumpled and sobbed in Kabir's arms.

The rickshaw driver pulled Mohan up, then held the two boys on either side as they walked back to Hari's house. Mohan kept muttering sorry but Hari refused to acknowledge him. As they drew closer, Hari saw that his father had come out of the house. He was dressed in a simple white dhoti, the large cotton sheet draped around his hips. His chest was bare save for the yellowed cord of his poonal across his torso. A barber had tonsured his father's head that morning before the cremation, and the shaved head made him look different, as if he were another man. Mohan fell silent at the sight of an adult in mourning.

"What's going on, Kabir?" Girish said.

"Nothing, Sahib, the boys were just…well, you know how hard it is for children."

Hari ran from Kabir's side, up the steps to the verandah. He buried his face in his father's chest, still sobbing. Girish ran his hands through his son's thick black hair.

"Take them home, Kabir," Girish said, indicating the other two children, and helped his son back into the house.

In the house, Girish led Hari into the puja room, where Hari's grandmother had slept. From one wall, framed images of deities smiled upon them. The pictures were arrayed around the large photograph of the statue of Lord Venkateshwara taken at the temple in Tirupathi, so holy to Hari's family. Hari remembered the time a few years back when he had taken the bus up the winding mountain road to the temple. The vertigo and nauseating diesel fumes had led him to vomit, and his mother had held his head outside the bus window.

He sat next to his father in front of the wall of images. Girish passed him the sandalwood round. Hari poured a teaspoon of water on it from a silver tumbler and scraped the fragrant anointing paste by rubbing a sandalwood stick in circles over the wet spot. His father took down each framed picture and wiped the glass with a damp muslin cloth. Then he dabbed a smudge of sandalwood paste on the forehead of each deity. A trace of red kumkum powder to the drying circle of sandalwood paste, slight adjustments to the plastic garland of jasmines around each frame, and he was done.

Below the myriad images of the gods, a framed photograph leaned against the wall on a shelf. This enlarged head shot showed a gaunt old man, bald and tired-looking, with a chin that seemed to quiver even in that frozen image taken in a photo studio years before Hari was born. This was his thatha, his paternal grandfather. He had passed away just after Hari's parents' marriage and his widow had occupied this room till her own death the previous night.

"Appa, will we get Paathi's picture framed now too?"

Girish nodded as he gave the image of his father an extra wipe with the damp cloth. He studied the image in front of him. "Yes, Hari, we'll enlarge that picture we took in the studio last year."

"Why do we put her image up with the gods?"

"Because she will be in heaven, looking after us."

"She's not already there?" Hari asked.

Girish sighed. "Ask your Kollu-thatha when he comes."

"Kollu-thatha is coming." Hari spoke this with excitement and fear.

Kollu thatha was the grand old man of their family. Hari's great-grandfather, he had arranged Girish and Savitri's wedding. Hari recalled how one day his paathi had let slip that Girish's father, the man in the photograph, had not been fond of Savitri. But Kollu-thatha had insisted on the match and Girish's father had no choice. But her husband was right, Hari's paathi had insisted, after all he had died within a year of Girish's marriage. What was that if not fate? Paathi's words rang in Hari's mind as he sat in the puja room scraping the sandalwood paste.

Girish broke his reverie. "He sent a telegram from Madras. He wants to come with us to Benaras."

"Appa, is Kollu-thatha your grandfather on your mother's side or your father's side?"

Girish smiled. "Why do you ask this now?"

"I never thought of it before."

"It's complicated," Girish said. "How does...how did Paathi call me?"

"Picchai," Hari said.

"And what does that mean?"

Hari was puzzled by the question, the word was simply a sound that his grandmother made to call his father, wasn't it? Then the meaning came to him in a flash. He had never given thought to the word before. He said, "It's what you give to beggars, isn't it?"

"Alms," Girish pointed to the framed photograph. "I was given as a baby to be raised by your thatha and your paathi."

"So you are adopted?" Hari raised his voice, forgetting his mourning.

"Your Kollu-thatha had two sons. I was born to his eldest son," Girish explained. "This photograph is of Kollu-thatha's younger son. When I was little, Kollu-thatha had them raise me as their child."

"So Kollu-thatha is still your paternal grandfather."

Girish nodded.

"But why," Hari asked. "Why did Kollu-thatha give you to his younger son?"

Girish sighed. "They could not have any children. My own father had three sons and one daughter, so it seemed unfair. Kollu-thatha could not bear the thought that his eldest son should have so many children and his youngest son should have none. So he asked my father to give me away as picchai."

"How old were you, Daddy?"

"Oh, I can't remember any off it." Girish shrugged. "Probably a year or so old."

"How come Paathi never told me?" Hari asked.

"Why would she?" Girish hung the photograph back in its place.

"But what about your real family?"

"They were not my family anymore," Girish said. "Hari, Kanna, I didn't know that they were my parents. I thought of them as my aunt and uncle. You know Shanthi Aunty, who is married to your Tangarajan Uncle?"

Hari nodded.

"When I was your age, I used to think that she was my cousin," Girish smiled. "But she's my sister, by blood."

It took Hari time to get used to this idea. Then he asked, "But what about Shanthi's parents? They must have felt bad, to lose their son."

Girish did not immediately answer. The question hung in the air.

"Maybe they did," Hari's mother answered from the door. "Now only Kollu-thatha knows, if he remembers. Shanthi's parents passed away soon after the adoption ceremony."

"They died in a train accident at Mangalore when Shanthi was very young," Girish said. "She was spending the summer with us in Salem. Her parents and brothers were on the train. They all perished."

"So Kollu-thatha was right," Hari said.

"What do you mean?" Savitri sounded surprised.

"Well, if Appa had not been given as picchai, they would have all been on that train," Hari said. The logic was unassailable in his mind. "Kollu-thatha saved both Appa and Shanthi Aunty."

"That's the stupidest thing I have ever heard," Savitri said.

Girish shook his head. "He may be right, you know. After all we are still alive, both his sons' lines have survived."

"Not bloodlines," Savitri countered.

"No," Girish said and nodded, "but they were never really separate, were they? After all, Kollu-thatha is our grandfather."

"Like Adam," Hari said, "our common ancestor."

Girish laughed.

"Strange ideas the convent teachers put in his head," Savitri grumbled. "Go get your panchapatram, Hari. You better practise your sandhi ceremony before Kollu-thatha arrives. He is your guru. What do you think he will say when he finds out that you have been eating fish and can't even remember your rituals? Adam, our ancestor. I think not."

And with that parting shot she headed back into the kitchen.

"It's all right, Kanna," Girish said as he tousled his son's hair. "She means well. Go get the things."

"Will she really tell Kollu-thatha that I ate fish?"

Girish shook his head. "No, neither of us will say anything. I promise. Go now, get the panchapatram."

"I can't do it by myself," Hari said, "I don't remember all the verses."

"I'll help you," his father said.

As he walked out of the room, Hari turned and leaned against the doorpost for support. "Appa, I am really sorry…about Paathi."

"We all are, Kanna," Girish said. "But it isn't your fault. Remember that always."

Kabir drove Hari and his parents to Nagpur Railway Station in his rickshaw. Three days had passed since the accident. Kollu-thatha, who had been a high official with the Railways before his retirement, had booked a first-class cabin on the Tamil Nadu Express from Madras.

At the station, Savitri sat at a bench and Girish arrayed the suitcases around her like the walls of a castle. He handed her the two silver urns in their cloth bag, but she flinched away from them.

"Don't give them to me."

"I can't put them on the platform. It's dirty."

"I'm not holding the ashes," Savitri told him firmly.

"Fine, just keep them on the bench next to you," he said, and set the two urns beside her.

She squirmed away from the urns, gaining a precious inch or two. Her anxiety amused Hari. She reminded him of the younger kids in school whom he and Mohan tormented by placing snails or frogs on the bench beside them.

"Come, let's go," his father told them. "I want to show you something."

As they walked towards the front of the platform where the signal lamp shone bright red, Hari looked back at his mother. She gently pushed the urns away from her towards the seat edge. Hari smiled and ran to catch up with his father. There was still a good half hour before the Tamil Nadu Express arrived. Father and son walked past the gathering crowds on the platform, past the large iron trolleys that waited laden with jute sacks bulging with large packages of mail. The crowd thinned near the edge of the platform. The concrete gave way to gravel.

"Do you see these?" Girish pointed towards the tracks.

Hari surveyed the railway yard. Vertical poles had sprung up beside the tracks since his last visit to the station the previous summer. They reminded him of Madras Central Station, where such poles held the electric wires high above the tracks.

"Is this what you are doing?" Hari looked at his father.

Girish nodded. "From here to Itarsi in the north and Balarshah to the south. Soon, the entire New Delhi to Madras line will be electrified."

"But the wires are not up yet."

"Not yet, but soon. We start wiring in the summer and hope to be done before the monsoon begins." Girish pointed to an incoming train and said, "Come, I want to show you something."

They walked across the gravel to the track upon which a train was pulling into the station. Girish squatted on his haunches and patted the gravel beside him for Hari to follow suit.

"Watch the tracks," Girish said.

Hari nodded, though he was afraid. The engine was loud, and as it drew closer, the driver honked the horn. It was a deafening sound. Hari's father merely raised his hand and waved. The engine rumbled over the tracks less than a yard from them. Hari watched the tracks bend and sag under the weight of the train upon them. Then the rails arced up as another section of the track took the pressure.

"It's the weight of the train," Girish said. "Something has to give."

Hari just nodded, beaming with pleasure at this new insight.

As they returned to the platform, Hari peppered his father with questions, about the tracks below, the catenated wiring above, and everything in between. Close to the bench where his mother sat, his father stopped him as the PA system crackled to life. A soft female voice announced, in that precise mimicry of the Queen's English so prized in Indian officialdom, the imminent arrival of the 2621 UP Tamil Nadu Express.

Hari ran up to his mother. "Our train is here!"

"Where did you two go?" Savitri was unmoved by his excitement.

"Appa took me to see how the tracks bend under the train," Hari told her. "Look, there it is!"

"That doesn't sound very exciting," Savitri said, getting up. She turned to Girish, "I thought you had taken him to see the inside of an engine."

"Perhaps some other time," Girish replied with a smile, hefting a suitcase.

Her reply was drowned out as the two diesel engines swept past the platform in a deafening crescendo, followed by rust-red coaches and striped orange-cream-orange coaches clickity-clacking their way past them.

Girish walked alongside the train, a suitcase under each arm. Savitri grabbed the cotton bags with their lunch and dinner, pointed at the silver urns, and took off. Hari gathered the bag with Paathi's ashes. The urns felt cool in the afternoon heat. Hawkers ran alongside the train, touting their wares, and large iron trolleys clanked and rolled along the rough concrete platform to the mail and carriage van.

A slim, bony hand waved from a window. Hari spied the wrinkled contours of Kollu-thatha's face in the compartment. He clutched the urns and ran behind the fleeting image. The train slowed to a stop. His parents were ahead, their pace slackening as they reached the coach. A grey-shirted attendant came down the metal rungs to help Girish carry the suitcases. Unlike the second-class coaches, where the passengers pressed against the doors trying to get in, calm pervaded the first-class cabins.

The coach felt dark after the station. Hari blinked several times in the passageway as he followed his parents into their cabin. He had never travelled first-class before, so he was surprised at the space allocated to them. They had a large cabin all to themselves. Kollu-thatha sat at one corner by the window. Savitri bowed in salutation and touched his toes.

"May your home and family be blessed forever," Kollu-thatha intoned in Sanskrit, laying his fingers gently over her head.

She began to sob gently at his blessing. A knot rose in Hari's throat.

"Shush," Kollu-thatha said as he leaned forward. "Death is a part of life. It is just another stage in this game the gods make us play."

Savitri nodded and pulled back from the venerable old head of their family.

"Your turn," Girish said, pulling Hari away from his intended destination, the other window seat.

Kollu-thatha grabbed Hari's arms as they reached towards his feet. "Come. Sit next to me."

Hari sat on the rexine-covered berth. His great-grandfather's hand remained on his shoulder, where the bony fingers tapped against him gently. His mother sat across them on the long wide berth. Despite the expansive berth, she sat at the very edge, wiping her eyes with the corner of her plain cotton sari as she took in the cabin.

"This is very nice," she then said.

"Sit back," Kollu-thatha motioned. "The attendant will bring some tea along."

"They serve tea?" Hari asked.

"In ceramic cups," Girish said. "And they serve lunch and dinner too."

"No need," Savitri said. "I have packed enough for all of us."

"Really," Kollu-thatha leaned forward. "What did you bring? You are such a good cook, Savitri, I can hardly wait."

Hari's mother smiled at this compliment. "Nothing fancy, just lemon rice with peanuts, bisibela bath, and curd rice."

"With poppadams and fried chillies," Hari added.

"Oh, that sounds delicious," Kollu-thatha said and nudged him. "What do you say, should we start already?"

Hari couldn't help smiling at this. But he shook his head. "Kollu-thatha, can I have a railway dinner please?"

"A railway dinner?" The octogenarian winked at Savitri. "But your mother is such a good cook!"

"But we always get to eat her food."

Girish laughed at this. Savitri just rolled her eyes.

Kollu-thatha nodded. "This is true. Very well, we'll ask the attendant."

With a lurch, the train resumed its journey. The people clustered along the water taps on the platform broke ranks and rushed towards the train. The undercarriage clanked and groaned as the wheels rolled over the switches in the massive railway yard, leading the train to the twin tracks headed north. Kollu-thatha peered out the window.

"What is all this?" he said. "I don't remember this slum. It's all over the goods yard."

Hari looked at the thatched-roof hutments, the tin sheds and the odd brick-and-tile structure that sat flush against the tracks. The timbre of the sounds generated by the wheels running over the fish-plates clickity-clack, clickity-clack changed as the train rattled past the mud- and dung-smeared walls of the tightly packed shantytown.

"What do you expect?" Girish said. "The railways have all this land and Nagpur is a growing city."

"It's not just any land. It's prime land right in the city centre."

"More reason for these people to move in," Girish said. "They are all illegal structures, of course."

"They should be razed to the ground," Kollu-thatha gestured. "Someone needs to stand up for the law here. I'll write to the divisional manager."

Girish shrugged. "Thatha, you do what you want to, but do you really think you can change anything? If the manager asked the municipality, the politicians will sign the order. The policemen will come and tear down the huts—"

Savitri spoke up, "While the politician stands with the evicted crowds of slum dwellers, raising speeches against the railways."

Girish nodded. "And six weeks later, you'll be back where you started. They build faster when it's the roof over their own heads, you know."

Kollu-thatha grumbled. "Back in the days of the British, they would never allow it." Flecks of spittle escaped his mouth and he wiped his chin with a cotton towel that hung about his shoulders.

"Don't let anyone hear you wishing back those days, Thatha," Girish said, laughing.

Hari extricated himself from his great-grandfather's side and sat across from him on the other window seat. They were now past the town, travelling through orchards of orange trees and fields of winter wheat. Although Hari faced the window, watching the scenery outside, his interest lay in the cabin and the uncomfortable silence that brooded over them. The two silver urns leaned against one corner of the berth opposite him. His father reached over to cradle them in his lap.

"Is that it?" Kollu-thatha reached out for them.

Girish handed them to his grandfather.

"So neat, and so little," Kollu-thatha mused.

"It's very efficient, the new electric crematorium," Girish said. "Two urns full only, always."

"Much better than the sandalwood cremations," Kollu-thatha said, handing back the urns. "There is always so much ash among the cinders and charred wood."

"Also so expensive," Savitri added.

Girish put away the two urns in the berth above him. "The ash is very fine, like dust. Not like old times."

"What do you mean, not like old times?" Hari asked.

Kollu-thatha smiled. "You'll see when you get to Benaras."

Girish sought to speak, but Hari saw his mother give him a look of annoyance.

"No need to talk to a kid about such things," she said.

"What things?" Hari asked. "I want to know."

Kollu-thatha raised his arm to quell Savitri's protest. "He's growing up. We might as well prepare him for Benaras."

"You know how we cremate our dead," Kollu-thatha turned and said to Hari. "Well, we light a pyre of wood, sandalwood."

Hari nodded.

"But even after burning for many hours sometimes, the body still persists. The bones get blackened but don't become ashes."

Hari wrinkled his nose at this image of charred bones and flesh among the embers of a funeral pyre. He had seen cremations on television but this was too real.

"But this electric crematorium is really quite good," Girish said. "Fast and efficient."

Hari turned away from them to look out his window. It seemed heartless to talk about his paathi this way.

The attendant came in with a brass kettle and poured out sweet milky tea in small cups of thick china. As they drank their tea, Kollu-thatha asked the attendant about dinner. Hari listened to them as he gulped his drink by the window. The dinner would be loaded in Itarsi, where they were disembarking. But the attendant suggested they eat at the railway canteen. There would be plenty of time before they caught their connection to Benaras.

"Hari," Girish said, rising from his seat after the attendant had left. "Let's get some air."

"What's wrong with the air in here?" Savitri looked up from the sweater she was knitting. Hari's old green cardigan was showing holes despite the mothballs in the mahogany cabinet. His mother had picked a bright red roll of yarn to knit the replacement on this journey.

"Nothing, we'll be back," Girish said, and led Hari out of the cabin.

Out in the small passageway connecting the cabins, Girish and Hari walked over to one end of the coach. The doors were open and the air swirled inside as the train sped over the Deccan plateau. Hari walked up to the door, where the vortices of wind pushed and pulled at him. Clutching the yellow door handles, he stuck his face out. The wind plastered his eye glasses against his face and his hair flew. He smelt the exhaust from the twin diesel engines; tiny particles of soot whipped past his face and buried themselves in his hair.

A reassuring hand clasped him across his tummy and Hari felt his father's body behind him, anchoring him to the train as it sped through the landscape. He inched forward, his feet at the edge of the linoleum floor, and leaned out into the wind. The train turned into a curve and for a moment he caught a glimpse of the rust-red diesel locomotives. Then his own coach entered the curve, and Hari looked back at the rest of the long train as each coach successively banked and then straightened out. Girish leaned forward, his face beside Hari's, sharing this sight.

Next to their train, keeping them company throughout their journey lay the other set of tracks for the southbound trains. On the far side of the southbound tracks, slim concrete poles stood at regular intervals.

"Did you put all these up as well?" Hari yelled into the wind.

The train passed a wire-fenced compound with large grey transformers and thick electrical cables leading into a small concrete building.

Girish pointed, yelling in return, "That's one of the substations that routes electricity from the main grid to the tracks. We'll attach the wires and hook them up to the grid and then we can run electric engines all the way from Delhi to Madras."

"Who makes these engines, Appa?"

"The electric engines are coming from Canada!"

"From Toronto?" Hari asked. His youngest aunt Kalyani and her husband Ramesh had immigrated there several years ago. They supplied him with the stamps that made him the envy of the other budding philatelists at school.

"Maybe," Girish replied. "It's a big country, who knows? All I know is that the engines are very fast. The trains will be able to reach a top speed of 140 kilometres per hour on this section once we finish electrification."

"How fast are we going now, Appa?" Hari had to project his voice even further to speak against the wind.

Girish pulled him back into the relative quiet of the vestibule. Hari could feel the dust and soot caked on his face and hair. His father handed his watch to Hari.

"Look at those poles," he said. "There are twenty-five poles to a kilometre, so count the poles that go by in one minute and see if you can figure out how fast we are going."

Hari nodded and leaned against the Formica-lined walls of the coach, watch in hand, as his father disappeared into the toilet. He was still counting when his mother interrupted.

"What are you doing standing at the door?" She grabbed him. "Come back."

Hari tried to shake free from her grip. "You made me lose count!"

The toilet door opened and Girish said, "What's going on?"

"How could you let him stand at the door?" She gestured to the toilet. "While you were in there. What if he'd fallen out?"

"He wasn't actually standing at the door, was he?" Girish turned to Hari for an answer.

Hari shook his head. "I only stand there when you are there, Daddy."

"See," Savitri said. "You're encouraging this. I don't understand why you two have to stand at the door."

"But the air is so fresh here," Girish said.

"Fresh?" Savitri pointed to Hari. "Look at him all covered in soot like a Chandala overseeing funeral pyres. Destroy my life, just go ahead. What do you two care? Get your fresh air. One of these days you'll both fall off the train and die. I'll be the one who suffers, in any case."

She stormed back into the cabin with this pronouncement. Hari smiled the same smile he shared with Mohan whenever they riled one of their teachers. Girish sighed and led Hari back into the cabin.

THREE

GETTING OFF IN ITARSI, Hari saw Kollu-thatha slip twenty rupees into the cabin attendant's hand. The grey-shirted man bowed in return and touched the money to his forehead before heading back into the compartment.

His father secured a red-shirted coolie. Hari watched as the coolie calmly raised three of the four suitcases atop his head, slung the bags over his shoulder and walked away without evidence of any strain. Hari ran to keep pace with the coolie's deft strides. Looking forty or fifty years old, the coolie, unlike the men in Hari's family who grew fat and potbellied, was thin with sinewy arms and legs. His skin was dark and sunburned. His moustache was white and wispy like his hair, except for the red stains from the betel leaf that he chewed as he walked. He slowed to let Hari catch up to him and the two walked up an overpass to the waiting room. Behind them, Hari's parents kept Kollu-thatha company as he strolled up the platform and the stairs, stopping often to look and ask questions.

In the waiting room, Savitri opened her food hamper so Kollu-thatha could eat. Girish took Hari down to the railway canteen where they served him dinner on a large thali. The stainless steel platter with indentations for dhal, vegetables, rice, curd, and pooris was so heavy that his father had to carry it to the table for him. The other diners in the canteen looked warily at Girish. With his tonsured head and white clothes, his mourning was obvious to all.

"I can't finish this," Hari said, at length, pushing the platter away. Small bits of rice and dhal stayed stuck to the fingers of his right hand.

"Don't lick your fingers," Girish said, "and eat some more. You can't waste so much food."

"You eat it," Hari told him, "I'm stuffed."

"Your eyes are bigger than your stomach," his father replied. "You know that I can't eat this anymore. It's eccil."

"You used to eat it before, when I was little," Hari said and sat back in his chair. "Why is it dirty now? It makes no sense."

"Don't be silly." Girish pulled the plate towards him. "You know better. You've had your poonal ceremony. You are a dvija, a twice born, now. That means you take care of yourself."

"I do."

"You are getting older, Hari. You can't keep being a child anymore." Girish stood up. "Don't give grief to your Kollu-thatha. He's getting old. Just do what your mother asks on this trip."

Hari pouted as he pushed back his chair. When he returned from the sink, his father was waiting by the canteen door. They walked in silence back to the waiting room. Kollu-thatha dozed on a wooden bench.

"Did you eat?" Savitri whispered.

Hari nodded.

Girish took the seat that Kollu-thatha had vacated and Savitri served him dinner. Hari pulled his satchel from under the bench where Kollu-thatha slept and fished out a book. It was George Eliot's *Silas Marner*, an old Penguin paperback. The pages were yellow and the words in small type crammed the page. He read, his attention broken by the intermittent announcements over the PA system as trains arrived and left Itarsi Junction. His parents chatted in low voices. After his father had finished dinner, his mother ate.

The coolie arrived at the waiting-room door. It was time for the Mahanagari Express. Girish roused Kollu-thatha and they headed to the platform. In the late evening dark, Hari could see the small point of light from the engine grow bright as the train drew towards them. The platform around them came alive as women herded the men and their belongings to the train. Their coolie clambered up the stairs into the coach before the train had even come to a full stop. He had already put away the suitcases under their berths in the cabin by the time they were in.

Girish paid the coolie and they settled in for the evening. The cabin attendant came to offer tea and apologies. Dinner had already been served. Kollu-thatha waved him away. Savitri took out her knitting and the needles made a quiet rhythmic sound, echoing the train wheels as they ran over the fishplates. Kollu-thatha lay drowsy and tired on his berth. Girish stepped out of the cabin, and Savitri made an impatient sound at his departure. Hari thought that the pace of her sewing had increased and the needles clacked against each other harder when his father was gone.

The landscape outside darkened. There was little to see save for the dots of light from the few houses spread across the land. Clouds covered the sky and hid the moon and the stars.

"Hari, go fetch your father," Savitri said.

"I don't know where he is," Hari replied.

"Shush," she spoke softly, gesturing towards Kollu-thatha, who lay asleep on the berth. "He's probably in one of the second-class compartments with low-class men. Maybe even in the pantry talking to the railway labourers."

"Ma," Hari protested.

"Don't start with me," she told him. "When you find him, just tell him it's time for bed. The train gets in very early in Benaras."

Hari nodded. As he stepped into the corridor he looked in either direction. There was no sign of his father. In the gangway connecting this carriage to the next, the heavy blue-black fabric enclosure trembled back and forth and side to side. The aluminium ramps under his feet grated against each other, and through a tear in the fabric, Hari saw the dark river of gravel churning under the gleaming tracks over which the train rumbled north.

He clutched at the thick fabric on either side as he walked over the ramps into the second-class coach. It was louder here; the cabins were open and people flowed easily from one cubicle to the next. He heard the uproarious laughter of men from somewhere in the middle of the coach. His father was among them; a card game was on.

Girish clapped him on the back as Hari joined him. Two young men sat across from his father, and an old fat man sitting next to the window on his side, his chest bare, held the deck on a briefcase over his lap.

"This is my son, Hari," Girish said.

"Want to join us, Hari?" the fat man asked. "You can take your father's side."

"No, no, he's too young," Girish said and turned to the thin, reedy young man across from him. "Come Bishun, play."

Bishun nodded. Girish patted the seat next to him and Hari sat to watch the game. He knew they were playing rummy and talking films.

"Mogambo...what kind of name is that?" Bishun said.

"It's a good bad-guy name. Say 'Mogambo', and immediately you think...what? Villain!" said the fat man, gesticulating with his hands. Hari could see the greying hairs of his chest under the many gold chains that lay strung around his neck.

"Anil Kapoor... such a good actor in *Mr India*. Too bad he was invisible in most of the fight scenes. He's a real film hero," Bishun said.

"What about Aamir Khan?" Hari said.

Bishun nodded; his eyes, enlarged by his glasses, seemed owl-like on his thin frame. He turned to his friend next to him with the round oily face marred by pimples, and said, "What was the movie from last year...you know...the one with Aamir in it? Do you remember the name, Omkar?"

Omkar smiled. "*Qayamat se qayamat tak*. What a name...huh...now that is a good name! Good songs too..."

"He is just a pretty face," the fat man said, dealing the cards out. "Someone a girl would pick."

Hari reddened. Omkar piped in, "If the girls like him, I sure wouldn't mind being him."

The men laughed in agreement. Girish tapped Hari on his knee, showing him his cards neatly spread out like a Chinese fan. Hari looked at the cards, familiar with the faces but clueless about the game. As he watched his father and the men play, he wondered where his father had learned to play card games. He knew that his mother would not approve; this was to be another secret between them, like the times they shared on the doorways of fast-moving trains.

As Hari drew close to his father, Girish said, "All these new heroes in Bollywood like Aamir Khan, Salman Khan, they are just cute and good for romances. That's where the industry is headed. Love stories and masala. No social messages, no religious understanding, no patriotism, no hope, nut-ting."

"Come on," the fat man said. "We were just talking about *Mr India*, national unity."

"Nah, that film is all fantasy," Girish replied, drawing a card from the deck. "No reality. So the hero has a watch that makes him invisible. Much better if the people get together and beat Mogambo with chappals. That way you see justice being done, none of this invisible nonsense."

"*Ram teri Ganga maili*...that was a good movie," Omkar said, and nudged his friend. "Powerful message, what do you say, Bishun?"

"Yes, powerful, if you mean Mandakini..." The fat man snorted as his hand curved through the air mimicking the heroine's titillating figure. They roared in laughter. The fat man slapped his thigh in amusement and nearly upset the cards on the briefcase. Hari blushed at his lechery.

"No, no," Girish said, laying a card down. "I mean real social messages like in the old films. They do that now only in the south."

"You mean, like the MGR and Anna movies?" Omkar asked.

"Yeah...where he gets up on the court stand and exposes the corruption, showcases the poverty; how he beats up the adulterators, the goons; when he raises a village's consciousness so the people become free. That is good cinema."

Hari watched Omkar shake his head in emphatic approval as his father spoke.

"Wait, isn't MGR the chief minister of Tamil Nadoo?" the fat man asked. "Isn't he that politician who is ill?"

"Yes, he'll recover though," Girish replied. "He's like a cat with nine lives."

"So he is also a philim star?" the fat man asked.

"The biggest in Tamil cinema," Omkar put in. "He's a real hero. Such a wonderful actor too...in *Engal Thangam* he appears as both Thangam and the chief minister in the first scene. In the film, like in real life, he is a minister doing good for the people...such a great idea. As a film star, he knows what the people want, and so, as a chief minister, he can do exactly what the people need. I used to belong to his manram in Trichy, before I came to Benaras for my studies, you know, when I was still finishing high school in Trichy."

"Manram? What's that?" the fat man asked.

"Manram? It's like a fan organization. Each film star has a fan club and ours was the best. We were the MGR manram, so it was our job to make sure that his films were well advertised. Not that it was difficult, mind you; you've probably heard the stories. People sold their blood to purchase tickets to his movies."

"No!" Hari said.

"Really," Omkar said, nodding his head. "That's how bad they want to see him in the movies. We also did a lot of social work besides promoting his films. Not like the other manrams who just sat and talked big about their actors. We did things—distributed water, soda to crowds—all kinds of good things. Anyway, when MGR decided to become chief minister, it was us, his fans from all the different manrams, that made up the new AIDMK party, ousted that old fox Karunanidhi from power and put MGR in office."

"Wow, that much power?" the fat dealer exclaimed.

"Arré, it's like that saffron-clad NT Rama Rao," Girish scoffed. "They voted him to power in Andhra Pradesh because he played the roles of gods in Telugu movies. He lives in Madras, too. They like to put their film heroes into political office in the south. Simple people! If he is a good man in the film, he must be a good man in office. That's all they think. Of course, MGR also had help. Indira Gandhi supported him."

Omkar now spoke up, his voice louder, "That's not true. MGR campaigned against the Congress party…"

"Arré, listen to me, that was later." Girish said. "First, Indira Gandhi helped MGR come to power and defeat Karunanidhi's DMK and then MGR turned on her. I don't know why. I think it has something to do with the conflict between the Tamil Tigers and the Sinhalese in Sri Lanka. Now that the Indian army jawans are down there, it's going to be interesting to see what MGR will do. After all, you know he let those Tamil Tigers set up training camps all over the state; now the snake bites the hand that fed it."

"Rummy," Omkar said.

Hari heard the defiance and pleasure in his voice as he laid down his cards. The others groaned and dropped their cards.

Hari clutched his father's sleeve. "Amma wants you to come back."

Girish shrugged at the men around and they took their leave after extended goodbyes. It was getting dark in the coaches as the passengers lay down to sleep and turned off the lights. Only the dim blue night lamps lit the corridor.

"Appa, I don't understand," Hari said as they walked back towards their cabin.

"What, Hari?"

"Back there, it seemed as though you liked Tamil films."

Girish nodded. "I do."

"But then you made Omkar mad later on."

Girish laughed. "I like Tamil films better than the Hindi ones they make in Bombay, Hari. But that doesn't mean that I want a film actor to become my chief minister. See, MGR is a good film hero and I like him in his films, but being a film hero is no qualification to be a political leader."

Hari nodded at this explanation.

"But don't talk about this in the cabin," Girish said.

"Is it because Mummy doesn't know that you play cards?" Hari asked.

"No," Girish said, giving Hari a short slap at the back of his head. "It's because your Kollu-thatha gets upset when we talk about politics in Tamil Nadu."

Back in the cabin of their first-class coach, they found Kollu-thatha stretched out over his berth. The cabin attendant had made the beds. Savitri was still knitting and gave them a reproachful look.

"Come here, Hari," she said, and measured the knitted piece against his back. "We'd better go to bed."

Girish helped Hari climb up to the berth above Kollu-thatha. Then he latched the cabin door and climbed into his bed.

The cabin steward woke them around four in the morning. It was still dark when they alighted at Benaras Junction and took a rickshaw to the math where they were staying: a religious hostel that specialized in services for South Indians. As they rode into the ancient city, Hari resolved to cleanse himself. He would ask forgiveness by entering the holiest of rivers and rinsing off his sins in its divine swell.

The cold of Benaras seemed to invigorate Hari's toothless, frail, and bony great-grandfather and he decided that they ought to head directly to the river to get an early morning plunge in.

Hari's mother looked at her Timex. "It's not even five in the morning and we have barely settled into the math," she said to Girish, afraid to contradict the elder.

Hari's father shrugged and pulled a cotton vaishti out of his suitcase to clothe himself for the dip. Savitri sighed, powerless, and held Hari's hand as they followed the two men, all of them walking barefoot through the narrow dirty streets of Benares towards the ghats that led to the river. Hari looked around him as his mother dragged him along. Billows of smoke rose from the wood fires and coal braziers on the street. Music from radios filtered down to the street from the tightly packed apartments above the closed shops. A young boy clacked loudly, herding his cattle through the street down to the river. The cows lowed and the bells around their necks tinkled. Hari and his mother flattened themselves against the iron shutters of a shop as the cows moved past them, grazing on rotting peels, paper, and plastic waste.

"Come, we'd better hurry," Savitri said, breaking into a run. "Your father and Kollu-thatha are so far ahead."

They hurried down the street to the ghat. Suddenly his mother exclaimed under her breath; she had stepped on a fresh cake of cow dung. She stopped, her face contorted at the feel of the warm squishiness under her feet.

"Perhaps we should have worn shoes," Hari said, trying not to laugh.

"No shoes. We can't bring footwear to the ghats. It's improper."

"But it's dirty," Hari said.

Without replying, she hopped the remaining way to the ghat. The river's surface glowed orange from the sliver of the dawn sun. Girish and Kollu-thatha were already at the bottom of the ghat, spreading their towels and about to enter the river. Hari's father motioned them to hurry. Savitri scraped her foot against the top step of the ghat, leaving a wad of soft green dung there. Hari clambered down the steps to the edge of the river. The water lapped against the sandstone ghats worn smooth by millions of feet over hundreds of years. Already there were some bathers in the river performing ablutions and early morning prayers to the rising sun. As Hari turned away from the river to remove his shirt and shorts, the sandstone walls and buildings of the holy city glowed in the saffron light of dawn.

The water felt warm and the steps of the ghat continued underwater. Hari stood on them, hip deep in the river. The promise of solid stone under his feet freed him to embrace the river and he pushed out closer to where his father and Kollu-thatha stood, the waters around their midriff, their poonal threads roped around their thumbs, offering the holy water to the rising sun. In the buoyant water, Hari felt light and caressed. Floating in the river, inches above the security of the stone steps, he thought: This is what being sinless and pure feels like.

Later that day, following the rites of sacrifice officiated by a Tamil priest at the math, they walked back to the ghat to take the noon boat. Hari's father wanted to scatter Paathi's ashes in the middle of the river. Hari stood numb at the ghat. The river, a sepia sludge, teemed with people washing near the ghats and small boats floating farther midstream. A huge sewer pipe poured the rich dark molasses of Benaras refuse into the river upstream of the ghat, where hours earlier he had so joyfully submerged his body into this river. Hari's skin began to itch from the memory of his early-morning dip. His mother prodded him on to the boat.

A group of men, sadhus garbed in old vermillion robes, their hair dreadlocked and unkempt, foreheads smeared with ash, walked down the steps to the river. The smooth wooden staffs they held gleamed with oil in the sun and their small brass lotas seemed lustreless by comparison.

Hari watched them, ignoring the ceremony in the boat. On the lowest step, the sadhus stopped and began disrobing, without thought to the men and women hurrying around them. Their wizened bodies revealed themselves to the crowds on the ghat until all that was left of their clothes was a thin thong of vermillion: muslin underwear that looped between the cheeks to form a string that ran around their hips.

The youngest sadhu in the group, having undressed early, stretched himself, as he laughed and talked with his disrobing companions. He reached with his hands to the bright white sky, his lithe body arching back, and then he dropped on his haunches, crouching on the balls of his feet so that the thin vermillion cord hung loose between his buttocks. Hari averted his eyes and watched his father recite the prayers.

"Kollu-thatha, why do people come to the Ganges to wash themselves clean when the river itself is so dirty?" Hari asked in English.

Kollu-thatha looked away from the head of the boat where Girish and the priest stood. "Who says the river is dirty?" he asked Hari.

"Well—" Hari pointed to the muddy waters around them.

Kollu-thatha raised a finger to silence him. "What does the river contain?"

"Water?"

"And what do we use water for?"

"Drinking...washing..."

"Yes, good, very good...and that is its job isn't it, whether we drink it or just wash ourselves in it, to clean us."

"Yes, but..."

"Listen to your elders," Savitri said and laid an arm on his shoulder to interrupt him.

"When we drink water, it cleans us from the inside and when we wash, it cleans us from the outside purifying us completely," Kolluthatha said, speaking in chaste Tamil. "Water takes all that is dirty and purifies it. But the water of the Ganges is the holiest of all holy waters; it cleans not only all the physical dirt but also spiritual dirt, the sins of our soul."

Hari listened carefully to parse out the glutinous words formed by his great-grandfather's tongue hitting his toothless gums. Beyond them, he could hear the rhythm of the Sanskrit verses chanted by the priest and his father.

"What happens to the dirt itself?" Hari asked. "Now it's in the water, isn't it? So doesn't the water become dirty? Then what happens to the next person taking a bath in it?"

"You are just seeing it with your physical eyes. It is the Ganges. Look with your mind's eye. Everything is transformed; even the dirt becomes holy and good."

"If that's true, then a fish living in the Ganges must be very holy, being born and living in these sacred waters."

"Hari," Savitri's voice was quiet, to veil her threat from Kolluthatha's ears.

Unaware of the circumstances surrounding Paathi's death, Kolluthatha smiled at his great-grandson's logic. "True enough," he said.

Hari avoided his mother's eyes and broached his question. "Then, we should be allowed to eat such a pure fish growing in this river, shouldn't we?"

Kollu-thatha's eyebrows came together, momentarily revealing furrows spread across his forehead. He put up his hand to silence Savitri's outburst and said, "It is not the purity of the animal flesh that concerns us. It is the intent of the flesh. Eating animal flesh creates animal passions within the body. As a brahmachari, these passions are not suitable to your quest for knowledge and perfection. As Brahmins we avoid foods and practices that distract us from our goal." The muscles of his face relaxed again and he leaned against the oar ring of the boat. "It is to aid your progress that we limit you from eating flesh, just like your paathi stopped eating onions and garlic following your thatha's death many years ago. To each station of life, there is an appropriate diet that suits its purpose. As Brahmins, we have no need for the passion and prowess of the Kshatriyas, the warriors, and so we keep ourselves away from flesh."

Hari could hear his ancient relative collect the saliva in his mouth and audibly swallow.

Then what of the fish bones that remain embedded in my throat? What other mischief would they concoct? Hari wondered, a scared, eleven-year-old, rocking on the wooden boat in the Ganges.

He looked back to the ghat, to the naked men who spun around on the steps, their hands clasped in front. The hair on their chests mirrored the black and grey of their beards as they stood, their eyes closed, their lips moving in silent prayer. Then, suddenly, they bounded down the steps and flung themselves into the river, laughing like young boys. They splashed in the brown water, among its floating collection of marigold and rose petals, then used their small brass pots to pour the holy water over themselves. The youngest sadhu let his lota float in the river while he cupped water into his palms and, raising them high above his head, recited verses to the noonday sun in the sky. The water dripped from his palms, leaking through the spaces between his fingers. When he tilted his palms to pour the sacrosanct offering back into the river, there were only a few drops left. He did not seem to mind. Around these playful men happy to be in the warm embrace of their holy Ganga-ma, the crowds surged into the fetid river.

Hari's father stood up in the boat and raised the earthen pot containing Paathi's remains over the river. The fine grey ash collected from the electric crematorium at Nagpur Hospital fell gently like a veil into the slow-moving river. But then a light breeze picked up the ash and fanned some of it over the boat. Hari's mother blanched and tried to escape but her mother-in-law, in death, managed to suffuse herself over them.

Savitri shivered the entire way back to the math and headed straight for the showers. That evening Hari's parents took the train to Gaya with the priest to complete the rituals for Paathi's safekeeping in the other world, leaving Kollu-thatha to care for Hari in Benares.

FOUR

KABIR'S RICKSHAW BELL rang from the street. Hari fidgeted as
Savitri inspected his school uniform: a white shirt tucked into grey
shorts; a pre-knotted tie hung from under the shirt collar.

"Study hard and behave," she said.

Hari ran down the verandah steps to the rickshaw where Mohan and
Anamika peered out at him.

"Arré, you are here after all," Kabir remarked genially from his seat.
"I almost decided to drive away, thinking you were still not back from
Benaras."

"You should have," Mohan told him. "Now we'll be late for school."

"Don't be mean," Anamika said, clearing space for Hari. "Come sit
here."

As Hari squeezed into the seat, Kabir pedalled the rickshaw down
the road for their ten-minute ride to school. Set up by Jesuit priests in
the 1910s, the school had originally been in the country but the city
had swallowed it along with the villages around as Nagpur grew.
Fortunately, an early principal had the foresight to purchase the small
pond and sacred grove of a village next to the school grounds. The
grove and pond now buffered the school from the noise and bustle of
the city.

"Study hard," Kabir said, as the three kids disembarked at the school
gates. "Hari, you especially have a lot of work to catch up."

Hari nodded and walked away with his two friends.

"I'll be here to collect you after school," Kabir called after them.

Kabir was right, Hari had missed a lot of school. A week had passed since his paathi's death and in that time Mohan had taken eight pages of notes in history, eleven pages of problems in mathematics, and six pages of grammar in English and Hindi each. Anamika's page counts were larger than Mohan's though she wrote in a smaller hand. To be safe, Hari left as many pages blank in his notebook as Anamika had written in hers and continued with the work in class.

"You can come over to my house and copy the notes later," Anamika said.

Hari shook his head. "I don't think my mother will let me come over to your house anymore."

"Then come to my house," Mohan said, putting his arm around Hari's shoulders. "You are my yaar, after all. Besides, if you come to my house, you will have less work."

"And his grades will also be less like yours," Anamika retorted, marching off to her desk.

Mohan laughed. "Man, she's so beautiful when she's angry."

Hari started upon hearing these words. "Where did you learn that line?" he asked sharply.

"Are you jealous?" Mohan looked at the retreating figure of Anamika among the other girls and smacked his lips together. "It's a line from a movie. My older brother took me to see it. Anil Kapoor says that when the heroine walks away from him, just like here."

Hari snickered.

"What?" Mohan asked and drew closer. "What's your problem?"

"Abe, we are eleven and in a convent school," Hari replied. "Not like your chotiya brother who is loafing around college, eve-teasing the girls."

"Hey, be careful of what you say about my brother."

"Me!" Hari spoke louder. "You are the one who constantly complains about how he beats you. Now suddenly you've changed your tune."

"Shush!" Mohan put his arm about Hari. "Why are you being so loud? If Sister comes in we'll be finished. Listen, you may be a kid, but I am growing up."

Hari tried to keep from laughing. Mohan looked so serious.

"Don't you. . ." Mohan seemed to waver, then continued, "Don't you feel…you know, like…"

Innocence, Hari decided, would make a good mask. He laid down his pencil over the blank pages of his notebook. "Feel like what?" he asked.

Mohan looked around, his voice dropping to a whisper. "When you are alone, thinking about…about girls…don't you…feel something?" Hands moving along his torso suggested upwelling.

"Girls?" Hari spoke a tad loud to pretend innocence, but the heightened pitch betrayed his act. "You mean like Anamika."

"Sure, and film actresses like Juhi Chawla, or Rekha."

"Don't forget Mandakini."

"Yes." Mohan smiled. "My brother says that she is almost naked in *Ram teri Ganga maili*. But my parents won't let me see the film."

"And you want to see her, without her clothes, in this film?" Hari asked.

"Saala!" Mohan's voice erupted in the classroom. A momentary silence followed the cuss word and then the students started chatting again. Mohan lowered his voice, "You monkey. You had me there for a while. Leading me around like you had no idea what I was talking about. I should have guessed earlier. You can awake a sleeper but not someone who is pretending to be asleep."

"And I guess you stand to attention when you awake, huh?" Hari grinned.

"Mohan!" The stern voice of Sister Mary came from the classroom door. "You wicked boy. I heard you out in the hallway. How dare you use rickshaw-wallah language inside these walls?"

Hari stepped away from where the blow would fall. Mohan blanched under Sister's eyes. She pointed to the hallway, and without a word Mohan walked past her, his head hung low. Sister Mary's stern demeanour melted into piety as she focused her eyes on Hari, saying, "Good to have you back, child. I am so sorry to hear about your grandmother. I will pray for her soul."

"Thank you, Sister." Hari gave her a little bow.

She smiled and hurried off behind Mohan. Anamika came up to Hari as they heard the sounds of the thrashing.

"What did you say to him?" Anamika whispered, "Why did he yell out 'saala'?"

Hari shrugged. "I dunno. We were just talking."

She looked at him, unconvinced. Hari knew that if he looked at her, she would start to cry. He pretended to copy out the notes, preferring to let her think he was an unfeeling beast. But his hand trembled each time he heard the cane landing on Mohan's backside.

The lunch bell rang. Hari collected Mohan's tiffin box along with his and ran to the office. Mohan stepped out from his morning detention, defiant and proud at having served his time.

"I brought your lunch," Hari said.

"What do you have?" Mohan asked as the two walked together towards the pond.

Hari opened his lunch container and peered inside. "Upma. You?"

"Roti with okra curry, wanna switch?"

Hari handed over his lunch box in reply. The boys made their way to the edge of the pond and sat under a neem tree. Most of the kids sat near the school building or beside the playgrounds. The sporty boys had already finished their lunches and set up a pitch to play cricket. Anil was there along with Bunty and the others, drawing up his team to get a quick inning during lunch.

Hari turned to Mohan. "I'm sorry about this morning."

"Don't worry about it," Mohan said. "Sister Mary just likes to see my bum."

Hari giggled. "She probably doesn't get to see many men."

"I bet it excites her to hit me." Mohan turned, and immediately regretted. His bottom was still sore from the thrashing. He continued, "She has these heavy breaths, you know, when she is done, like she ran ten kilometres or something. Except she hasn't, so I figure she has the hots for me."

"Shut up!" Hari pushed him away. "That's just gross. Besides, if someone hears you, then she'll have the hots for you again."

The boys snickered under the neem tree.

"Man, it hurts," Mohan complained.

Hari walked up to the water's edge and lay on his stomach. The pond was green, overrun with water hyacinth. Further from the shore, a small clump of water lilies held out against the chokehold of the hyacinth; reeds of water chestnuts rose in slender shafts from the water surface. Hari remembered the biology teacher's lament that the hyacinth was killing the pond. He grabbed a fistful of hyacinth and tugged at it. It resisted, but after a few pulls, he tore away a section. He looked at the bulbous plant in his fist, the water dripping down his forearm. Laying it in the sun to shrivel, he reached in again into the dark waters of the pond to drag out more of the hyacinth.

"What are you doing?" Mohan stood next to him, adjusting his shorts to prevent the painful caress of cloth against cut skin.

"Sister Agnes said that the hyacinth is bad for the pond, so I am pulling it out."

"What's the point? You can't pull all of it out."

"Sure I can."

Mohan pointed to the centre of the pond. "What about there? You can't even swim."

"But you can."

Hari looked up from where he squatted; the sun was behind Mohan and Hari squinted in the bright light.

"I am not going to swim in there to pick slimy plants," Mohan said. "I have a better idea, though."

Hari watched as Mohan looked around. Satisfied they were alone, Mohan pulled down his shorts and leaned over the edge of the pond. He lapped the cool water over his cuts, letting out exaggerated sighs of contentment. Hari laughed and rose, standing sentinel over Mohan.

"Get up," he said in a low voice. "Anamika is coming."

"Really?" Mohan fumbled with his shorts.

Hari ran to head her off. When they returned, Mohan was skipping stones over water. He turned to them as if they had interrupted this pleasing routine.

"How are you?" Anamika asked. She avoided looking at his shorts. "Does it hurt?"

Mohan shrugged. "No big deal. If you were a boy, you'd understand."

"Shall we go to the woodapple tree?" Hari said.

Anamika hesitated.

"Come with us," Mohan said, "it'll be alright."

The three of them walked around the edge of the pond to the dark sacred grove. Inside, they stood in the shade of the tall peepal tree and watched, in awed silence, the hundreds of bats hanging torpid under the noonday sun. The bats swayed in the breeze, menacing despite their great height. Anamika cowered and Mohan put his arm about her. She let him, and Hari knew that it was his right that day.

Hari walked ahead past the spectre of the bats to the woodapple tree. High above him, the hard-shelled fruit hung off the tall branches. He flung pebbles and stones at them. Most missed their mark, but one or two hit a fruit. Mohan joined him. Anamika walked around them, trying to find any fruit that had fallen among the leaves at the bottom of the tree.

When the first bell to announce the end of lunch rang, the boys had felled two and Anamika had found three woodapples. Pleased with themselves, they made their way back to the school, their pace quickening as they realized they were late.

"Peck-tin," Mohan said, spittle flying out of his mouth as he aspirated the word. He held the woodapple high like a hunting prize.

Hari's mother had taught him that word. She made a delicate jam from the fruit and Mohan prized his ability to contribute to that sweet confection.

Weeks passed and school became routine again. Hari knew now that both he and Mohan loved Anamika, just as he knew that they were both going through the change. This knowledge comforted him. Mohan was still his best friend, not a rival. Anamika continued to treat them as equals. And though his mother was not happy about Hari's visits to her house, her prohibition had lapsed over time. The only real change was that Mrs Mukherjee no longer fed him or Mohan when they visited.

The day after the full moon in March, Hari tore through his cupboard looking for the shabbiest set of clothes he could find. Behind him he could hear his mother's nagging voice addressed to his father.

"We are in mourning, for God's sake," she said. "And you want him to go out and play with coloured water."

Girish drew out buckets of water from the tank at the back of the house. As he carried the buckets through the house to the front verandah, sloshing water in the hallway, he said, "Savitri, he is just a young boy. How can you expect him to sit in here while all of his friends are out celebrating Holi?"

"So what if he is young, it doesn't mean that we ignore our duties."

"Fine, we'll sit in here and mope, but I won't let him waste his childhood just because his grandmother is dead."

Hari heard his father walking out into the verandah. As he changed,

Hari knew what his mother had in her mind, that it was his fault that Paathi was dead. But he knew she couldn't bring herself to say that. It would hurt his father too much. Without saying goodbye to her, he slipped out of the house. Girish had laid out the coloured powders for Holi in neat piles next to the buckets.

"Happy Holi!" Mr Mukherjee greeted, arriving at their gate. Anamika followed him, carrying a dish covered with cloth.

Girish brought his hands together in salutation.

"We know you aren't celebrating this year," Mr Mukherjee said. "But the missus wanted you to have some sweets."

Anamika handed the gift to Hari. Without thinking, Hari pulled the cloth aside to reveal rassogollas swimming in rose syrup. He grinned at his father, pleased with his discovery. Mr Mukherjee laughed.

"Say thank you," Girish instructed as he took the dish inside.

"I'm not a baby," Hari hissed.

"So are you ready?" Mr Mukherjee asked, appraising the powders and the water in the buckets.

"I was just making the colours," Hari said. He displayed his spray gun to Anamika, but she had a squirt pistol loaded with green dye buried in the folds of her skirt. She squeezed a shot at him, colouring him, before he could put up his hands to shield himself.

"Wait, I am not ready yet," he said.

"That's your problem, isn't it?" Mr Mukherjee grabbed a fistful of pink rice powder and rubbed it into Hari's hair.

Within seconds, the front of the house was smeared with a rainbow of colours as Hari retaliated. But a shriek stopped them all.

"Hari, no!" Savitri cried out. "Not in the house. Go outside and play."

Then she pulled her plain sari over her head and bowed to Mr Mukherjee. "Thank you for the sweets. Where's Lata?"

"She's off with the other women. Left me in charge of the girl." Mr Mukherjee ran his hand over his daughter's head. "Says it's her day off from the family."

While they talked, Hari poured his colour crystals into the buckets of water, preparing his arsenal of red, green, and blue coloured water. Anamika joined him and together they reloaded her squirt pistol and filled up his water gun. Then, in a coordinated swoop, they fell upon Mr Mukherjee. As soon as the first drops of the coloured spray hit him, he ran out of the garden into the laneway, pursued by the two children.

Mohan and his brother joined them, and they all ran together squirt-
ing and shrieking at each other.

Shouts of "Holi hai!" rang out from parts of the colony and the children followed the sounds trying to find the action. As the sun rose high
that spring morning, their faces grew unrecognizable from the colours
sprayed over their skin, hair, and clothes. Mr Mukherjee stayed back at
Mohan's house, where the men had gathered to dispense colour and
drinks among themselves. Halfway through the housing development,
the children ran into the women, who squealed in delight and yelled in
mock anger as the children pelted them with spray and powder.

A large woman, dyed black and blue all over, grabbed Hari and
pressed him against her sari. "Tell me, Hari," she said, "where are the
men hiding?"

Hari recognized Mrs Mukherjee's voice, and as she pushed him
back, the children and the women around him laughed. Hari felt the
back of his head with his hand. When he looked at the hand, it was
bright yellow.

"Why should I tell you, if you tricked me?" Hari said to Mrs
Mukherjee.

She looked odd, her white teeth and pink gums ghastly against the
green and black of her dyed face.

"I only did it to make you look even prettier this spring," she replied.
The women laughed aloud.

"They're at my house," Mohan said.

"Who's that?" Mrs Mukherjee asked. "Is that you, Mohan? Come
give me a hug."

"I don't think so," Mohan said, stumbling away from her.

Hari realized that there was something different about the women
this day. The layers of colour had changed them. They seemed frivo-
lous and carefree, but also powerful and assertive. He watched as they
charged en masse towards the men corralled at Mohan's house, talking
and laughing loudly. Some of the older kids followed the women to
watch them make sport of the men, but Hari walked down the lane
towards his house. Mohan and Anamika ran after him.

"I need a refill," Hari said and shook his empty water gun at them.

"So do I." Mohan fell into step.

Anamika sprayed them with the leftover water in her squirt pistol.
The boys did not even flinch, letting the water run over their backs. The

warmth from the afternoon sun began to dry them. Their hair stood out in stiff spikes, and their clothes stuck to their bodies in places.

"All done?" Girish asked the three children as they came in.

"Hey, Hari's dad," Mohan said, reaching for Anamika's squirt gun. "Spray him!" he shouted.

"No," Anamika pulled away from him. "It's not right."

"I'll get you some clean water to wash up," Girish said and disappeared into the house.

"They are in mourning, you moron," Anamika whispered.

"Oh," Mohan turned to Hari, "sorry."

"It's all right," Hari said, filling his canister with the thick green water. "But you must let me spray you now. No spray back."

"That's not fair," Mohan said but he did not move, only put up his hands as Hari sprayed him, emptying the entire canister.

When Hari turned to see what Anamika thought of this trick, he found her crouched by the jasmine shrub. She was squatting, one hand on her head, the other pushed low against her stomach.

"What's wrong?" Hari asked, running over to her.

"Nothing," she said, and looked away.

Water splashed in the verandah as Girish came out. "Savitri!" he bellowed, when he saw the children, and ran towards them.

"What's wrong?" he asked and crouched near the girl. Then he stood up again. "Come away, come away," he said, leading the boys away.

The tears flowing down Anamika's face turned black as they washed the dye down her cheeks. Hari's mother stumbled out of the house and ran to Anamika. She spoke to her in hurried tones. Then she looked at Girish and, without saying a word, she helped Anamika up. The two walked around the house to the back.

"Appa, what happened?" Hari asked.

"Nothing," Girish said, looking at the dye on his clothes from grabbing the two boys. In a futile gesture, he brushed the coloured stains with his hand. He sighed, "Just women's business."

Hari looked at Mohan, who seemed to know more about this.

"Do you know where her mother is?" Girish asked.

"My house," Mohan said. "That's where they were headed."

"Mohan, be a good boy, please, and fetch her."

Girish headed back to the verandah.

As Mohan sprinted off to find Mrs Mukherjee, Hari started walking towards the back of the house, following the trail of coloured footsteps Anamika had left on the flagstones.

"Where do you think you are going, mister?"

Hari stopped. "I was going back to wash up."

"Use this," Girish pointed to the bucket in the verandah. "You are staying here."

Hari shrugged and splashed the water over his face, trying to scrub out as much of the dye and powder as he could. He was almost finished when the gate swung open and the Mukherjees ran in. Hari would have laughed at the sight of two adults doused in a myriad colours running through the streets, had they not looked so anxious.

"Where is she? What happened?" Mrs Mukherjee gasped for breath after each question.

Hari's father put out his hands to calm her. Then he spoke to the two of them in a quiet voice so Hari could not hear. The Mukherjees looked at one another and Hari was sure that they smiled at each other. Girish pointed to the path beside the house, and Mrs Mukherjee charged down to the back. Hari watched her wistfully, wondering yet again why she was allowed there while he wasn't.

Mr Mukherjee was shaking his father's hand. He seemed embarrassed. "Well, I guess it's a good thing we brought you the sweets today," he said.

Girish laughed. "Let me bring them out."

"No, no," Mr Mukherjee stopped him. "They are for you. Enjoy them. Some Holi this turned out to be, no?"

Girish looked over his clothes and shrugged. "Seems like Holi wanted to come to this family, whether we were ready or not."

Mr Mukherjee laughed loud and long at this comment. He sat on the stone steps of the verandah and washed his face with the little water that was left in the bucket.

"Hari!" Mohan beckoned from the gate. "Come here."

Hari ran out and followed Mohan, who gestured him to be quiet. Mohan led him around the neighbours' house into their back garden. The house was empty; the couple who rented it were celebrating at Mohan's house.

"What are we doing here?" Hari whispered.

"Shush," Mohan put his finger over his lips, "just come and see."

Hari wanted to laugh. Mohan looked like a little rakshasha, a demon, his clotted hair sprouting wildly in all directions over his black face and arms. They approached the thick bougainvillea-covered hedge separating the houses. Beyond the hedge, Hari could hear the sounds of his mother talking to Mrs Mukherjee.

"What's happening?" Hari leaned close to Mohan's ear.

"I think that Anamika became a woman today."

"Wasn't she always?"

Mohan whacked him on the head. "Don't be stupid. She was a girl, and now she is a woman."

"How do you know?"

"You know how we go pee-pee," Mohan whispered. "Well, blood is coming out of there for her today."

"Shut up." Hari was revolted by the thought of Anamika bleeding. "Girls don't even have a pee-pee like us."

"It's the truth," Mohan said. "My brother told me."

"Your brother is a liar."

"No, I swear, scout's honour," Mohan said. "That's where babies come from."

Hari scoffed, "That's not how babies are made."

"How do you think they are made then?"

"Do you remember the story of how Brahma created the world by growing a lotus flower from his belly button?"

"So what?"

"My cousin told me the story about how babies are formed. You have to pee into a woman's belly button, and then just like Brahma's lotus, a baby grows in her womb."

Mohan's body shook in quiet laughter. "Brahma's lotus. You are a first rate imbecile, Hari."

Hari shrugged and turned to look at the hedge. "I like my way much better than yours with bleeding and whatnot. I wish we could see through this hedge."

"You want to?"

Hari looked at him. "What do you mean?"

"Come," Mohan said and scrambled a few feet past the curry bush, to where the hedge thinned. From here they could peek into the back garden of Hari's house. In the tottam, his mother, her plain sari streaked with colour, and Mrs Mukherjee, still completely doused in colour, stood over the crouched Anamika. Hari's mother was scrubbing Anamika's hair, while Mrs Mukherjee was washing her hands. Anamika was naked, but neither Hari nor Mohan could make out her features, drenched as she was in the colours of Holi.

"Come, we shouldn't be watching this," Hari said, pulling Mohan back.

"Funny, that's exactly what she said," Mohan replied, sitting on a flat stone.

A tendril of fear coursed through Hari's body. "Who?"

"Anamika." Mohan laughed. "I brought her here the night you ate that fish and your grandmother died."

Hari was speechless in shock.

"We saw everything…" Mohan pointed towards the women. "Not like today. There was no paint to hide your nakedness that night."

With a howl, Hari fell upon his friend. They rolled over the garden, mud and dirt sticking to their bodies as Hari tried to kick and punch Mohan.

Mohan grabbed Hari in a bear hug, trapping him. "Shush. Shut up, for God's sakes."

The women in the tottam had gone quiet at the noise of their fight. Then Hari heard his mother calling for his father in a loud voice, "Girish! Come see who is behind the hedge!"

"Run," Mohan whispered.

The two boys fled towards the front of the house.

"Where should we go?" Hari asked as he ran alongside. United against the fear of discovery, they were best friends again. Hari laughed as they scrammed out the gate.

"Anamika's house."

Hari was so shocked by this statement that he came to a momentary halt. Mohan stopped too. "It makes perfect sense," he said.

"It does," Hari agreed. Snickering once more, he ran past Mohan, past the holy basil bushes on the side of Mrs Mukherjee's house into her back garden. There he leaned over, his hands on his knees, and panted for breath.

"If they had caught us…" Mohan grinned like an idiot, his face a riot of colours. "That was stupid of you."

"Well, you should not have spied on me."

"Big deal, like I have never seen you naked before."

"Not you," Hari said, "Anamika!"

Mohan considered this for a while. He nodded. "I suppose you are right." He stuck out his hand. "I am sorry for that."

Recalling an American film, Hari spat on his palm and shook Mohan's hand.

II
Kodumai (cruelty)

FIVE

SUMMER HOLIDAYS SPLIT up the trio. Mohan travelled to Gujarat, to his grandparents near Ahmedabad; Mrs Mukherjee took Anamika to Calcutta to her relatives; and Hari and his mother booked their tickets to Madras on the Tamil Nadu Express. Due to the ongoing electrification of the tracks, Girish would spend weeks away from home, living with the technicians along the route, and Savitri did not fancy living in the colony, which thinned out as people fled the hot Deccan for the months of May and June.

"You know that your uncle Mani will be in Madras this year," Savitri said as they packed.

"Mani-uncle is coming, from New York?" Hari dropped his shirts in a heap on the bed. "Why did you not tell me before?"

"I'm telling you now." Savitri took up the shirts, folded them, and packed them inside the suitcase. "Sit down, Hari."

Hari looked at her, puzzled.

"He is not coming alone...he's gotten married."

Hari opened his mouth and let out a breath of pleasure. His mother's hesitation meant only one thing.

"Mani-mama had a love marriage." Hari drew out the words to prolong scandalizing his mother.

She sighed and nodded.

"Is she Indian?"

Another sigh. This was juicy gossip. Too bad, Anamika and Mohan had already left on their summer vacations, Hari thought. He had an American aunt and no one to share the news with. Unlike his mother, who seemed apprehensive about having an American for a relative, Hari was quite pleased with this news.

"What does she look like?" he asked.

Savitri started putting away the clothes faster now, packing them tighter. "I don't know. Mani has sent pictures to Thatha and Paathi. My mother says that she is very pale with a long bony face and dark curly hair."

"Do you know her name?"

"Sarah."

"Sarah...doesn't Appa want to come to Madras and see her?"

"Your father has a job to do. He can't just go running down to Madras because his brother-in-law has brought home an English girl."

"English? I thought she'd be American."

"It's all the same. English, American, what difference does it make? She is not Indian."

"Did he get married in a church?" he said, now toying with his mother.

"Why would he?" Savitri looked annoyed. "He's not Christian, and neither is she as a matter of fact. He writes to say that she is Jewish. They got married in city hall—a civil marriage."

"Is Thatha mad?" Hari tried to imagine his maternal grandfather, the bald rotund man with horn-rimmed glasses, with a scowl on his face.

"Your paathi is furious." Savitri pulled the suitcase shut. "Sit on it."

Hari climbed atop the suitcase and his mother fastened the clips. Then she locked it with a set of small keys that jangled from her key ring.

"All I can say is, thank God my youngest sister Kalyani got married before this nonsense. Otherwise who knows what might have happened."

"But Kalyani-chitti and Ramesh-chittappa live in Toronto, why would they care if Mani-mama married an Indian girl or not?"

"Everyone cares." Savitri struggled as she hefted the suitcase to the floor. Hari pushed it along the tiled floor to the front door. Behind him his mother continued, "We know him. If he had an arranged marriage we can look for a nice girl and make sure that she comes from a good family. There are many things that make a proper match. What does Mani know about finding the right wife?"

Hari kept quiet. He wanted to say much, but his mother would rule his views contrarian and that only meant a long lecture. Besides, he would have ample opportunity to learn more once they arrived in Madras. Hari stood in the verandah and watched the street. Bleach-white light from the hot sun parched the soil and turned the asphalt soft. The heat was unbearable and the trees rustled noisily as the dry leaves brushed against each other.

Madras was hot, too, but the sea breezes from the harbour tempered the heat in the afternoons. Unlike Nagpur, however, the air here was humid and the sweat never really evaporated, coating everyone in a thin sheen of perspiration. His grandparents' old house in T-Nagar, a suburb of Madras, was surprisingly pleasant and cool. The three-storied mansion was ancient, built before the First World War, and occupied a sprawling lot. Hari's grandparents lived on the main floor, with tenants on the top two floors. Their maid, Sivagami, a fixture in the house for half a century, had two rooms on the west side.

"Thatha," Hari said, "I want to go to America like Mani-mama and Ramesh-chittappa when I grow up." They were in the tool shed in the back garden. Hari cleaned and oiled the garden tools while his grandfather sharpened the shears.

"Un-huh, but you'll have to study hard to go there..."

"But I do study hard. Ask Amma, I am always in the top ten of the class..."

"Top ten, but not the top one always." Thatha flicked the wiping cloth at Hari.

"Mani-mama once said that I could stay with him and do college in New York. He thinks my grades are super-duper."

"Well we'll see what Mani-mama thinks now that he is married," Thatha said. "Soon he'll have his own kids to worry about."

"Amma and Paathi seem upset that he married an American." Hari tried to sound nonchalant.

Thatha looked at him. "Since when do you care about such things?"

Hari shrugged.

"They think they have a right to be upset," Thatha said, running his fingers along the sharp edge of his shears. "Mani was a good catch, a proper Brahmin boy with a job in America. Families with marriageable daughters would have lined up for miles outside our door. Your grandmother and your mother would have ruled the roost, causing all sorts of troubles for such girls and their matchmakers. They had planned it for so long, being the centre of all that fawning attention that…well, perhaps it is all for the best."

"Thatha, is arranged marriage really the best?" Hari asked.

Hari's grandfather shrugged. "What do I know, Kanna? I've only known one kind of marriage." He looked curiously at Hari. "Why are you asking? Are you in love already?"

"No," Hari blushed. "It's just what Amma was saying about Mani-mama's love marriage."

"Hari, I want you to do something for me," Thatha said and waved the shears at him. "I want you to listen to your Paathi and your Amma."

Hari's face fell.

"Listen to them, and then when Mani and Sarah get here tomorrow, I want you to observe. See for yourself if the women's talk in the kitchens is really true." Thatha put down the shears and stood closer to Hari. "It's time you started making up your own mind about some things."

Hari nodded and looked serious. "I can do that. I'll be in the kitchen anyway, because I have to learn to cook."

"Learn to cook?"

"Thatha, you are not listening. I want to go to America, and if I am going to study there, I should know how to cook."

"Oh!" Hari's thatha said. "Don't worry, we'll send a nice wife with you so she can cook for you. That way you can pay attention to your studies."

"Thatha!"

"What?! Otherwise you'll get married to a memsahib, like Mani did; and your grandmother will have another heart attack. By then she will be too old to survive such a shock."

Sivagami arrived at the door; it was time for afternoon tiffin. "Come, child," she coaxed, "don't potter about in Ayya's shed." She held her hand out.

"Go away, Sivagami. I am busy."

"Come, my little prince, let's go before something breaks."

"Nothing except your head is going to break if you don't leave me alone." He shook a screwdriver at her.

"Don't talk to Sivagami like that," Thatha reproved.

Sivagami laughed. "O...o...the little master is pouting! He is angry at his old crony!" She stroked his face with the dry, lye-cracked skin of her palms, letting him feel the warmth of her loving caress.

It was impossible to remonstrate with or to threaten her. This small dark woman, half her teeth missing, her skin wrinkled and leathery with age, with her head of patchy white hair, ruled over the house in her servitude. Not only had she weaned Hari's mother as a child, she had also welcomed his grandmother to this house when his grandfather, then still a young man in his late teens living at home, had married. This long association had made Sivagami more family member than valued servant.

In fact, Hari's grandfather had taken charge of Sivagami's brother Sundaran after he lost his job in the strike actions at the textile factories of Coimbatore during the Emergency years. Thatha helped Sundaran buy a motor rickshaw, which he now plied through the streets of Madras. Sundaran repaid this favour by mooring his rickshaw outside the house and starting a rickshaw stand. Over the years, the rickshaw stand had grown, but Sundaran would not let anyone else ferry members of Hari's family as long as he was there.

As he walked over the stone pathway to the house, Hari wondered why he knew more about the lives of the people who served his family than about his grandparents, or his parents. Close to the kitchen door, he heard his mother's voice inside.

"...imagine what Kollu-thatha is going to say when he finds out that Mani is bringing home this white witch?"

"Come, child," his grandmother said to Hari, and pointed to the plate. "I made you some dosais."

Hari breathed in deeply the tangy smell of sourdough crepes griddled in peanut oil and rubbed his hands in delight.

"Wash them first," Savitri pointed at his hands. She was sitting on the floor, chopping spinach on an old wooden cutting board next to where his plate was laid out. White coconut chutney, red chutney powder, and a cup of lentil sambhar were arrayed around the browned crepes.

Hari rinsed his hands in the kitchen sink. His grandmother held out the edge of her sari for him to dry his hands.

Savitri spoke up, "How long are they staying here?"

"Here?" Hari's grandmother turned away from the stove to respond to her daughter. "They're not staying here. Mani insisted that we get them rooms at the ITDC hotel near Parry's corner."

"I suppose that makes sense."

"Nonsense. Suddenly after all these years, this house his grandfather built is not good enough for him. Mark my words, you mark my words. . ." Paathi shook the spatula at them while Sivagami stood in the doorway nodding solemnly. "If it hadn't been for this white witch, he would never have stayed at that expensive hotel. She probably drinks, too!"

"Amma, how do you expect them to stay with us," Savitri said loudly, "in this crowded house? Already Hari is sleeping on a mat in the living room. Where do you intend to put them up?"

"Oh, so now the way we sleep is not good enough? What's wrong with the palmyra mats? For generations we have slept on them..."

"Forget I said anything. Besides, Amma, think of the toilet. She is probably used to that ceramic sitting toilet, you know with toilet paper..."

"What toilet paper... why does she have to read the paper in the toilet?"

Hari snickered. "No, Paathi, not to read, to wipe her bottom."

"What! She uses paper to clean herself? No water? But how? That's just dirty. How can you clean yourself without water?"

"And they pay good money to buy the paper too...only the Parsi shops and those Mount Road merchants carry them. Fine imported paper for fine bums," Hari's mother let out, and they all collapsed in laughter in the kitchen.

Late that night, after everyone had fallen asleep, a loud racket on the street woke the household. Someone was singing a Tamil film song loudly and banging against the wrought iron gates to keep time. Hari watched his grandfather turn on the lights and step into the courtyard. Sivagami ran from her side of the house and intercepted him.

"Ayya, please forgive him," she pleaded. "It's just Vishu. Just go back inside and I'll take him home."

"Is he drunk?" Thatha asked.

"Yes, I am drunk," Vishu called out from the gate. "And what are you going to do about it? Let me in!"

"Shut your mouth!" Sivagami called out, then again turned to

Thatha. "Ayya, please, just this once, forgive him. . ."

She fell on her knees in front of the old man. Thatha stood at the gates in front of the drunken son of his maidservant, as Hari watched from the verandah with his mother. His grandmother came out, sighed at the scene, and disappeared into the kitchen in the back of the house.

"Sivagami, get up." Thatha pulled away from her. "This is not a film, stop being so melodramatic."

"No, Mother! Stay!" Vishu yelled out. "This is a Tamil film. Stay and protect your son from the evil Brahmin landlord!"

Hari would have laughed at Vishu's theatrics, but the lights and grumbles of complaint from the tenants' apartments above shamed him.

"That's it!" Hari's grandfather unlatched the gate, pushed Sivagami to one side and dragged Vishu into the courtyard. Without a support to lean against, Vishu stumbled and fell. Hari's grandfather locked the gate and kicked the drunken young man who was lying on the flagstones. Sivagami sobbed where she lay.

"Look at her," Thatha said. "Look at your mother. See what you are doing to her? Is this all you can do? Watch films and drink away your mother's earnings?"

"Ayya please. . .," Sivagami pleaded.

Hari's grandfather grunted and spat at the crouched figure on the ground.

"You have money and power; rich relatives coming from Amriika and faraway places," Vishu spoke, his voice catching. "We poor people only have our drink."

Sivagami scrambled over to her son and slapped him hard. She beat against him with her fists. "How dare you speak back to Ayya? He's like your father."

Thatha leaned and pulled Sivagami off her son, saving him this time.

"You keep thinking that you are part of their family," Vishu sobbed. "You're deluded. They treat you like a servant and you treat their children better than you treat me."

"Take him home and put him to bed," Thatha said to Sivagami and returned to the house.

Sivagami crept back to her son. Cradling him in her arms, she rocked him back and forth on the ground.

"Come, Hari, let's go in," his mother said.

"You go. I'll come in."

Hari watched Sivagami help Vishu up. They hobbled past him to her quarters. Vishu was crying and clutching his ribs where Thatha had kicked him.

The following morning, Sivagami led Vishu to Hari's grandfather as he pruned the roses in the front garden. Hari was grafting one rose variety onto another. He listened as he slit an opening in a green stem with a razor blade.

"Ayya," Sivagami called softly and gestured towards her son.

Thatha wiped the pruning shears with the cloth around his shoulders and threw a look at Vishu.

"Ayya, please forgive me," Vishu said, his hands held together, and his head bowed low. "I made a mistake. I should have never gone to the toddy liquor shop last night."

"Is that what you think you did wrong?"

"Ayya, you watch over me like a father. Please don't punish my mother—"

"Shut up," Hari's grandfather interrupted, waving him away. "Like your behaviour reflects on your mother. Idiot. Watch your mother and learn from her. Why don't you try and find a job and work instead of loafing around with that damned film club of yours? You went drinking with those film club friends of yours, didn't you?"

"Ayya, it was only because the new MGR film came out—"

Sivagami whacked him on the head. Vishu scowled and Hari giggled.

Hari's grandfather said, "What do you want me to do for him, Sivagami?"

"Just forgive him, Ayya. Without your blessings, how can he be successful in this world?"

"Fine, tell Sundaran to keep an eye on him and make sure that he leaves that damned MGR film club. That man's a damned nuisance." Hari's grandfather turned his back on the pair.

When the two left, Hari said, "Thatha, isn't MGR the chief minister of Tamil Nadu?"

"Yes."

"So how can he act in films like a film star and be a chief minister at the same time?"

Thatha laughed. He came over to inspect Hari's work. Taking a thin strip of plastic, he helped Hari tie up the slit on either side of the new scion.

"Even a young boy like you knows enough to ask that question, but no one seems to want to know the answer," Thatha said. "Come, let's see if lunch is ready."

The rest of the day passed in a blur. The anticipated arrival of Mani and Sarah's flight late that night from New York masked the upheaval from the night before. Thatha would take the taxi alone to the airport to greet the midnight flight and accompany them to their hotel. They would arrive for a late lunch the next day, having slept in. Nonetheless, Hari's grandmother and mother worked themselves up into a frenzy. They brought in an older Brahmin woman, a professional cook, opened up the out-kitchen in the backyard and supervised the making of sweets and savouries. The house smelled divine, as if the festival of kartikei or pongal had occurred in the middle of May.

Sivagami cleaned and scrubbed the floors with such vigour that Thatha crumpled his newspaper in annoyance and marched off to his tool shed, though lunch had not yet been served. Hari followed him.

"Cooking like there is a wedding happening," Thatha muttered. "So this is how they hope to get their revenge."

Hari munched on a warm murukku, the swirls of rice pastry breaking off and leaving crumbs wherever he stood. "I thought they were angry?"

"What?"

"Paathi and Amma, I thought they were angry at Mani-mama," Hari repeated.

"They are."

"Then why are they cooking all these dishes to welcome him?"

Thatha shrugged. "To make him feel guilty." He settled at his desk and began sifting through his tool box, organizing it.

Hari leaned against the door of the tool shed and watched the women in the out-kitchen. Fumes rose from the huge wok where the cook fried murukku, thenguzal, and thattai. At the kitchen threshold, his mother mixed the fried boondi with sugar syrup and fried cashews to form round sweet laddus. It was a happy exercise, the three women gossiped and laughed through the afternoon as the sun descended in the sky and the sea breezes cooled the city.

Despite Thatha's words, Hari was pleased that the women were making such elaborate preparations for Mani-mama's arrival. Aunts, uncles, second cousins were expected to come and see Mani; even Kollu-thatha was expected the next day, with Tangarajan-uncle and Shanthi-aunty. Hari was especially looking forward to seeing them. For now, he contented himself by presenting himself to his grandmother to taste samples of the snacks being prepared.

"He's going to have diarrhoea if you keep feeding him," Savitri warned.

Paathi waved her complaints away. "He's just a child. Let him enjoy it."

SIX

HARI WOKE UP in the predawn darkness and shuffled into the kitchen. MS Subbulakshmi sang the suprabhatam over the radio in that husky, granular voice that had earned her so much acclaim around the world. His grandmother smiled at him; behind her, steam rose from the kettle on the stove as water boiled for the morning coffee in the kitchen.

"Why didn't you wake me last night?" Hari asked, rubbing his eyes.

"Whatever for, Kanna?"

"I wanted to see Thatha off to the airport."

Paathi laughed gently as Hari yawned. "Go fetch the milk by the front gate," she told him. "It's alright, your Mani-mama will be here soon enough."

Hari nodded and walked barefoot through the living room to the front of the house. The cool air in the verandah was drenched in the sticky sweet aroma of the coral jasmine flowers, which had fallen overnight from the low branches. He knelt to observe the big black ants gathering nectar from the small orange-stalked flowers. Carefully, he stepped around them to grab the milk bags dropped off by the government milk truck.

When he returned, his grandmother mumbled a few prayers and poured boiling water over the coffee powder packed in a small stainless steel filter to prepare the dikasin, a thick almost syrupy coffee base. She then apportioned it into three tumblers. The milk now went on the stove to boil in its turn.

A low rumbling noise began in the backyard as Hari's thatha returned, having started the pump to fill the underground water sump. Every morning, before dawn, he peered into the tank to see how much municipal water had flowed in overnight, and almost always he had to turn the pump on to fill the tank from his own bore well.

He joined them in the kitchen as Hari's grandmother poured the boiling milk into the coffee tumblers.

"You're awake," Thatha said, sitting down on a well-worn palakai, a wide wooden stool barely three inches high.

"Tell me, what happened?" Hari asked.

Although Hari was now eleven, in the summer of 1987, his grandfather still poured his coffee for him, letting it fall from one tumbler into another. Slowly the distance between the two tumblers increased and the coffee fell from ever greater heights in a thin stream from the tumbler stretched far above his head and frothed in the other, held centimetres off the ground.

As he frothed the coffee, Hari's grandfather narrated the details of his drive to the airport and the long wait at the reception hall. The flight arrived an hour late and by the time Mani and Sarah had passed through customs, it was nearly two in the morning.

Satisfied that the coffee was now cool enough to drink, Thatha set the tumbler in front of Hari and began swirling his own tumbler. Hari's grandmother had no such pretensions for her coffee, hopelessly addicted as she was to the drink. She gulped it down, her throat rising and falling with each gurgling swallow, and then reached into the fridge to pull vegetables out for Thatha to chop. The suprabhatam was followed by the news on All India Radio and Hari's grandfather alternated between making approving noises and grunting in dismay at the different bits of news as he chopped and diced the vegetables for lunch.

Later that morning, they heard hurried knocking on the door. Thatha napped on the couch in the living room, catching up on lost sleep, so Hari opened the door. Sundaran came in, wringing his turban cloth in his hands.

"Ayya, do you have any whitewash?" he asked, waking Hari's grandfather.

"What's wrong?" Thatha said.

Sundaran motioned towards the compound wall outside. Noises could be heard from what seemed like a restless crowd on the other side. Thatha, tired and half asleep, yawned and stretched his arms and then walked out with Sundaran. Hari followed them barefoot. Outside the gate, on the cream-coloured walls that faced the street, someone had splattered red paint and written some words in the curvy noodle-script of Tamil. Hari, having grown up in central India, was familiar with Hindi and its Devanagari script but illiterate in his mother tongue.

"Thatha, what does it say?"

"Here live Hindi speakers," Thatha read. He surveyed the people gathered on the street and said, "You'd better go inside, Hari."

"Why?"

"Just do as I say."

"He is the one," someone said. In that mass of people it was difficult to identify the voice.

Hari could feel the eyes of the crowd upon him. He hung his head low and walked into the house, his pace quickening.

"What are you all staring at?" Hari's grandfather said to the crowd.

They muttered among themselves.

"Go on, get back to your work. Sundaran, get some lime and white-wash this wall."

Sivagami was washing the floors when Hari ran into the living room. "What's wrong, Kanna?"

"Thatha is mad at me because I speak Hindi." Hari wanted to cry.

Sivagami laughed. "Why would he be mad at you for speaking Hindi?"

"Because someone painted something on the wall."

Sivagami looked to the doorway. Hari's grandfather was back.

"Hari, come here. I want to talk to you," he said. "I am not angry with you. They are just some silly people who still think that Hindi should not be spoken in the south."

"But it's the national language."

"That it may be," Thatha said. "Nevertheless, from now on, I don't want you to speak Hindi outside the house. That includes the gardens. Can you do that for me?" Hari's grandfather held out his hand.

Hari looked at the large hand in front of him. Instead of shaking it, he said, "Can I speak English still?"

Hari's grandfather sighed. "Yes, you can speak English and Tamil, but I would prefer it if you just spoke Tamil, all right?"

Hari nodded and put his right hand into his grandfather's.

"You know what, I'll teach you to read and write Tamil like everyone else in Madras," Sivagami said.

"And when are you going to do that?" Hari's grandmother asked. She had stood in the kitchen corridor, ladle in hand, listening to the conversation.

"In the afternoon, when the electricity goes off."

"That's when you take a nap."

"What do I need a nap for?" Sivagami said and turned to Hari. "We'll begin today, right after your lunch. We'll walk through the gardens talking so loudly in Tamil that no one will believe that anyone who speaks Hindi lives here."

Hari grinned at the small dark woman crouched on the floor next to her bucket of dirty water.

"So who was it?" Hari's grandmother asked.

"Probably somebody from one of the political parties, miscreants," Thatha replied.

"You don't think Vishu had anything to do with this, do you?"

"No, Ayya, Vishu would never do something like this," Sivagami said.

"He's out helping his uncle whitewash the walls right now," Thatha said, shrugging his shoulders, and returned to the couch.

And so at lunch time, when Mani-mama and Sarah-aunty arrived at the ancestral home, they found the compound walls glistening with a wet coat of whitewash in the noonday sun. Sundaran, his clothes covered in lime, bowed deeply to Mani and his pale American wife, while Vishu, clutching his brush, observed them with a sneer on his face. Hari, washed and wearing new clothes, stood next to his thatha, behind the women. From his half-hidden post, he observed Vishu's contempt as Sundaran struggled to pull out the large suitcase from the taxi trunk.

"She does look pretty in the shalwar-kameez," Savitri whispered to her mother.

Hari's grandmother nodded. The two women had dressed in heavy Kancheevaram silk saris despite the summer heat. Sweat poured off them and darkened their blouses at the armpits as they lit the camphor and performed the aarthi to welcome the prodigal son home.

No recriminations, no snarky comments, just smiles, hugs, and kind words filled the moment. From within the house, the tape deck blared classical Carnatic music. Outside the gates, people crowded to watch, and above them, the tenants flung open the windows to peek at the arrivals.

"Appa," Mani said, laughing, "you didn't have to paint the compound walls for us."

"We didn't," Thatha replied, turning to head back into the house. Hari knew it was the public spectacle that annoyed him. But he also saw that his grandfather's terse reply had stung the visitors' ears. Sarah's eyes turned to her husband in momentary alarm.

"Come, let's go inside," Paathi said, putting her arm around Sarah, leading her new daughter-in-law into the cool interior of the house.

Sundaran followed them with the heavy suitcase. Sivagami shut the door behind them. Inside, Hari scrambled to lay down on the floor large sections of banana leaves for lunch.

"Hari, put down a silver plate for Sarah," Thatha instructed in English. "It'll be easier."

"No no," Sarah put her arm out in protest. "I want to try eating out of the banana leaf, like everyone else."

"Are you sure, honey?" Mani said. "It's quite a challenge."

Hari stood rooted to the floor. This was the first time he had heard someone use the term "honey." The term aside, the sweetness in Mani-mama's voice was so different from the way his own parents talked. How could they be so openly affectionate, he wondered.

"Don't just stand there, lay out the plate for her," Hari's grandmother exclaimed, bringing in the brass pot filled to the brim with steaming sambhar. Behind her, Savitri brought the rice and poriyal.

Sarah hesitated. "I'll eat with you, after the men have eaten," she said.

Paathi laughed at this. "Where did you learn that? Has Mani been coaching you?"

"Me coach her?" Mani said. "She knows more about our culture than I do. She's studying Tamil history and film at Columbia."

"No," Paathi put her hands on her lips as she smiled. "Why didn't you tell me this before?"

Sarah blushed. "That's how we met." She directed this remark to Hari's mother.

Hari could see that Mani's statement had gone some way in placating his grandmother. She beamed proudly at his grandfather and gestured to Sivagami, beckoning her in.

"She can even speak Tamil," Mani volunteered the information like a proud parent.

"Stop it, Mani," Sarah said in English.

Paathi's smile fell; she seemed taken aback. Savitri made a quick movement, as if to raise her hand to her mouth, and exchanged a loaded look with her mother. No matter how Sarah tried to ingratiate herself, she was still a foreigner. Even Hari knew that it was improper for a wife to address her husband by name when others were present.

Thatha cleared his throat to quell the silence. "Speak a little," he said in Tamil to encourage her.

Sarah bent her head in shyness, spoke slowly, "I can only speak and write a little…"

They marvelled at the strange accent. Hari's grandmother covered her mouth with her hand to stifle a laugh.

"That's still better than our Hari here," Sivagami cackled from the kitchen door where she stood listening.

When Mani explained the joke to Sarah, she smiled kindly at Hari. He shrugged and sat down at the largest banana leaf plate. Savitri helped her mother serve lunch and time passed as questions flew back and forth. Hari listened to everything, but his eyes flitted again and again to the large suitcase that Mani-mama had brought along. In it, Hari was sure, had come the gifts from America.

After lunch Sarah helped the women clear the plates and stayed with them in the kitchen where they ate. Mani sat in the wicker chair in the living room, while Thatha lounged on the wooden swing, gently swaying. The postman arrived with the mail. A letter from Anamika and a postcard from Mohan were addressed to Hari. He read them in the shade of the verandah.

The postcard was a quick affair. Mohan had enlarged his usual writing to fill the small space. Barely three sentences long, it was a perfunctory note stating that he was having fun and that he missed Hari. With a smile, Hari put away the yellow postcard and opened the blue inland letter that Anamika had sent from Calcutta. Crammed with closely spaced words, her long letter described an outing to Darjeeling, the crowds on the Hoogli River, and an altercation with an older cousin, who she described as a mean and vicious creature. Hari read and reread the letter.

"Hey, champion," Mani-mama stood at the door. Hari turned at the sound. "Do you want to see what we brought for you?"

Hari gathered up his postcard and letter and stood up with an alacrity that made his uncle laugh. Inside, the women had returned from the kitchen. Paathi brought out her betel box and prepared her paan, stuffing a betel leaf with lime, a tinge of tobacco, and fennel seeds, as Mani dragged the suitcase to the centre. Like a conjurer about to perform, he threw his bag open with a flourish. There were toys for Hari, and a DeWalt drill for Thatha, with a transformer for the 220-volt lines in India. Sarah pulled out a bottle of Chanel No. 5 for Savitri, and gave her mother-in-law a beautifully wrapped vase of Hungarian cut crystal.

Hari was pleased with his gifts, a remote-controlled car and a computerized chess set that beeped every time he made a move. Mani-mama showed him how to operate the car and it whizzed around the room. But Hari's grandmother soon complained about the noise it made.

Hari dropped the remote on a chair and slipped off to his mother's room. Sitting at her old school desk, he wrote his first letter to Mohan, describing his new American aunt and the toys she had brought him. As he sealed the brief note, he listened to the soft murmur of voices from the living room. The letter to Anamika was more personal. Hari made no mention of the toys, instead he wrote about Vishu and the slanderous accusation under the whitewashed walls. He knew Anamika would understand. After all, she could only speak pidgin Bengali, just as he spoke rudimentary Tamil. Their time in central India had left them both bereft of ability in their mother tongues. He read over the letter carefully, corrected a misspelling and then licked the flaps shut.

Walking past the adults in the living room, he donned his rubber sandals and stepped into the hot sun. The streets, never deserted, were quieter in the afternoon. Sundaran, sitting under the shade of a road-side tea shop, waved to Hari. The large red pillar box beside the tea stall was hot to touch as Hari posted the letters.

"Sending letters, little master?" Sundaran asked.

"Sundaran," Hari said, coming up to the rickshaw driver, "why is

Vishu always so angry?"

The tea-stall owner laughed at this. Sundaran also smiled, but his smile was tinged with sadness.

"He's like Amitabh Bachchan in *Sholay*," the stall owner said. "Typical angry young man."

"But he needs to settle down," Sundaran put in, rolling the glass tumbler of tea in his hand. "And learn to respect his elders. Did you know he was drunk two nights ago and insulted Ayya?"

The stall owner leaned forward as he exclaimed, "No!"

Hari nodded. "I was there. I saw it."

"Oh dear," the owner drew a glass of tea from his kettle and brought it to Hari. "Here you go, little master. It's on the house. Your grandfather is so good to us. You must know that we won't let anyone else do that kind of stuff here anymore." He pointed to the bright white newly painted wall of the compound.

Sundaran shrugged. "At least we'll try. But our own children no longer know the meaning of loyalty."

"It's the Kali Yuga, everything is inverted," the owner commiserated. "Look at your Vishu; he thinks people like him should be the lords of the land, not Ayya and the others in those houses."

"Don't talk to me about him and his democracy," Sundaran said and spat on the dry dust of the roadside.

"But Sundaran," Hari told him, "we live in a democracy. In school, my teachers say that you have as much a right as my father or grandfather."

Sundaran smiled and bowed his head. "That is all very well for you to say, little master. It is a very kind thing to say. But what do we know about politics and government? I failed grade four and my father put me to work." He pointed to the tea-stall owner. "Kutty here has never even seen the inside of a school. What do we know about who is good and who is bad?"

Kutty nodded his head solemnly in agreement. "Yes, he's right, little master. Your grandfather and your family are all educated people. They know what is right and what is wrong. If something goes wrong on this street, what do we do? We take it to your grandfather and he sets everything right. No need to go to the police or complain to the municipality."

"Look at where Vishu's democracy has led us," Sundaran said.

"Power cuts every afternoon, and each year less water flows in the Cauvery and into Madras. Only long speeches and rallies, those we have no scarcity of."

Hari sipped his tea as they chatted. It was sweet and milky, spiced with cardamom and ginger. Hari, sitting on the long wooden bench of the tea stall, thought about what he had learned in class and what the men said. He believed what he was taught in school about the independence struggle, about the Mahatma's idea of equality, Nehru's vision of a pluralistic democracy. Yet he was also pleased to hear that Sundaran placed his trust in Thatha. It was a feudal trust, lingering from the past, but in his mind, Hari saw no conflict in the lives of these two men.

He finished his tea and thanked the stall owner, then made his way to the house. On the way, he recalled Sivagami's offer to teach him Tamil. He walked around the house towards the back. The door to Sivagami's quarters was open.

Hari peeked inside, his pupils adjusting to the dark. The quarters were small: a cot in one corner, worn-out pictures of deities hanging on the wall beside the old mahogany cabinet which had been brought here from his grandparents' living room. Sivagami had no kitchen because she ate leftovers from his grandparents' kitchen.

Hari started. In the dim darkness he could make out Vishu in his mother's bedroom, pocketing the gold bangles that Hari's grandmother had given Sivagami for her fifty-fifth birthday.

"What are you doing?" Hari said, stepping into the room. "Where's Sivagami?"

"What do you mean, what am I doing here?" Vishu sneered. "This is my house. What are you doing here? Just because my mother works for your family doesn't mean that you can come in here whenever you like. Don't they teach you in your fancy school to knock on the door and wait for someone to answer?"

"Sivagami asked me to come, she is going to teach me Tamil."

"And I suppose your mother is paying for that?"

Hari shook his head. The topic of money for the lessons had never come up.

"So, you people are willing to pay through the nose when it comes to Inglis education, but when it comes to learning your own mother-tongue, you can't afford a penny." Vishu continued, mimicking to himself, "Let's just find a servant to teach our son Tamil, but if a foreigner comes then we'll dance like monkeys until we drop from exhaustion."

Hari shouted, "Shut up, you thief!"

"Come here," Vishu said.

Hari turned to run out, but Vishu was faster. He caught Hari by his arms and dragged him over to the cot. Hari glared at him as the young man pushed him down on the thin mattress. "Get off me, you drunk," Hari yelled.

Vishu raised an eyebrow. "Is that what you think? I am a drunk and a thief, is that it?" Clapping his left hand over Hari's mouth, Vishu moved his right arm lower, clawing Hari's torso. "If you ever come in like that again, or tell anyone what you saw here today. . ." Vishu grabbed him by the crotch. Hari sucked his breath in and yelped as Vishu squeezed his genitals, a quick short squeeze followed by a longer harder crush. "I'll make sure that you can't even pee out of this miserable little dick."

Vishu stood up and then snickered at the bulge in Hari's shorts. "Look at you, aroused by a man's touch." He spat to one side.

Hari sat up and covered his crotch with his hands. Silent tears began as he ran out of the room into the back garden. He made his way through the trees to the small space behind the tool shed. There he collapsed, ashamed that his body had betrayed him even as Vishu had violated him.

Hari cupped his hands around his balls. The pain ebbed away. A tabby cat walked atop the compound wall. She came to a stop, looked at Hari and meowed. The top of the brick and concrete boundary wall running around his grandfather's house had sharp pieces of broken brown, green, and clear glass bottles sticking out. They were designed to prevent thieves and robbers from climbing over the wall. The cat, however, was unfazed by the dispersed pieces of broken glass. She grew bored of watching Hari and walked along the wall towards the house.

Hari looked down at his crotch. The bulge was gone. He unzipped his shorts to take a quick peek. There was no blood. He zipped them up and headed back inside.

SEVEN

THAT AFTERNOON, Kollu-thatha came to visit with his grand-daughter Shanthi and her husband Tangarajan. Hari's paathi super-vised the women as they made vadais and bondas in the kitchen for afternoon tea.

"We were married in 1982," Shanthi was telling Sarah. She held an arm out to Hari as he walked in. "Just the day after Hari's sacred thread ceremony. Do you remember me, Hari?"

He nodded shyly at her and retreated to his mother's side.

"Five years, already," Hari's grandmother said. "When are you two going to have a child?"

Shanthi coloured at this.

"Are you trying?" Savitri asked.

Paathi spoke up, "Of course, they are trying. What is the point of marriage if not to produce children?" She addressed Sarah, "You and Mani better have children, lots of them. After all he is the son and our line continues through him."

"Ma!" Savitri's tone was reproachful. "And what about Hari here? Is he not your line too?"

"Of course he is," Paathi's voice was soothing, conciliatory. "But you know it is different with Mani's son."

Sarah stood quietly listening to this exchange.

Paathi looked around her and spoke to Hari, "Go, Kanna, and see if you can find Sivagami. I don't know where she is. I need her to do these dishes."

Hari nodded and headed up the stairs. He arrived panting on the roof, but there was no one there. Wet saris and shirts hung on the clothesline in the hot sun. The roof itself was scorching hot so Hari quickly retreated downstairs. Outside the house, he kept to the shade as he sidled up to Sivagami's door. He didn't dare enter. Inside her quarters, he heard a flurry of movement and then sobbing.

"Sivagami?" He peeked, yet again, into the darkness of her rooms.

She was squatting on her bed, her hand wrapped around her knees. Clothes lay haphazardly on the floor. Seeing Hari enter, Sivagami moaned, "Aiioo, just let me die."

Unprepared for such misery, Hari ran out and into the arms of his grandmother.

"Where have you been?" Paathi asked, on her way towards Sivagami's quarters. "Where is she?"

"No, don't go in there!" Hari cried.

She turned to look at him, her brow furrowed. Then she heard the sobs coming from inside and firmly entered. Hari heard loud crying amidst the exchange of words. His grandmother's tone was forceful, Sivagami's supplicating. Soon his paathi emerged back into the sunlight. "Get your thatha, Hari."

Hari nodded and went unwillingly to the living room. When he returned with Thatha, Mani-mama, and Tangarajan, Hari's paathi described the theft.

"It has to be Vishu," she said.

"We don't know that for sure," Thatha replied.

"Look at her face," Paathi pointed to Sivagami. "She knows it. That's why she was hiding in here, crying. If I hadn't come in, she would never have told us that her own flesh-and-blood had robbed her."

Thatha sighed and turned back. Tangarajan put his arms about Hari's shoulder and they followed him back to the house. Mani-mama helped Paathi take Sivagami into the kitchen. As they reentered the house, Thatha said, "Hari, go get Sundaran. Come, Tangarajan, let's go back inside."

Hari gulped at this command, but nodded nonetheless and ran to the front. His pace slowed as he neared the gates, recalling Vishu's anger and warning. He unlatched the gates, wondering if Vishu would kill him, even if he had nothing to do with the discovery. By the time Hari reached Sundaran's stand, his blood thumped in his ears and his voice quivered in a falsetto.

"Thatha wants to see you," he said to Sundaran.

Sundaran and his nephew sat crouched beside the rickshaw, next to an open box of tools. Vishu, a wrench in hand, smirked at Hari from behind his uncle.

"Finish fixing the rickshaw, will you?" Sundaran ordered Vishu. He stood up and wiped his hands on a dirty rag.

"Mama, I have to be at the Villayam Talkies soon!" Vishu said.

"It'll just be a few minutes. I'll be back soon," Sundaran replied, leading Hari back towards the house.

"Come in, Sundaran, have you heard?" Thatha said without preamble. "Vishu has stolen Sivagami's bangles."

Hari's grandmother stood at the door to the kitchen. Sivagami squatted beside her, flanked by Hari's mother and Shanthi. Kollu-thatha sat on the swing, slurping his tea, while Tangarajan paced the living room. Mani-mama and Sarah-aunty sat to one side, as if to observe the proceedings. He translated the scene in a low voice and she looked anguished at the site of the ancient Sivagami crying uncontrollably.

Sundaran, his voice trembling, joined his hands together in front of Thatha. "Ayya, I have no idea what you are saying."

"Where is he?"

"He's at the rickshaw stand, fixing my motor, Ayya. He was going to the new MGR film in Villayam Talkies but because you called me, I had him watch over the stand, Ayya."

"Sivagami! What did I tell you? Did I not say no more of that damned film club?"

"Ayya, he tried," Sivagami said. "He went yesterday to break with them. But you know what happened afterwards."

"What happened afterwards?" Kollu-thatha asked.

"They painted graffiti on the compound walls this morning," Hari's thatha said.

Kollu-thatha nodded in the silence that followed. "Films have replaced religion for following nowadays."

"The new opium for the masses," Tangarajan joked, but no one laughed.

"Why worship gods, when we can worship the actors who play celluloid gods," Kollu-thatha said. "We should get rid of the whole damned lot."

"Ayya, please don't call the police," Sundaran pleaded.

"No? Why not?" Thatha asked. "If he is part of that MGR fan club, can't he get himself out? What is the point?"

"Oh, he is part of a political organization," Kollu-thatha waved his bony arm at Hari's grandfather. "No, no, we shouldn't get the police involved. It'll only complicate matters."

"Yes, but he stole from his own mother," Hari's grandmother said.

"But we still don't know that for sure, though." Tangarajan opined.

"It doesn't matter," Kollu-thatha said. "He is politically connected—even if he is just a petty film-club member. It's just inviting trouble home."

"Oh, come on. Who else could have done it?" Thatha said.

"Where is he now?" Kollu-thatha asked.

"Minding the rickshaw, shall I get him?" Sundaran replied.

"No, no. Not yet. Let's first decide what we are going to do."

"Ayya, please don't send him to the police," Sivagami begged.

"What can I do?" Thatha raised his hands in a gesture of futility. "He doesn't seem to have changed at all. He doesn't have a job, and he hangs out with that film club of his. What do you want me to do?"

"Send him somewhere, away from Madras, where he can get a job," Kollu-thatha said, turning to Tangarajan. "Let's ask DM, your father. Maybe he can find Vishu a small job in the Railways; send him somewhere safe—Dindigul maybe or Coimbatore."

"I have a better idea," Tangarajan said. "Sundaran bring your nephew."

When Sundaran left to fetch his nephew, Tangarajan explained his idea. He had just finished when a sullen-looking Vishu came into the living room, pushed by a rather fierce-looking Sundaran. Vishu glowered at Hari, who looked away at the tiled floor, afraid to meet his eye.

"Good that you are here. Tangarajan here is related to Savitri's husband," Thatha said, pointing him out to Vishu. "And he is offering you a job."

Vishu's face brightened. "Ayya is very generous. Where is this job?"

"At the Ashok Leyland factory in Ennore," Tangarajan said.

"Ennore? Ayya, can I not stay in Madras?"

Thatha strained to keep his voice calm. "Vishu, it is a good job.

Tangarajan doesn't even know you, and he is offering you a job in a factory. It is just an hour north of here. You should accept it."

"But I can't leave the city. I have to take care of my mother and Sundaran-mama's rickshaw stand."

"We'll manage," Sundaran told him. "I am here to watch out for your mother."

"This is just a scheme to get me out of the city and away from my family," Vishu said.

"Shut your mouth, you thief!" Hari's grandmother shouted. She stepped into the living room and knuckled Vishu on his head. "Shame on you! Stealing from the woman who bore you in her womb for nine months."

Vishu's face darkened with anger at her outburst. He rubbed his head as he stood obdurate in front of the men.

"What is your name again?" Kollu-thatha asked.

"Vishu."

"And where is your father?"

In the uncomfortable silence that followed, Vishu stood defiantly. He glared at the old, withered man on the wooden swing who had posed the question. Kollu-thatha waited for his answer.

"He's dead," Vishu finally said.

"No! Don't say such things," Sivagami said. She turned to Kollu-thatha. "He left us. When Vishu was born."

Kollu-thatha focused on Vishu. "Did you steal your—"

"I don't steal," Vishu whined. "I am not a thief."

"Very well, did you take your mother's gold bangles?"

"So what if I did? Who are you to get involved? What business is it of yours what happens between a mother and her son?"

Sivagami rushed out from her spot next to the wall and slapped Vishu, then pummelled his back with blows until Sundaran intervened and pulled her away. She broke into loud sobs.

"Keep your bloody mouth shut," Sundaran told him. "And listen to your elders, you ingrate."

"Okay, here is the deal," Tangarajan broke in. "You return those bangles you stole from your mother. We'll all forget that this ever happened. You can get a clean start again. I'll arrange for a job in the factory for you. You can get away from your film club and get another shot at making a man of yourself."

"So you can all feel pretty good about yourselves."

"Goddammit!" Thatha said, "we are trying to help you here."

"Why do feel so responsible for me?"

Hari felt the exasperation in his grandfather's voice.

"You are so cocky because you think that if I get the police to arrest you, you can get your film friends to release you. I know how the film business is linked to politics. But I can lock you in the cellar here and you'll rot under this house. No one will even know you existed."

"Vishu-kanna, please, for my sake," Sivagami pleaded from where she sat slumped on the floor. "Take the offer and go to Ennore. They will look after you. Don't worry about the bangles. Just go."

As he listened to the plaintive broken voice of the old maid, Hari wanted to run and hide somewhere. He slowly inched back till he felt the solid wall behind him. Then his knees gave out under him and he slid down the wall to the cool, tiled floor. His hands folded around his knees, Hari buried his head in his lap to block Sivagami's distress.

"Harry?" It was Sarah, kneeling next to him. "Show me the garden."

Hari shook his head.

"Please?" She cocked her head at him.

They walked out of the room, leaving the mess and drudgery of life behind. The afternoon sun had sunk behind the house, so they walked in the shade as he showed her the rose bushes. Sarah bent close to the roses and inhaled deeply.

"You shouldn't smell them," Hari said.

"Why not?"

"Paathi uses them for her puja. They are offerings to the gods. If we smell them, they are spoiled."

She nodded uncertainly, then pointed to the whitewashed compound wall. "What happened there?"

Hari lowered his voice, a concession to the mob. "They don't like it that I speak Hindi."

"I thought the language riots were over," she said.

Hari looked puzzled. "What language riots?"

"You don't know?" She seemed surprised. "But I suppose you are too young. I studied it in a history course. The southern states rebelled when the federal government tried to make Hindi the national language."

"But it is the national language."

"In name, yes," Sarah nodded. "But there are still so many other languages around. And that is good thing, I think."

They walked back to the house. Hari remembered that Anamika spoke Bengali at home; Mohan spoke Gujarati. Hindi and English were their languages of communication.

"I'm sorry about that," Hari gestured to the house. "That was not the welcome we had planned."

"Overwhelming," she said. Her eyes strayed back to the compound wall. "But why are you sorry about it? It's not your fault."

"Everything is so messy," Hari said, leading her to the back garden. "Not like the families in the English books. I wish we were like that."

She laughed. "I would give anything to have your family, Harry."

"It's pronounced 'hurry,'" he told her, "not Harry."

"Oh, I'm sorry."

They stood under the mango tree contemplating the green fruit hanging among the leaves.

"I've never seen a mango tree before," she said.

Hari reached to pull a leaf. It tore. He smelled the fragment and offered it to her. She sniffed the astringent essence of unripe mango with approval, and crumpled the leaf so that the fragrance lingered in her hand.

She sat on a large stone and arranged the kameez around her knees. "Shall I tell you a secret?"

Hari came closer.

"Soon you will have a cousin," she told him.

Hari looked at her tummy. "You're pregnant?"

She laughed. "No, not I. Your aunt Kalyani in Toronto. She's going to have a baby around Christmas."

Hari nodded without feeling. The baby was abstract, an idea in his mind. Kalyani and Ramesh had been gone for four years. Toronto was a faraway place, their faces a dim memory.

"They were supposed to come with us for the summer, you know?" Sarah continued. "To ease my introduction. But now that she's pregnant, she'll be coming in December to have her baby. I have to fend for myself."

"Do you love my Mani-mama?" Hari asked, as he pointed out the coconuts hanging in bunches high above them.

"How old are you?"

"Eleven."

"And what do you know about love?" The question was gentle, the tone cajoling.

Hari shrugged. "My mother says that it comes later in an arranged marriage."

"She disapproves of Mani marrying me," Sarah said, her hand straying to the silver anklets that Savitri had given her as a gift.

Hari looked to the house. The evening rays of the sun painted the back walls orange. "Thatha thinks that she just misses not being involved...in marrying Mani-mama off."

Sarah cupped her face in her hands and watched Hari. "You are telling me what other people think," she said. "What do you think?"

Hari suddenly felt shy. He retreated to the trunk of the coconut tree and let his hands graze the grooves. "I think that you are very nice."

She smiled at this, and Hari noticed that her teeth were large, white, and straight, like a movie star's.

EIGHT

AT THE END of the summer, Hari's return to Nagpur coincided with the arrival of the monsoon. Thick black clouds arriving from the south west horizon darkened the landscape. The birds fled to the safety of trees, cawing and chirping at the lightning and thunder overhead. Then, just before the first raindrops arrived, pungent petrichor rose up from the parched earth. This interlude of sounds, sights, and smells turned the season. For the next few weeks, it rained. Curtains of water fell from the sky and washed away the clay and mud—beaten to dust in the summer heat. As the water soaked through the dirt and swelled the soil, it drove up, first, bright red earthworms and, later, small green shoots.

Through all this, Kabir came each morning. His rickshaw, now covered with thick plastic, ferried the kids to a new year of school. The three children squirmed together trying to remain in the centre, away from the rain that lashed against them in all directions. Kabir, a rubber cap atop his head, wore his usual cotton kurta over his stained pyjamas. Girish bought him a cheap set of plastic raingear; Kabir wore it once and then set it aside, complaining that it made him feel too hot.

During the first weeks of school, the three children entertained each other with stories from the summer. Hari won the game of one-upmanship with tales of his new American aunt. Mohan envied his remote control car and Hari let him play with it while Anamika taught him chess moves. Anamika had changed since the holidays, Hari realized. He had also grown over the holidays; wisps of hair had sprouted under his armpits and between his legs, though not yet on his chin. But she seemed more mature, felt older. Sometimes, the two boys seemed to annoy her, other times she mothered them so much that Mohan would stomp off to play with the other boys. At such times Hari felt that their time as a trio was coming to a close.

The end came on Gokulashtami, the birthday of Lord Krishna, when Hari's mother kicked him out of the house. She was busy cleaning the house and drawing tiny imprints of child-size feet on the tiled floor. Later that evening Hari would trace these child steps from the door to the puja room, enacting the arrival of Lord Krishna to their house.

He sauntered down the laneway towards Anamika's house, his hands stuck in his shorts, trying to whistle. She laughed at the wheezy sounds from his puckered lips.

"Come, here," she said, holding his hand and dragging him to the side of the house.

In the shade between the two houses, under a young papaya tree, the contents of a first-aid box lay spread among the grass and dirt.

"What are you doing?" Hari said, as she sat down.

"It's a hospital. Remember how you said you wanted to be a doctor?"

"But we are too old to play doctor-doctor," Hari said.

"But this is not just any old clinic. It's a field hospital," Anamika told him. "You're an army doctor and I'm the nurse."

Hari laughed. "Well, then there isn't much to do. We need a patient, Anamika. I'll get Mohan."

"No," Anamika said. "Can't we just play, the two of us?"

"Did you fight with him again?" Hari asked. He squatted down, flushed with burning pleasure. She had chosen him.

"I'll be the patient," she said. "Here, record my heartbeat with your hand here."

Hari looked at where she placed her hand, between the twin mounds that had risen over the summer on her chest. He shook his head.

"Give me your hand. I saw this on TV," Hari said; taking her wrist in his hand, probing. "There are these doctors in Ladakh who can diagnose everything just by listening to the pulse."

"What's wrong with me, doctor?" Anamika spoke in a false voice, sounding tremulous, in mortal fear.

Hari recalled the deep voice of Dr Gupta. "My dear girl, your problem is that you are dead. There is no pulse."

"Be serious," she said, after they had recovered from their laughter. "Let's play properly. Say that I have rheumatoid arthritis."

"What's that?" Hari asked.

"My grandmother has it," Anamika said. "She needs injections of penicillin. Every six months."

"Okay," Hari shrugged. "You have room-a-toyed art-right-is. I'll have to poke you with a needle, little girl." Dr Gupta's voice had returned.

"Here." Anamika handed him a thin bamboo twig.

Hari leaned forward to stick the needle in her arm.

"No," Anamika said, "that's not where you stick needles for arthritis."

Hari's hand trembled. The fever in her voice boded ill. She turned to face him and lifted her skirt to reveal the fair skin of her thighs underneath, then the flash of white panties. He looked up at her. Her eyes were fixed at him, determined. She hooked her thumb underneath the soft fabric and began pulling the panties down.

Hari dropped the needle and fled, his chest heaving. She called out his name, but he fled without looking back towards the maidan where the boys played cricket. Among them, he would be safe. At the pitch, Sameer was bowling and Bunty was batting. Mohan stood up from his wicketkeeper's crouch as Hari ran onto the field and fell on the ground, gasping.

"What's wrong?" Mohan asked, rushing up to his friend.

"Water," Hari gestured to the bottles laid behind the stump.

He drank as the boys gathered around him, upset at the interruption.

"Sorry, I just ran all the way," Hari said. "Can I play?"

Sameer and Bunty looked at each other.

"C'mon, let him play with us," Mohan said to Bunty, who was the leader.

Sameer nodded. "Yeah, take him."

Bunty didn't look happy. But he shrugged and pointed to the far corner of the maidan. "Outfield," he said.

Hari nodded and walked off. He needed time to think, perhaps even to talk to Mohan. Running away was a bad idea, he thought, but what could he have done instead? He wished he had known what to do. It felt wrong, but out in the field, watching the game, Hari wanted to be back there, in the dark shade among the houses, next to Anamika.

Mohan was yelling and waving the bat at him. Hari ran up to the pitch.

"Your turn to bat," Mohan called. Then he drew closer and muttered, "Don't embarrass me."

Hari nodded, took the bat, and stood in front of the wicket. Sameer rubbed the ball against his shorts. It was a regular cricket ball, not a tennis ball, like they used at school. He became nervous of the red ball, it was heavy and could hurt.

Sameer ran up to his lone wicket and bowled. The ball flew towards Hari, bouncing off the hard ground. Hari brought his bat up like a shield, the ball clipped it and tumbled off to the side.

"Swing at it," Mohan hissed from behind the wicket.

Hari turned to nod, but his gaze was diverted by a group of men marching in formation at the far end of the field. They were dressed in white shirts and starched khaki shorts, like policemen. Except for the two older men who led them, they all looked college-aged. Each carried a laathi, like the sticks carried by policemen.

Behind him, Hari heard Sameer groan. Slowly the boys out in the field herded towards the pitch and Mohan stood up, stopping the game. The boys drew close in their group and watched the invaders.

"They were here two days ago too," Bunty said.

The men spread out and began exercising with their laathis, mimicking blocks, thrusts, and blows. One of the older men kept time in military style with short bursts of a whistle while the other walked around the troop inspecting their movements. He beckoned to the kids and came striding towards them.

"We're playing," Hari said.

"Play if you must." He waved away Hari's protest. "Play that British game...or, if you like, you can join us in some Hindustani exercises like these patriots." He spoke in chaste Hindi and pointed to the uniformed men behind him.

"Who are you?" Mohan asked.

"And what are you doing on our playground?" Sameer said.

"The maidan belongs to the municipality," the man said, speaking like a teacher. "It belongs to all people. It is not meant for little kids to dig up with their cricket stumps. Now look at those men, don't they look dashing in their uniforms, and strong, performing together?"

Hari nodded. He felt the allure of their coordinated movements. It reminded him of troops on parade. He looked around and saw the other boys watching the men practise with the same awe. Mohan tapped his arm and pointed. Anamika stood at one edge of the playground, beckoning to him.

Hari walked reluctantly up to her.

"It's the RSS," she said, shaking her head towards the intruding men.

"I know," Hari said, avoiding her eyes.

"My mother says they are very bad. They killed Mahatma Gandhi, you know."

"Is that Mohan's brother?" Hari looked over.

"You're not listening." She stamped her foot.

"I am." Hari turned away from her, looked at the troop closely. "Listen, I think that's Mohan's brother with them. It can't be that bad if he's in there."

She looked at him closely. "You won't say anything, will you?"

Hari shook his head and returned to the group. The man was speaking to the boys.

"We train young people like you to be strong and ready to serve the nation should something bad happen. Be ready to fight and help out if something like Sri Lanka happens here or if Pakistan decides to do something foolish."

"Are you going to come every day?" Bunty asked.

"We will practise three days a week here. Come, you kids can exercise with us. It will build your strength."

"But we don't have laathis or uniforms," Hari said. He looked back towards Anamika. She was walking away.

"You don't need laathis and uniforms, not yet, anyway. Right now I just want strong souls. Come, practise with us. Use your bats and stumps if you like."

A mad rush ensued for the stumps and bats, then the boys ran behind the man. The young men in uniforms stopped their movements and smiled as the former cricketers took positions behind them and began mimicking them. Hari's face fell as he realized that Mohan's brother was not part of the group. Rajaram, the man who had invited the boys to join, now moved among them, helping them take up the proper postures and movements.

Despite what he knew about the RSS—that it was a right-wing Hindu organization, that one of its members had assassinated Mahatma Gandhi, that it often stoked the communal riots and fights which broke out periodically throughout India—Hari felt happy in that little troop of men exercising on the maidan. He felt a sense of belonging despite the ragtag assortment they were as a company. There was a unity in their purpose and a certain grace in their movements that he found enjoyable.

But it came to an end all too soon. Mrs Mukherjee's voice carried out to the kids. She raced towards them in her bright yellow starched Bengali sari, her face dark with rage despite the festive decorations on her. Her sari lost its grace from the careless speed at which she bore down on them.

"Chalo, Hari, Sameer, Mohan, come on everyone, time to go home. Let's go, let's go," she said and shepherded the kids away. The short bursts of the whistle stopped, and the young men, interrupted in their drill, turned to look at this woman, wild despite her festive garb.

Rajaram joined his hands together. "Namasté, Maaji."

"Don't you Maaji me; I know what you are doing here." Mukherjee-aunty stood in front of Rajaram, her arms spread out like a fence separating the kids from him. She had spoken in English. Rajaram's face darkened.

"They are just exercising, soon it will be finished, then you take them home," he replied in Hindi.

"Exercise," said Mrs Mukherjee. "You only build strong bodies with weak minds."

"Madam, no need to insult," Rajaram said in a heavily accented English, then reverted to Hindi. "You don't hear me making comments about godless communism in Bengal."

Mrs Mukherjee seemed taken aback for an instant. Instead of replying, she turned her back on him and pushed the young boys away from the playground, towards the colony.

"A festival is not just about making rossogollas and sandesh and eating sweets, one must also follow one's duties to one's religion everyday," a young man in the troop called out.

Mrs Mukherjee turned red in the face, but kept walking. "Chalo, hurry, hurry. We should all get back home. It is not safe here anymore."

Back in the colony, she dispersed the children. Hari walked back home with her, for she lived three houses past his. She led him up the verandah, where his mother, sitting on her haunches, was drawing a kolam on the floor. Her hands were white with rice powder, and Hari thought that she looked beautiful, dressed in her deep red Kancheevaram silk sari with its foot-high gold border.

She looked up and smiled guardedly at Mukherjee-aunty.

"Savitri, you wouldn't believe what happened just now," Mukherjee-aunty said.

"What did he do now?" Savitri's smile vanished.

"Hari? Nothing, but the RSS is here."

Savitri stood up and peered out into the lane. "Where?"

"Not here, Savitri. In the maidan," Mrs Mukherjee said. "They were trying to recruit the children."

"What do you mean?" She turned to Hari. "What were you doing?"

Hari explained.

"First it is discipline, they say. Then they start spewing their bad philosophy," Mrs Mukherjee interrupted. "Savitri, we have to stop them."

"I don't know, Lata. This kid could use some order in his life. Maybe the discipline would be good for him, you know?"

"No, no...I cannot believe you would even think about such a thing..."

"Why not?"

"They are a bunch of religious fanatics, that's why."

"Oh, don't say that, Lata. You are just saying that because..." Savitri trailed off, and she changed topics. "Look at your sari, Lata. Such a beautiful sari all crumpled from worrying and marching around. Enough with the rallies, no? Secularism will thrive, despite our festivals and foolishness."

"Sending one's child to them is like pushing it in front of a truck." And with that parting shot, Mrs Mukherjee stormed down the steps.

Savitri sighed and pointed to the gate that Mrs Mukherjee had left unlatched on her way out. "Go close the gate, Hari."

A few days after this confrontation, Hari turned twelve. Waking up that morning, Hari hurried to the verandah where Girish was reading the morning paper.

"Happy birthday, champ," Girish said. The paper rustled as he folded it and held out his arms.

Unwilling and awkward, Hari let his father hug him. "Dad, can I ask you something?"

"Sure."

"Will you give me thirty rupees?"

Girish leaned back in his chair. "Why?"

"I want to take Mohan to see *The Towering Inferno* at Lakshmi Talkies," Hari said.

"But I thought you are having a party here this evening," Girish replied. "Your mother is already in the kitchen preparing."

"Not today," Hari said. "Later this week, maybe Friday."

"What does your mother say?"

"You know she'll say no. Please, Daddy."

"Hari, I am very busy now. You know that we are having problems with the electrification." Girish's voice sounded reasonable, tinged with regret. "I don't have time to take you to the movies."

"You don't have to. Kabir can drive us from school to the cinema and then back home."

Girish laughed. "I don't think Kabir enjoys American films."

"He doesn't have to see it then," Hari said.

"And what are we going to tell your mother?"

"I'll tell her that I will be at Mohan's house for the evening," Hari smiled, "studying."

Girish shook his head as he drew a twenty-rupee and two five-rupee notes out of his wallet. "No good will come of lying to your mother, Hari."

"Just a little white lie," Hari assured him, pocketing the money. "Thanks, Dad."

On Monday, Hari announced his plans in the rickshaw.

"What about me?" Anamika said, crossing her arms over her chest. "How am I supposed to get home?"

"You can go home in Sameer or Bunty's rickshaw," Mohan answered.

"Why can't I come with you?"

"No, no," Kabir broke in. "It's not right for a young girl like you to go to the movies with boys. People will talk."

She pouted, and Hari shrugged. "Kabir," he asked. "Do you think we'll have enough time to go to Haldiram's restaurant before the movie?"

"What time is the movie, Baba?" Kabir turned, letting the rickshaw coast on the road.

"Seven, I think," Mohan said and turned to Hari for confirmation.

Kabir wiped the sweat off his brow as he braked the rickshaw. "Should be all right...but what am I to do when you are in the theatre?"

"You can come and watch the film," Hari said. "I'll pay for your ticket."

"No, Baba," Kabir said and shook his head. "I don't understand those Inglis films. Now if it was a good Hindi film, then I would definitely come with you."

"What about *Ram teri Ganga maili*?" Mohan said, turning to Hari, "Let's go to see that instead!"

"We can't go see that film, it's rated U/A," Hari replied.

"Well Kabir is an adult, he can buy the tickets and take us in," Mohan countered.

"It's a good movie," Kabir said, "I've seen it many times. Much better than any Hollywood film. And it's playing at Metro, right next to Haldiram's."

"What do you say?" Mohan asked.

Hari shrugged. "If you want..."

"I'll tell your mother," Anamika spoke up from her corner. "I'll tell her that you are going to see a dirty film."

Hari pounced on her and pinched her. As she yelped, he whispered, "And I'll tell Mohan about the dirty patient."

She rubbed her arm to ease the pain. Biting her lip, she looked out the rickshaw away from them. Kabir had turned too late to see Hari's attack, and as Anamika refused to respond to his questions, he could do little but drive on.

Mohan pointed to the billboard advertisement for *Ram teri Ganga maili* as they rode to school. The film, playing for over two years to packed crowds everywhere, was ostensibly about the river Ganga. The title invoked Lord Rama complaining that his holy river was polluted. But the beautiful woman dressed like a courtesan belied this suggestion. Mandakini, the heroine of the movie, seemed more like a prostitute than a penitent on the billboards.

That Friday, the two boys drank the sweet, milky tea and ate the hot chole-baturas at Haldiram's restaurant. They were excited not only because of the film but also because they had both lied to their parents. Mohan was spending the evening at Hari's place, while Hari was doing homework at Mohan's as far as their mothers knew. In their excitement and nervousness, they barely ate the large baturas that Haldiram's was famous for.

Kabir waited for them by the Metro Talkies, an old art-deco theatre, a holdover from a grander age of Indian cinema. Mohan and Hari grabbed their tickets and ran up the large, curving staircase to the balcony section, oblivious of the ornate beauty of the cinema house. At the balcony level an elderly man in a faded uniform stood slouching by the door. He punched their tickets and led them to their seats with the aid of a pencil flashlight.

In the dark theatre, the boys sat enthralled by the musical drama unfolding on the screen. They laughed at the young hero's antics in the foothills of the Himalayas as he fell in love with the naïve mountain girl Ganga. The pleasure Hari felt when Ram, the hero, married Ganga gave way to worry as he left her alone and returned home to Calcutta. Then, during the scene where the heroine was tricked into a brothel in Gangotri, Hari shrank into his seat, afraid for her. Mohan must have felt the same, because he reached out and clasped Hari's knee. Hari flinched and pulled his friend's fingers off his leg. They held each other tight until the harsh notes of the music faded and the next scene began. Hari let Mohan's hand fall and it lay over Hari's thigh. When the heroine finally escaped and got on the train to Benaras, Mohan leaned over and whispered into Hari's ears, "Your leg feels nice and cool."

Hari nodded and smiled. "My thigh is always cool. It feels good to run my palm across it and under my calf during the summer."

"Really? Mine isn't." Mohan's hand remained on Hari's thigh.

Hari recalled the episode in the shade with Anamika. His attention was divided between the film and the warmth of Mohan's palm on his thigh. He squirmed a little in his seat and the hand moved higher until it touched the hem of his shorts. An unnamed desire swelled through him and Hari felt his penis stiffen within his shorts. Hari sat up to hide his excitement but Mohan's fingers gently brushed over the bulge in Hari's shorts as he withdrew his hand to the armrest.

Hari held his breath, unsure if the fondling was deliberate or accidental. He dared not look at Mohan; instead, he stared straight ahead at the screen. The heroine, now trapped in a brothel in Benaras, danced across the screen in a skimpy costume. Mohan's leg rubbed against Hari's. Hari turned to look at Mohan, but his eyes were fixed on the screen. Hari let his hand fall on Mohan's leg. It remained there, unmoving for the rest of the film.

Below the two boys in their balcony section, Kabir sat in the crowded cinema floor among the rough-and-tumble men. A few days' growth on their faces, they sat tightly packed on the wooden benches, smoked hand-rolled bidis, and adored the clean-shaven, slim hero in his alpine hat and suede leather jacket. The labourers and peons laughed with the hero, cried out at the villains, and whistled at the heroine, aping the filmi image of manhood. Mohan and Hari, entranced by the same scenes, feeling the same exultation as the crowd below them, remained unable to voice it in their chaste, upper balcony. Instead, they merely played with their hands and fingers in the darkness, in the rexine-covered, coir-filled seats of the family section.

III
Pacam (attachment)

NINE

IT WAS CHRISTMAS EVE, 1987.

At Nagpur Central Station, the soft female voice over the PA system announced the arrival of the 2622 DN Tamil Nadu Express. As the announcement was repeated in chaste Hindi and vernacular Marathi over the loudspeaker, Hari came down from the overpass, through the bustle of people preparing to depart. He found his mother on the bench where he'd left her, splayed across their luggage, her sari askew, exposing her navel, reading *Femina*. She looked at him for a moment and returned to her reading.

"So, did they let you climb inside an engine?" She flipped a page.

"Not this time."

"Not ever…when will you learn?"

"Dad promised that one day he would make them take me."

"Your father's promises…when will you learn not to take him on his word? Besides, you are growing up. You can't keep scampering around the station."

Hari shrugged and stood at the edge of the platform, waiting for the train that would take them to Madras. His aunt Kalyani had returned from Canada to have her first child.

"Do you think she's brought toys like Mani-mama and Sarah aunty did?"

Savitri pushed against the suitcase to stand up. "Kalyani? Probably. But don't go asking her. She was probably very busy dealing with her pregnancy."

"I wrote to Sarah-aunty, you know," Hari said. "I asked her to send a remote-controlled plane with Kalyani-chitti. I hope she remembered."

"You didn't!" His mother sounded angry. "You don't ask for gifts. That's rude. She'll think that we are beggars, asking for this and that."

"No, she won't," Hari said. He left out the fact that Sarah had asked him to send her his wish list. It would be pretty cold up there now, he thought, what with Christmas tomorrow. If it hadn't been for Christmas vacations at his school, he couldn't have travelled with his mother on this unexpected winter vacation to Madras. His father, yet again, could not come along for the trip.

"Where is that damned coolie?" Savitri looked up and down the platform.

The coolie, who had carried their luggage to the platform, was bound to return, for he would not be paid till the luggage was settled in the carriage. Hari craned his neck and watched the gently sloping nose of the brown engine bend away from the main tracks and curve towards the platform.

"It's here," he said, hurrying towards his mother.

The coolie came strolling along the platform. He bent down and swept up their suitcase on to his turbaned head, Savitri's agitation having little effect upon him. Hari gathered the remaining bags and rushed alongside the slowing train. The coolie walked and chewed with the same ferocious calmness, striding deftly past the knots of chattering people and baggage congregated on the platform, while Savitri and Hari struggled behind him.

At the door of their bogie, he waited for Hari's mother to scan the lined sheet of paper printed with the names and reserved berth numbers of the passengers.

"Are your names on…" the coolie asked, nodding towards the list.

"Four and five," Hari's mother said.

He found an opening through the disembarking crowd, clambered up the stairs, and disappeared inside. Their way in was blocked by an ample woman, fat bulging through her tight cotton blouse. As she negotiated the steps down the train, she rasped, and with a rolled magazine batted away the impatient crowd trying to get in. Behind her, the coolie stood waiting for them, his hands refashioning his long red cotton scarf into a turban to help carry another load.

Their berths were in the ladies' cubicle.

It was a small enclosed space—a long berth seating three on either side—located within a regular second-class sleeper coach. It had two windows facing the outside, and a door which opened to the side corridor running along the length of the coach. This door could be locked from the inside. The door and windows came equipped with shutters to afford privacy, especially to traditional, burkha-clad Muslim women travelling in the trains. Usually one would have to request such a berth, but since they were travelling without adult male escort, they had been afforded the privilege by a thoughtful ticket clerk.

Hari could care less, as long as he had a window seat. He looked at the two other occupants in the cubicle. They looked like a mother and daughter. The younger woman, dressed in a blue shalwar-kameez, sat in the window seat across from Hari. Her knees folded on the berth, her arm resting on the window sill, her face stuck against the window bars, she watched the platform and ignored the two new arrivals. The mother sat next to her daughter in the middle of their berth. She grabbed the shawl closer across her shoulders and smiled at Hari and his mother as they stumbled in with their luggage. She stretched out her hand to support Savitri's hand basket.

"Careful, dear," she said. "You might spill it."

Her accent gave her away as a Punjabi, the way her Hindi was soft and sprinkled with diminutives. Hari's mother thanked her before setting the basket, more slowly this time, on the red linoleum floor of the coach.

"Ahh," Hari's mother sighed and spoke in Hindi, "...so nice to settle down and finally get going."

"I know," the woman said, nodding. "Thank God the train is running on time."

"Have you been travelling long?"

"All the way from Delhi and down to Madras."

Savitri puckered her lips into an O and sucked in air in a gesture of sympathy.

"My son is in the hospital," the woman said. "What can I do, Béta? Life is so cruel to us?"

"What happened?" Savitri laid down her *Femina*.

"Ceylon," the woman said. "My son Suresh is a captain in the army. He was in Jaffna with the Indian Peace Keeping Force there."

"Oh," Savitri leaned forward. "I heard in the news that the LTTE rebels broke the ceasefire in Sri Lanka and began fighting in Jaffna."

The woman nodded her head. "That was it. My son was stationed there. They shot him." She started sobbing. "He goes there to keep the peace, and they shoot him."

"Ma," her daughter turned around and stroked her head. "It's all right. He'll be fine. Don't cry."

"Is he hurt seriously?" Savitri asked the daughter.

The young woman shook her head. "In the leg," she said.

"Madras has the best hospitals," Savitri said to the woman in a reassuring voice. "You'll see. He'll be fine in no time."

"That's what Suman says too," the elderly woman pointed to her daughter. "But I won't be happy until I bring him back to Delhi with us. Home is home after all."

No one could argue with that. Suman smiled wanly, then stared out through her window onto the busy platform. Hari's mother nodded in silence and reached below the seat to retrieve their thermos. Hari shook his head when she proffered it, so she lifted it and, raising it above her mouth, without letting it touch her lips, drank some water. It was their way.

"You're Brahmins," the woman said.

"Ji," Savitri acknowledged.

"We're Hindu Punjabis," the woman said and looked at Hari. "What's your name, Béta?"

"Hari," he said, looking around their little cubicle. There were two free seats. Outside the cubicle two folding seats formed a side berth in the corridor. Hari noted the trunk and suitcase shoved under the side berth, suggesting that someone had occupied that seat.

Hari's mother reached past him to toggle the fan switch. Nothing happened. There wasn't much light inside either.

"They were working before," the Punjabi woman said.

"It'll turn on soon," Hari said in English. "They are switching the twin diesels with an electrical engine."

"Such a smart boy, no?" the woman said. "He seems to know a lot about trains."

"He is in love with the railway," Hari's mother said, shaking her head. "Thank God he no longer wants to grow up and be an engine driver or a station master. You know how children are."

"Hello," Hari said, waving his hand in front of his mother's face. "I'm right here. Do you mind not talking about me like I am not here?" He spoke in English.

Suman turned and laughed at his protest.

"Don't put your hands in front of me," Savitri said irritably. "It's rude."

"Well, it's rude to talk about people like they don't exist," Hari replied, crossing his arms over his chest. He looked away from his mother and out the window. Through the corner of his eye he could see Suman still smiling at him. He wasn't sure if she was smiling at his perceived childishness or at his discomfort. Suddenly, her eyes were drawn away from him. Hari turned and craned his neck to look in the same direction. Through his window, Hari could see much of the platform. There really wasn't anything out of the ordinary.

"What were you looking at?" he asked Suman.

"Me?" she looked surprised and shook her head. "Nothing."

A young man came and took his seat on the berth outside their little cubicle. He was dressed in black from head to toe. Hari had never seen anyone dressed so completely in black before. It seemed as if his intent was to draw attention to his body. He reminded Hari of Mohan's brother, who was in college and constantly talking about girls. But unlike Mohan's brother, who still looked silly despite the pomaded hair and expensive clothes, the attire accentuated this young man's looks.

His jet black hair was glossy and wavy. He had a pleasant clean-shaven face, with rugged features sharper than the soft boyish faces of the pretty Bollywood stars. His shirt was of a material that glimmered despite its darkness. The top button was undone and Hari could see the rise of the clavicles, the thin gold necklace that hung between them, and the hair that rose from under the shirt.

Hari's mother snorted. "Does he think he is a film star?" she whispered.

Suman snickered. She leaned forward and replied in a low voice, "He's been on the train since Gwalior, takes out a comb every half hour to style his hair."

"What?" Savitri said. "Not enough Brylcreem?"

The two women laughed.

Hari wasn't sure how to respond to the women's mockery. He studied the man. He must have been a gymnast to have such a body. It was not heavy and overdone with blocks of muscles, like a wrestler's, nor was it effete and feline like those of the Bolshoi ballet dancers, who had appeared on national television earlier that year, performing at the Festival of the Soviet Union. His body was appropriately filmi—the rising sloping pectorals, the triangular torso that curved down to a small hip, and muscular legs which bulged against the tight fabric of his pants. This was a young man aspiring to be a Bollywood hero and imitating the galaxy of stars that included Amitabh Bachchan, Mithun Chakraborthy, Anil Kapoor, and Aamir Khan.

The man looked up from the Bollywood fan magazine in his hands and gazed into their compartment. Savitri turned away from him and spoke to the Punjabi woman, "It is difficult travelling alone nowadays…"

"Everything is difficult for us women alone," the woman, whose name was Mrs Sharma, replied. "Ever since Suman's father passed away three years ago, I have realized how much a man takes care of, and how he protects us from the vagaries of the world."

"Oh! I am so sorry to hear that. What happened?"

"Béta, don't ask. Life is so cruel. Rioting…poor man. We're Hindu Punjabis, not even Sikhs, but still they killed him two days after Indira Gandhi died," she said, her eyes tearing.

"Revenge," Savitri nodded. "People say that the government gave out the addresses of Sikhs to Hindu mobs. I find that hard to believe."

"Believe it, Béta," Mrs Sharma slapped the seat for emphasis. "Pure evil times they were. Suman's father was returning from the store; we had a clothing shop in Connaught Circle then. Suresh was a lieutenant in the army, but he could do nothing to save his own father. They beat him to a pulp with their laathis…they didn't care…"

Suman turned to put her hands around her mother as she broke down. The woman dabbed her eyes with her shawl and smiled. "It's okay, Béta," she said. "I'll be fine…what can I do, first He takes away my husband, and now my only son is lying in hospital. God is trying me, what can I say."

"One cannot do anything when fate intervenes," Hari's mother leaned forward to squeeze the old woman's knees. "And politics is just madness."

"Yes, you are right." The gold bangles on the woman's arm rattled as she caressed her daughter's hair. "Of course it would have been so much better if Suresh's father had handed Suman off in marriage before he died, poor girl."

"Ma," Suman said.

The lights came on, the fans began spinning, and a slight jolt backwards signalled the arrival of the new engine. Within minutes, the PA system came alive to proclaim the imminent departure of the train. The people queuing around the water coolers on the platform broke ranks to mass around the few taps as they sought to fill their thermoses. Then the train glided along the tracks, gathering speed behind the electric locomotive, without the perceptible jerks produced by the older diesel engines. His face against the rust-smelling window bars, Hari watched the platform disappear behind them. One by one, each adjacent track merged with theirs, accompanied by the loud clanking of the wheels. Soon they were beyond the rail yard, just the two tracks of the main line heading west, then south.

TEN

PAST THE RAILWAY yards of Nagpur, the train trundled through hutments and slums. Hari recalled Kollu-thatha's outburst. That trip to Benaras, barely a year old now, seemed so long ago.

"This is our third train trip this year," he said to his mother.

She looked at him, "So?"

Hari shrugged. "I just realized that." He returned to the scenery outside his window. The sweet stench of garbage and wood smoke from the shantytowns cleared as winter crops of wheat and cotton and groves of orange trees filled the landscape. Sometimes, without warning, a train barrelled past on the far side of the coach, where the UP tracks ran alongside theirs. At the noise, Hari would turn to look through the window on that side, next to the filmi man. Sometimes it was a long goods train, the rust-red and tan-green cars fleeing past in a blur of colour, at other times it was a passenger train and for a fleeting moment Hari would get a look into other coaches, at the travellers making their way north.

Hari turned away from the window to look at his mother dozing, her magazine open at the same page she had been reading on the platform at Nagpur Central. The filmi man got up from his seat and walked towards the middle of the coach. Hari slid into his shoes, leaving the laces untied. Mrs Sharma looked up as he slid out into the corridor. Three steps later, he was in the vestibule. The sounds of the train were louder here and the wind whipped in from the open doors on either side of him.

Then, he saw her. Her arms were slender and fine, though her skin was very dark. Her thick hair was pitch black and tied into a neat bun at the back, with coral jasmines braided around it. There was a trace of red kumkum powder where the furrow of the parting met her forehead, and under the kumkum, a short greyish white stripe of holy ash on her forehead. A small golden earring dangled from an earlobe. An electric blue sari was draped loosely on her thin frame, over a blue cotton blouse. She squatted atop a small red suitcase, next to the toilets, in the corridor that led to the umbilical linking the coaches. A woven bamboo basket stood next to her.

"Oii, look at this young lad staring at me. Want a little suckee?" She spoke in coarse Hindi, little drops of betel juice flying out of her mouth, the skin around her eyes crinkling as she laughed. Her hands reached up into the air towards Hari, and her palms came together in a clap, fingers extended. It was the typical gesture of the hijra.

Hari stepped back as he realized that she was a eunuch. Her disguise perfect, he had failed to notice the man in the pretty woman. Here was a man more feminine than masculine, more dark than fair, more comely than muscular, and despite all this, he found her rather pretty. He stared in confusion at her, noticed the smell despite the jasmine flowers braided in her hair.

"What are you, dumb?" She beckoned him with her hand, "Come here, laddie."

Hari shook his head. "I'm not stupid. I know who you are."

"He speaks," she announced, looking around as if at an imaginary audience.

"What are you doing here?" Hari said.

She frowned. "What? Is this your father's train? What do you care what I do here?"

Cowed, Hari leaned against the Formica-lined wall. "I didn't mean anything."

"If you didn't mean anything, then keep your mouth shut," she said and turned away. "Maybe it was better before he started speaking," she announced.

He wanted to come out with something caustic but words failed him. This bizarre wretch was permitted her idiocies because she was a hijra—impotent, castrated—neither male nor female, her head filled with superstitious nonsense as she was simultaneously revered and reviled.

He looked through the door where he had intended to stand. The coach swayed from side to side as the train flew past a tiny mud post next to a small road crossing. A gaunt man in a ferocious white moustache stood stiffly to attention as the train passed. The guard wore a khaki Gandhi-cap and a khaki shirt over his shorts, green and red flags rolled under his armpits. He was barefoot. Smoke rose from under the thatched roofs of a settlement. Cows reclined on dung-layered clean courtyards chewing cud, oblivious to the train thundering past them under the catenated wires.

Hari sighed and returned to his cubicle.

Savitri looked up at him as he entered. "Where did you go?"

"Nowhere."

"Don't lie to me," she said. "You were standing at the door. I've told you before not to do that. What if you fell? How can you be so cruel to your own mother?"

He let her wear herself out. Her censure, so oft-repeated, had begun to lose all meaning. Instead, crouched by the window, Hari watched the posts of concrete and steel fly by the tracks. The posts, labelled zero through forty-nine, whipped past for every kilometre travelled, containing the train and controlling its movements: the live wire above, the tracks below, the odd numbered girders for the UP track and the even numbered for the DOWN track. Parameters that allowed some engineer sitting in an air-conditioned building in a city somewhere to know where they were on their long journey south.

ELEVEN

SAVITRI CONTINUED TO GRUMBLE. She had confined Hari to the ladies cubicle. Hari decided to pay no mind to her prohibition; he hadn't stood at the door so she had no right to punish him, he thought.

The train continued its steady run south through the Deccan. The rocky landscape flew past them and dust rose from the fallow fields. Tamarind trees, large cacti, scattered palm trees, and thorn bushes were the only vegetation among the thick rock outcroppings. High above, on a hill far away, a small temple in white flew a saffron flag. Below the smooth rock face, huts sprawled about the base of the hill. Arid soil and boulders interspersed by thin dust paths lay between them and the temple.

The afternoon warmth gathered in the coach and the women around him dozed in the comfort of the swaying carriage. Hari waited until he was sure that they were asleep. Then he stole out to the corridor, intent on finding the filmi man. He passed by cubicles with old men stretched out on berths, women curled up next to windows, a few young men reading or napping. Near the middle of the coach he heard the soft noises of men chatting in Hindi. An old transistor radio sang an ancient film song, the tune marred by scratches as the train drew away from the local transmittor of All India Radio. In a cubicle the filmi man was playing cards with two other men.

"Are you playing rummy?" Hari asked, coming up to them.

The filmi man looked up from his cards and smiled at Hari.

"Can you play?" the dealer asked. He held the remainder of the deck on a Samsonite suitcase over his lap.

Hari shook his head.

"Make your move, Mukund," the third man addressed the filmi man. He was young, about twenty, and dark skinned. There was no hair on his face, which was angular and long, like a horse's. A gold crucifix hung on a thin chain around his neck. He looked like a Syrian Christian, probably headed home for the holidays.

"Sit here," said Mukund, clearing a space next to him.

Hari sat down next to the filmi man, his heart fluttering as he observed the game. The dealer, who seemed the oldest, had a thick black moustache. His hands were stained brown with tobacco; dirt had collected in his nails. The books that Hari read would have described him as swarthy.

"What I don't understand, Mukund-mian," the dealer said, "is if you are interested in films, why you are going to Madras instead of Bombay?"

"I don't know anyone in Bombay," Mukund said. "My mother's second cousin works for a film company in Madras, assistant to the cameraman. So I thought I could stay with him and maybe he'd help."

"Can you speak Tamil?" Hari asked.

"No," Mukund shook his head.

"Don't worry," the thin young man said, "that's the magic of cinema. Deaf, dumb, or blind, they can put you on screen and no one would know."

"Listen to our Joseph," the dealer quipped. "He knows everything."

Joseph ignored the sarcasm. "You know, MGR, the biggest hero in Tamil cinema, he's not Tamil either."

Mukund almost dropped his cards. "Really?"

"He's a Malayali like me," Joseph said. "In fact he was born in Sri Lanka."

"Is that why he let the Tamil Tigers set up camps in India?" Hari asked, recalling something his father had said earlier.

Joseph glowered at him, but before he could answer, the dealer spoke up. "You know there is a full company of army jawans headed south on this train. Two full bogies, I saw them."

"Who cares about politics," Mukund said, brushing away the topic with a gesture of the hand. "Tell me more about MGR. So does he speak

Tamil?"

"Of course," Joseph said, but as Mukund's face fell, he added, "But you know, after the shooting, his voice had to be dubbed as well."

"What shooting?" Hari asked.

"Oh, you don't know about this? Well there was this other actor named MR Radha. He used to play the villain in MGR films. They say he was unhappy about the roles he played. Anyway, one day MR Radha comes up to MGR and shoots him. I think he was drunk. One of the bullets hit MGR in the throat and his voice became muffled. So they started dubbing his voice in films."

Hari looked around, surprised that the other two did not ask a question.

Joseph continued, "That's why they call him thrice-born. Unlike the twice-born high castes, MGR was born, then he was born again after the shooting, and then just two years ago, he had this paralyzing attack that could have killed him and he was born for the third time. See...thrice-born, that's what makes him so special."

"Wait, so you are telling me that he can't speak?" Hari asked. "And he is the chief minister?"

"Arré, you are a small child. You don't understand these things," the dealer told him. "So what if he cannot speak. He is still the same person. People know and recognize him. They trust him, so he is in power."

"So you don't think that language will be a problem?" Mukund asked.

"I don't think it will be," Joseph said. "I mean, you should try to learn to speak Tamil, of course..."

The radio hissed and scratched as the train moved beyond the range of the station. The dealer switched it off. A shrill voice came from the far end of the coach.

"Chakka, chakka, chakka," the hijra said, clapping in time with the palms of her hand. As she walked towards them, her limbs pranced under her sari, as if swaying to music that only she heard. The coach grumbled to life as people stirred awake. The dealer gathered the cards and put them away, then the men leaned forward to watch the hijra make her way down.

She avoided the women, instead teased the men till they coughed up money. Hari watched her progress, fear mounting as he realized that she was between him and his cubicle. If he had stayed with his mother, he wouldn't have to deal with this. Mukund leaned against him and said softly, "Don't be afraid. They can smell fear. Just be quiet and I'll take care of it."

Hari looked at him and nodded. The men around him in the cubicle grew quiet as they tried to look busy. Joseph opened a book and started reading while the dealer stared out of the window.

"Aiii, see these strapping young men, such a show of masculine strength, all gathered here…" the hijra said, sauntering into their cubicle. Without further ado, she began her routine. "Okay, come on; give me a fiver or ten. God will be very happy. He will make you big and strong and your sperm virile. Lots of boys when you marry. Chakka, chakka, chakka."

She appeared bored as she clapped her hands. Mukund rose slightly and slid a hand into his back pocket to pull out a ten-rupee note.

"Here, this is for the boy and me," he said.

"Aren't you a sight for sore eyes," she replied. She took the money and reached over to stroke his cheek. He bent away from her hand, discomfort apparent in his face, but did not protest.

"Now the rest of you, come on now, be good like this boy," she laid a hand on Hari's shoulder. He cringed, but a warning shove from Mukund let him know that he wasn't to resist. She fixed a glance of amused surprise at Hari, watched Mukund for a moment, then continued, a hint of vehemence in her voice, "Come on, give me your donations and let me be on my way. Remember, I can curse you with impotence as easily as I can bless you with sons."

The dealer fumbled with his wallet and deposited his money in her hand. She unrolled his five-rupee bill, folded it around Mukund's ten, and lifting her blouse, slipped it under her bra. She turned to the dealer again. "Hey, you, come on. Fork over some more and you'll get back more than you can dream off. Don't be a greedy miser now. Remember, donations here earn you credit up there," she said, her hand stretching towards him, her fingers flicking upwards.

"Arré, I just gave you money."

"Come, come and don't waste my time. Just be a good man and give me more."

"Hey, leave him alone," Joseph said. "Why don't you find a job? Do something useful instead of extorting from others."

"Oooh! And who do we have here? What's your name, hen-some?" She leaned forward to stare at him, her face inches away from his.

Joseph batted her away, his face filled with anger. "Don't you dare touch me, you…"

She stood up, and the smile disappeared from her face. "I just asked your name. There is no reason to be impolite. You could just let me know what your name is. Here let's start again, my name is Radha. What's yours?"

"Joseph."

"Joseph, I scc…," she intoned. "Well, Joseph, my blessings help everyone, not just Hindus. Muslims and Christians too…everyone. Joseph, don't you want a nice son like Jesus? With my blessings, this time it'll be your sperm that begets him."

He started at this. "You whore."

Hari giggled at the hijra's comment but stopped when he saw the fury on Joseph's face. Mukund stood up and put his hand on the young man's shoulder. Hari could see Joseph's hand trembling. The dealer also rose from his seat, proffering a twenty-rupee note to the hijra.

"Just leave, okay," he said.

She grabbed the bill, gave a small laugh and walked out. The dealer and Mukund restrained the student, who was screaming as though insane.

"It's just dhandha, don't get all spoiled," the hijra said, her desultory voice breezing down the corridor. Hari watched her hurry to the end of the corridor and disappear into the next carriage. She did not stop at any of the other cubicles, where curious faces leaned out to watch Joseph's fury.

"Hari…"

His mother stood at the far end of the coach, a worried crease on her forehead as she beckoned him. Hari shrugged at Mukund and walked back to the ladies' cubicle.

"What was all that about?" his mother asked in English, her gaze still fixed on the scene behind him.

"Nothing."

The seat was wet and warm due to the sweat from her neck, and Hari wriggled to wipe it dry with his cotton shorts.

"Listen, you need to be careful," Savitri said, lowering her voice even though Suman and her mother were awake, staring at them. "You can't just sneak out every time I doze off. You're old enough to know better. Have some responsibility. It's dangerous to go walking about on your own."

"I was still in the same coach, just a few cubicles down."

"Fine, I don't want to get into an argument with you again, all right? Why can't you just read your book? Or sleep like the rest of us?"

Mukund popped his head in through the door and smiled. "Joseph is madder than a bull seeing red," he said in Hindi.

"What's wrong with him?" Hari's mother asked.

Mukund shrugged. "Just religious, I guess."

Savitri turned to Hari. "You hungry?"

"Can I have a cutlet the next time the attendant goes by?"

"Sure, we also have to ask him about buying a dinner for you."

"Wait, you don't have your dinner ticket yet?" Mukund said.

"Why? Has he already been by?" Savitri asked.

Mukund nodded. "He came in when we were passing through Itarsi and took the orders."

"Itarsi?" Hari said. "But that would have been too early in the morning."

"He sold both lunch and dinner at that time. Maybe he will come back again to book the dinners."

"And what if he doesn't?" Savitri asked. "Hari, I told you we should have packed dinner along. But no, railway dinner, railway dinner, that's all you think about."

"How was I to know they don't take bookings after Nagpur?" he replied.

"Well, we'll figure out something. Otherwise I suppose you'll just have to starve. It'll be a lesson for you."

Hari rolled his eyes and stared out through the window.

The coach became warmer as the afternoon progressed and Savitri lay down again to sleep. Mukund lay down on his berth in the corridor, outside their cubicle door, and flipped through his film magazine, slumber slowly descending upon him. Hari watched the landscape as it fled past. Beyond the slope of the embankment, the sparse fields of cotton and grain momentarily lined up in orderly rows before disappearing into the chaos of leaves.

Even when the fields receded and the shrubbery and thorns of the wild took over, a narrow path followed them, ochre mud beaten down by countless footsteps, dry grass and bramble on either side. Such a path could snake along for miles alongside the train, turning and twisting until suddenly without warning, it hurled itself against the gravel bed of the tracks and disappeared. Sometimes it slid down the embankment to a small bridge and merged with a gully or a dirt road under the tracks.

Savitri nudged against Hari's thigh in her sleep and grunted. "What time is it?"

"Almost five in the evening," Hari said, watching the red hues in the western sky. She got up and began rearranging her sari.

"Did the chaiwalla make his rounds?" she asked, her hands rising to adjust her hair.

"I am sure he will be back again," Mrs Sharma said, nodding sleepily at Savitri. She sat with one knee folded against her breast, the other leg tucked underneath her. She looked petite, her body knotted together in that comfortable position. She had dozed fitfully throughout the afternoon, resting her head on the raised knee, looking up at the slightest sound, smiling at Hari as he walked in and out of the cubicle. She would raise her head ever so often and look at her daughter, a few times reaching over to graze a hand over the sleeping figure. Suman, oblivious to the cares of her mother, slept, one arm on the window sill over which she had laid her head.

"Where are you going now?" his mother said, as he got up to leave again.

"Nowhere..."

"Why can't you sit at the window like normal people?"

"Maybe because I am abnormal..."

"Well, at least tell me if you want some tea...," Hari heard her say as he fled. The Punjabi woman commiserated in Hindi, unaware of the details of their English conversation, but drawing the unmistakable conclusion of paltry conflict from the tones of their voices.

"Boys will be like that, dear, always doing their own thing."

"This one is special," his mother replied in Hindi. "But he is still too young..."

"What did he say?" Mukund leaned towards the cubicle door and asked, also in Hindi.

Hari's heart sank. Mukund did not understand English. So what if he was good-looking. He could not understand English. Hari's affection for him ebbed away. How could he not have noticed?

En-route to the vestibule, Hari saw the hijra's wooden basket and froze. But neither the hijra nor her red suitcase sat next to the toilet. The toilet door opened and the dealer came out, smiled weakly at Hari, and walked back into the coach.

Hari went and stood at the outside door, keeping well away from the steps as he watched the scenery rushing past.

TWELVE

A ROAD CROSSING approached; men on bicycles and women carrying baskets atop their heads stood among the tracks as the train rattled past them. Jeeps and buses waited behind the yellow and black barrier which had been lowered for the train's passage. The Tamil Nadu Express slowed past the crossing and began rolling by walls covered with political graffiti. Leaving the main tracks, the train drew up to the knots of people waiting on the platform at Balarshah station. Men began crowding in the vestibule to get off the train, and Hari inched back into the coach. The ladies' cubicle was empty.

Hari wondered where everyone was. Outside the window a vendor warmed small oval patties of spiced potatoes on a large tava. Suman rushed in, her hair awry, wiping her hands on her gauzy churidar, crumpling the fabric. She looked at the empty berths and turned to Hari as if about to say something. Instead she took her berth across from his and peered out the window.

"Balarshah," Hari said.

"Accha, are we in Andhra Pradesh?"

Hari shook his head, "No, but almost there."

"Oh!" she said. "So are we still on time?"

Hari shrugged.

Mukund peered in, patted his hair down and grinned sheepishly at the two. He turned to head off.

"Mukund," Hari said. He stood up and put his hand into his pocket.

Mukund waited. Hari drew out two five-rupee notes and held out one towards him. "For earlier," he said. "When you paid the hijra."

Mukund laughed. "It's alright, you don't have to pay me."

"I want to," Hari said.

"No," Mukund countered, "I can't take money from you." He walked away down the corridor.

"What was that about?" Suman asked.

"Nothing." Hari folded the two notes and put them back into his pocket. He sat down again by the window.

Suman smiled at Hari. "You like standing at the door, don't you?"

Hari shrugged.

"I saw you," she said, "at the door, before we entered the station. You should listen to your mother. It's not good to stand at the door. One unlucky moment and that's it. Khattam."

Hari's mother walked in.

"Where were you?" Hari said.

"What! You can run away whenever you like, but I have to tell you when I go? Seems a little crazy to me."

"It's not the same," Hari's voice cracked.

Savitri smiled. "Don't get upset. I just went to the pantry car to see about your dinner."

"What did they say? Did you…"

"No. They aren't taking reservations anymore. The clerk has already left the train with the orders. There may be one or two extra casseroles and the man said he'll get something if he finds anything. If we are lucky there'll be someone selling a few meals on the platform in Warangal."

"I am sure we'll get food in Warangal," Hari said. "That's where they load the meals anyway."

"Yes, but it'll cost me more to buy the same meal on the platform," she said. "I have to shop in the black market because of you!"

Outside the window, a vendor's cry approached. "Vadai, Masala vadai. Hot, hot. Get them now. Vadai, Masala vadai."

"You hungry?" Savitri asked, digging into her purse. "Stop him when he comes."

Hari flung his hand out the window and waved down the vendor. Hari's mother leaned over next to him to inspect the vendor's wares.

"Tazza hai kya?" Savitri asked and without waiting to hear his reply, she nodded towards Suman and asked, "Do you want some too?"

Suman shook her head.

"Yes, yes, hot and fresh. Just removed from the oil," the vendor chanted, nodding his head and motioning carelessly to a building behind him.

Hari's mother harrumphed but ordered two plates anyway and settled back to delve into her purse for change as Hari took charge of the small paper plates loaded with vadais and dollops of coconut chutney. The train began pulling away as she passed him the money. The vendor walked along the train, his pace quickening as Hari slipped his hands through the window bars and dropped the money in his outstretched palm. They were off again.

"You must have been tired, you've slept well during the afternoon," Savitri said to Suman.

Suman blushed, pulling her leg up on the berth, and playing with the rings on her toes. They were made of silver, two on the second toe and one on the fourth. Her toenails were polished purple.

She said, "I guess it's just the rhythm of the train. I always seem to doze away in a train, especially if it is warm."

"I know exactly what you mean, and with the breeze coming in, it's just so nice to take a nap. So did you always live in Delhi? Are you from there?"

"Ji, my family is from Amritsar but my father had his business in Delhi. Clothing, you know."

"Really? My husband lived in Delhi when he was studying engineering. But I have never been there, never seen the bloody capital of this country that I've lived in for thirty-three years. How old are you?" Hari's mother asked, waving a vadai piece at her, the coconut chutney sticking to it.

"Ji, twenty..."

"You know, I was just around your age when I had this little brat," she said, pointing at Hari.

"I'm still here, you know," Hari said as the two women laughed.

Savitri ignored him. "So are you studying?"

"Ji, BA in political science."

"Nice...political science...good, good. So what do you want to do after that?"

"I don't know. My brother Suresh wants me to try out for the IAS but

I think Ma won't allow it. She's already worried about marrying me off but Suresh-bhaiya wants me to study more."

"That's nice of him. It's a wonderful thing. You should study...marriage will happen. You're still young. Besides nowadays a woman civil service officer should have no problems getting married. Lots of men want to marry them...maybe you'll find a higher ranking officer to marry you, huh?"

"Amma," Hari said, "stop embarrassing yourself."

"What is there to be embarrassed about?" Savitri replied. "It's the truth. Talk all you like about modernization and whatnot. I believe in it too, but I'd be a fool to think that everyone's come around in the past fifty years."

"I guess so," Suman said. "Suresh-bhaiya just wants me to be independent...you know, have my own career, stand on my own feet, that sort of thing. But you know I really want to work in a nonprofit field. Start women's cooperative movements, bring literacy to girls. Can you believe it? They are still burning widows in Madhya Pradesh...and marrying off ten-year-old girls in Rajasthan?"

Savitri waved her hands to stop her. "Wait, wait...yes, I know all about that, but you have to listen to me. Listen, it's very nice that you want to do all these things, but you must think of your family. Your brother is supporting your education and wants you to be independent...a laudable sentiment. What will happen if he decides to change his mind and become one with your mother?"

"But why would he?" Suman said.

"Listen first. If you want to be successful and not be married off to the first Sinha, Sharma, or Verma your mother finds, you're going to have to choose...now I don't know your brother, but if you tell him that you are going to tramp through villages in backward areas, what is he going to think? A young unmarried woman in such places...no, no, no...he'll rather see you married and embroidering clothes at home, am I right? What will he do?"

"You don't know my Suresh-bhaiya," Suman said. Her voice was low and defiant.

Hari's mother nodded at this. "True enough, but all I am saying is that you have to be careful. Just be reasonable. We women can't have everything we want. Little battles, little victories. Just bide your time till you are ready to do what you want, not before."

"You are asking her to lie," Hari said, pleased at having discovered this side to his mother.

Savitri crumpled her empty paper plate and leaned past him to slip the trash between the window bars. "Shut up. Don't listen to others' conversations."

Hari watched the paper fly off behind the train.

Suman stood up to help her mother as she hobbled in, her hand leaning against the door, then the top berth. The elderly woman looked at Hari's plate of vadais, smiled, and turned to her daughter. She spoke in Punjabi. Suman nodded and pulled out a large, cylindrical aluminium container from under their berth. She settled it between her legs and pried it open using her fingernails. Inside was a smaller stainless steel container sitting on a huge pile of puris.

As Suman struggled to get the smaller container open, her mother brought out two plastic plates from a wicker bag, one neon green and the other electric blue. She shoved the plates toward Hari and his mother. "Have some."

Hari's mother inspected the open bin and the stainless steel container, with its mass of spiced potato-sagu for the puris. Hari was tempted, even though he still had an entire vadai on his paper plate. Savitri nodded, "I had some of the vadais. It looks very nice though, you eat."

They did.

The sun had set and the wind was cool by the time Hari finished his vadais. His hands were covered with coconut and grease. Outside, the sky had lost its vermillion hue and now favoured the deeper shades of blue, violet, and black as he rose to go out and wash his hands at the little basin in the vestibule, by the door. Hari wasn't allowed to lick his fingers, so he waited till he was in the vestibule to begin sucking them, one by one, from the little finger to the thumb. He even managed to give his palm a good lick before he reached the stainless steel sink with its push-in tap.

"Hey, you got some money?"

Hari turned at the sound. He'd forgotten about the hijra. She sat atop her red suitcase, this time further back, almost at the edge of the swaying aluminium ramps between the coaches. In the dark, Hari had missed her. He spat out the water from his mouth, the iron taste lingering on his tongue as he shook his head.

"What happened to the money you took in the afternoon?" he asked.

"Saala, he took it all."

"Who?"

"That motherfucking ticket collector. May his balls shrivel up and rise within his belly."

"Don't you have a ticket?"

She spat on the floor. "As if holding a ticket would make a difference. Baba, it doesn't matter what we poor people do. They always find a way to squeeze the little we have out of us."

"Aey!" a grey-shirted vendor yelled. "Come on, clear the way, chaia…chaiaaa…" He came in behind her from the next compartment and pushed past, cradling a line of plastic cups in the crook of one arm and lugging a stainless steel container in the other.

The hijra sat back, adjusted her sari and began fixing her hair. Suman came up to them, holding her two plates to wash at the sink. Hari avoided the hijra's eyes, gave his hands a final rinse and nodded shortly to Suman before heading back into the cubicle.

A large red moon hung low in the sky and the small pools of water they passed shone like shards of glass flung on the hard plateau by a giant's hand. The engine hooted, and in the far distance, small points of light moved slowly along the dark shadows of the land. Hari read for a while, pausing to look out the window. The carriage windows cast small rectangles of light outside, forming an ephemeral sheen of travelling portraits on stone, gravel, and thorn bushes. Pursuing the layered image of his window outside was a tall image cast through the door: the silhouette of a man.

Hari's mother nudged him with the portable chess set that Mani-mama and Sarah-aunty had given him last summer. Already, a small piece of a toothpick stood in for a lost rook. Hari turned away from the window, and they set up the pieces. Suman leaned over to help.

"Shatranj," her mother said. "My father used to love the game. I watched him play in the courtyard of our village when I was a little girl."

Savitri nodded to encourage the older woman.

"Now even that village near Lahore is gone," Mrs Sharma said and let her head fall against the seat. "After Partition, the village became part of Pakistan. Everything, they took it all away from us." She sighed.

"It's the same old story," Suman said. "She tells it to everyone she meets."

Mukund lay on his berth, watching them from the open cubicle door as they moved the pieces from hole to hole across the board.

"Can you play?" Hari asked.

Mukund shook his head.

"Shush," Savitri said in a low voice. "He can't come in here. It's the ladies' cubicle, remember."

Just then the ticket collector arrived, his name printed in white on a small black plastic badge attached to his stained black coat. He sat next to Savitri in the cubicle, checked the four passengers' names off his list and slashed a line across the tickets.

"Do you know if there are any extra dinners?" Savitri asked him.

"Ask the pantry clerk," he said.

"Is the train on time?" Mukund asked.

The ticket collector peered into the darkness outside.

"Looks like it," he said. He returned their tickets and disappeared down the coach.

"How could he know just by looking? It's completely black out there," Hari said.

"He goes back and forth on this train a thousand times," Savitri replied. "He knows. Just make your move."

Savitri and Hari played a game; then Suman and Hari played. Hari grew tired of playing and offered the set to Suman and her mother. The elderly woman's eyes brightened at the offering and Savitri leaned over to watch them. Hari walked out of the cubicle to the doors in the vestibule. A surly-looking young man wearing a dirty white kurta over his pants leaned out of the door where Hari had previously stood. There was no sign of the hijra. His usual post taken, Hari unlatched the door on the opposite side of the carriage to peer out. It was better this way because his mother couldn't catch sight of him dangling out of the train.

A small paved street ran alongside the train. Long fluorescent tubes drooped over and cast patches of thin bluish-white light on the road. They were approaching a town. The train slowed. After a slight jump and the brief rush of metal scraping against metal, a new set of gleaming tracks strode out from underneath them to run parallel with the train. In turn another set of tracks budded off the sister track. A signal station appeared and Hari saw the dark silhouette of an engineer holding a small green lantern in his hand as he stood against the rail of the balcony. In the lit room behind him, a row of levers became visible, their large handles gleaming a bright red. The levers were as large as the man standing at the railing. The dot of red that was his cigarette flared a bright orange each time the man drew on it.

Farther beyond the railway yard, a small ochre-painted government bungalow carried a lit semicircular metal-plate arch over its doorway: Warangal Sub-divisional Headquarters. Ahead, where the train was headed, Hari could make out the corrugated aluminium and concrete of the platform roofing and the long fluorescent lamps above the large yellow station posts.

Someone cried out in the ladies' cubicle.

Hari turned and saw the young man, who had been standing at the opposite door, drop down from the train. He had been riding on the steps, leaning forward, holding the long yellow door handle with a single hand. In the split second following the cry, the man let go and fell onto the gravel. Hari rushed across to look; a woman wailed in the ladies' cubicle. As Hari leaned out, stretching his neck to look for the fallen figure, and trying to think how the accident had happened, the train slid onto another set of tracks and began to pull up.

Away in the distance, among the silent, dark, empty, goods train carriages, he saw the man running wildly. Inside the carriage Mukund, the filmi hero, came sprinting behind Hari and almost shoved him off the train as he surged out of the door. Howling like an enraged animal, he waved his clenched fist at the departing figure. Hari began to feel queasy as he recognized his mother's voice in that unnatural wailing from within the coach.

The dirt and mud of the yard gave way to the concrete of the platform as the train rolled into the station. Air escaped with a loud hiss from underneath the carriage as someone pulled the emergency cord. Hari heard two short whistles followed by a long hoot of the engine signalling trouble. The locked wheels squeaked loudly in protest. Hari walked back slowly, unwillingly into their little cubicle. A knot of people had gathered by the door, murmuring and trying to squeeze through the metal frame to catch a sight of the chaos within.

He pushed through the small crowd and found his mother bawling amid the two other women. Mrs Sharma and her daughter were trying to console her, holding her hand and patting her shoulder. The chess pieces lay scattered all over the red linoleum floor of the cabin and the aluminium shutters on the twin windows were pulled down and clamped shut. The only light in the coach came from the two small incandescent lamps, one dim yellow and the other blue.

In that scant light, Hari saw the red chain for the emergency brake hanging loose, rattling high above their heads. His mother, squeezed between the two women, cried out to all in the different languages she knew.

"…oh, my wedding necklace, my thaalli, my mangalsutra…"

Hari took in this entire scene, stunned at the drama which had unfolded. That man was no platform snoop trying to determine which side the train would slide into the station. He was a necklace snatcher and had taken the opportunity presented by the slowing train to reach into the window beside the door and grab his mother's thick gold wedding band. Having yanked it from around her neck, he had run into the safety of the shantytowns that encroached every railway yard in the country.

A welt was developing where the gold chain had bit into his mother's neck before the clasp broke and came free.

THIRTEEN

HARI'S MOTHER TREMBLED as she recounted the surprise and sudden pain that had paralysed her.

"I was just playing chess with Suman and Mrs Sharma here. Then, I felt his hand through the window bars, here. . . . No, I didn't really feel anything until he pulled, Then I choked, unable to breathe."

"Look at her neck," Mrs Sharma said, pointing out the welt to the khaki-shirted policeman who had come to investigate. "She could have died."

"Instead, the clasp broke and the necklace just left me," Savitri said, sobbing. "I wish he had slit my throat, my shame is unbearable."

"No, no, don't say that," Suman said. "Think of your son."

Hari sat motionless, afraid that he would be blamed for the thief's actions. Had he only remained in the seat by the window, his mother would have been safe, he thought. The policemen and all these people wouldn't be here. He berated himself for going to stand at the door, and silent tears dripped down his cheek. Suman reached across and patted his knee.

The crowd outside their door were a wall of gazing eyes watching with interest as the policeman scribbled onto the long FIR in his tin file holder, recording details of the robbery.

He looked up from his file. "So you were sitting by the window…"

"Right there," Savitri pointed.

"…and he grabbed your mangalsutra. These things happen. The

window is so close to the door, someone can just reach in and take a wedding band. You should be more careful. Not sit by the window…"

"Arré, how would we know such a disaster would occur?" Suman said. "Why don't you people do something if you know such things happen? Especially in a ladies' cubicle!"

The policeman shrugged. "What can we do, Miss? We write up our reports, but it is the engineers and big officers who build the coaches who have to change the way window bars are in place. But they cannot be bothered to read every complaint lodged at the railway stations."

"Béta," Suman's mother said. "Why tell us about the faults of the big officers? What have we to do with their lives, huh? Tell us how you will find the wedding necklace…just bring it back and we shall all bless you."

Hari heard the hijra's voice from behind the crowd. "Move away, you vultures."

The men drew away from the door at this shrill call. Radha stood at the door and nodded with sympathy towards Savitri.

"What are you doing here?" The policeman asked her.

"Why do you ask them about the thief?" she said. "Ask me, I'll tell you. He was standing at the door when he stole the necklace. Do you think respectable people like them travel in the vestibule?"

"Watch your tongue," the policeman said. "Do you have a ticket to be on this train?"

"Who cares about the ticket." Suman beckoned her in. "Ask her about the thief."

Radha bared her teeth and squatted on the floor. "I'll tell you, Miss. It was that guy in the white kurta who did this. I knew he was up to no good. Why else would someone go from one coach to another, leaning out of doors and peering into cubicles? All afternoon long I see him…"

"Did you see him take the necklace?"

Radha's face fell. "No, Miss. I was not there…but if I was, I would have clobbered him with my chappal."

The policeman snorted.

"Do you know him?" Savitri asked.

"Name? No. I don't know his name. But I know where he is. He told me that he works in Warangal. And he lives near Champak Lane."

"How do you know this?" The policeman asked.

"Have you no shame? Will you make me tell in front of respectable women, with all these men gawking?"

"Chi, chi," Mrs Sharma covered her face with a corner of her shawl.

The men at the cubicle door laughed and the policeman squirmed. In the distance, the engine hooted.

"Accha," the policeman said. "It's time for the train to be on its way. You, come with me to the station. I will take your testimony there."

"Arré, but I am going to Madras. I can't get off the train here. I've been travelling long."

"Without a ticket, but that doesn't matter. You'll take the next train."

"Maaji, please, Miss. Help me." Radha looked to Hari's mother and then to Suman, her hands held together. "I have to be home for my mother's funeral. Take pity on me."

Suman sighed. "What more can she tell you? Hasn't there been enough damage without having to take her off the train?"

"Be quiet," Mrs Sharma said, tapping her daughter's knee. "Let the policeman do his work."

"But mother, why should she have to get off the train? She was trying to help, and for that she'll be punished."

"Yes, yes. Let her remain," Savitri said. "What has happened has happened."

The train lurched and decided the matter. The policeman shrugged and squeezed past the crowd in the corridor to jump off the moving train. With the train in motion, and the policeman gone, the crowd too dissipated. Slowly the men returned to their seats through the train, taking the story with them.

"That's it?" Radha said. "Saala, he won't ever catch the thief. Maaji, don't expect a report from this policewallah. The necklace is gone and that's fate, what can one do?"

Hari's mother started crying again

"Enough of your talk," Mrs Sharma said. She opened her large bag and fished out her small clasp purse. She offered a ten-rupee note to the hijra. Radha stuffed the proffered money in her bra and thanked the Punjabi woman. But she made no move to leave; instead she sat on her haunches on the floor and watched them.

"So when did your mother pass away?" Suman asked.

"Who? My mother? She's still alive, that witch."

"Didn't you tell the policeman you were going home to your mother's funeral?"

"Just a little lie, Miss."

"Chi, chi. You shouldn't lie to policemen," Mrs Sharma said.

Radha made an appropriate face of contrition and the older woman appeared mollified.

"Maaji, you know how it is with poor people. If we don't take care of ourselves, these policewallahs and u'ffcers will suck us dry."

"Amma," Hari said, "stop crying." He reached over to comfort her, but she shied away from his touch. "Why don't we just get Thatha and Paathi to make a new wedding necklace in Madras? Paathi loves to shop for jewellery."

Savitri wiped her tears with a corner of her sari. "That one will not be blessed by my in-laws."

"But you never even liked them."

She said in Tamil, "Don't say that! Without the blessings of my in-laws, how can I have a happy marriage?"

Radha, who had till now spoken only in Hindi, said in Tamil, "That is true. Kanna, don't bug your mother like that."

"Oh, you speak Tamil?" Hari's mother looked at the hijra with renewed interest.

"Oh yes. I am from a small village about two hours south of Kumbakonam..." Radha noticed the two other women looking at each other and switched to Hindi. "The village I come from is very small. No electricity, no toilets; just a dirt road, and some small houses and huts; a village temple to Draupadiamman, its pond, and the temple fields. My family tills the temple fields. Once a week, the state transport bus stops along the highway four kilometres from the village, that's how remote our village is."

"But you speak good Hindi," Suman's mother said. "Did you learn in eskool?"

"No, no. Hindi I learned from films, when I moved to Bombay. When I was small, every month my family—all of us—took the bus to the neighbouring village of Charitur with our parents for their village fair. All the people from the zillah would come to do business. We used to sell small toys, chettiar dolls, and kites at the fair. I used to paint the dolls. I'm pretty artistic, you know."

Hari watched Mukund, who was sitting on his berth in the corridor. He looked morose as he stared at the floor, but Hari knew that he was listening. Mukund smiled at Hari when he caught his eye. Hari turned away from him to watch Radha. Her manner was subdued, unlike her blustery self earlier that afternoon. As the train sped south she kept up a steady chatter.

"At this fair, they used to have the travelling talkies. A man would bring a projector, set it up under a palmyra hut and they would put up a big white bedsheet for a screen," Radha said, her arms spreading wide. "Then after the day's work was complete, we'd see a film. Sometimes it was a Hindi film from Bombay, but mostly they were Tamil films. That's where I first saw all of MGR's old films, *Nadodi Mannan*, *Kanavan*, *Rickshawkaran*. Did you see them?" Radha turned to Hari's mother.

Savitri nodded and managed a small smile before raising her hand-kerchief back to her face.

"Oh! So many films that I can barely remember... Sometimes they showed a film with Shivaji Ganesan or some other actor, but then my parents didn't wait and we took the evening bus back. If it was an MGR film, though, my father always insisted that we stay for it and then we would return home with the rest of the village in a shared jeep."

"You, hanging out a jeep?" Hari said. He shook his head.

"Do you think that I dressed like this then?" Radha laughed. "I was young then, just like you." Turning to Savitri, she asked, "Is your family from a village?"

"No," Hari's mother said. "My family has lived in Madras for many generations now."

"Too bad," Radha said. "You might have big theatres and cinemas in the city, but it's not the same as in the villages. I still remember the troupes of performers who put on the therru-kuttu street theatre. They enacted scenes from the *Kampan Ramayana*, or from *Cilappatikaaram* during the festivals of Kartikei and Pongal."

"What's the *Cilappatikaaram*?" Hari asked.

"You've never heard the story of Kannaki and Kovalan?"

"What is this story?" Suman asked.

Radha sighed. "What is the point of being educated if you don't even know the stories of your people? What do they teach you north of the Vindhya Mountains anyway?"

"Fine, be that way!" Hari leaned back on his seat and looked away.

"No," Radha cocked her head and said. "You must have heard this story, you know, about the woman who destroyed Madurai, the capital of the Pandyan kings."

"Oh! That one!" Mrs Sharma spoke up. "Doesn't she break her bangles and curse the city to burn…"

Savitri smiled. "Not her bangles, her anklets."

Mrs Sharma nodded. "Right! And rubies come out…"

Hari caught Radha giving Suman a look of satisfaction.

"Yes, rubies instead of pearls."

"But I forget why…"

"Tell us the story," Radha said to Savitri.

Savitri shook her head.

"Come now," Suman leaned forward and patted Savitri's knee. "It'll make you feel better."

"I don't remember all of it," Savitri said.

"Fine, I'll start," Radha said. "You can finish the story."

"Long time ago, the Cheras, Cholas, and Pandyas ruled the land south of the Vindhya Mountains. In the Chola capital of Pukaar lived a happy young couple, a sixteen-year-old lad named Kovalan and his twelve-year-old wife Kannaki, a ship-owner's daughter. But one day, Madhavi, the greatest and most beautiful courtesan in the king's court, sees the beautiful Kovalan and falls passionately in love with him. Kovalan, ensnared by her charms, abandons his wife to live with Madhavi. They even have a daughter, Manimekalai, together. But as months pass, Kovalan becomes jealous of Madhavi's role as a courtesan dancer in the king's court and after a sudden quarrel during the New Year celebration, he leaves her."

"Just like that?" Hari said.

"Well it was really just a lovers' quarrel," Savitri said. "Madhavi keeps hope that he'll return."

"So, does he?"

Savitri picked up the story. "Well, Kovalan has spent all his money buying trinkets for his mistress Madhavi and not paid attention to his business. He is now ruined and penniless. So he returns to Kannaki in remorse. Kannaki, the loyal wife, welcomes him back and gives him her silver anklet—cilampu—to raise money so they can begin a new life. They leave the Chola kingdom and travel to Madurai, capital of the Pandyan kings. In Madurai, Kovalan leaves his wife in the care of the shepherds just outside the city walls and goes into the city to find a jeweller who will help him sell Kannaki's anklet and raise money for a new life." She gestured to Radha to continue.

"In the city, however, fate had other ideas in store," Radha began and sighed. "The royal jeweller was a crook. He'd stolen the queen's anklet. So when Kovalan shows him Kannaki's anklet, the royal jeweller accuses him of theft in the king's court. The king, eager to please his queen, pronounces his judgement, 'Put the man to death and return the jewel to the queen.'"

"Oh! I remember now," Mrs Sharma said. "So that is why he dies and Kannaki returns in rage to burn the city!"

"Soon, but not yet." Radha nodded before continuing, "The soldiers drag poor Kovalan to the executioners so the death sentence can be carried out. But even the executioners see the innocence on Kovalan's face and cannot bring themselves to take his life. A drunken soldier, an instrument of fate, sees the king's writ done. It is said that when Kovalan's body hit the ground and his blood seeped through the soil, the earth shuddered in horror and grief."

Suman interrupted, "So this is when Kannaki comes into the city…"

Savitri nodded and continued, "and she runs to the Pandyan court to prove her husband's innocence by shattering the other anklet, revealing the rubies inside unlike the pearls of the queen's own anklet."

"So what happens then?" Hari asked. "How does the city get destroyed?"

"Well," Radha said. "The king sees the rubies clattering in the court and dies in shock and remorse. The queen faints with sorrow. Kannaki's wrath now turns upon the city that failed to protect her innocent husband. She twists off one of her breasts and hurls it at the city, setting it ablaze. Then she breaks her bangles and leaves the city for the land of the Cheras to the west, where she performs a penance of remorse until a divine chariot appears with Kovalan and together they both ride off to heaven."

"…and they lived happily ever after," Suman said. "But wait, she really threw her own breast to burn the city? I don't believe you."

"Why not?" Radha said. "What does she need her breasts for, now that her beloved husband Kovalan is dead? Think of the nurturing power of the breast, how it makes babies grow strong. So if a woman decides to use it as a weapon, just imagine the scale of destruction she can wreak!"

The elderly Mrs Sharma added, "Even the gods cannot stand against the fury of an enraged woman."

"Yes, but you don't have to believe me." Radha gestured to Suman. "You can go to the town of Vanci and see for yourself that her breast is missing."

"Fine, fine, that's all good in stories and legends," Hari said, "but it's not really true. Kannaki can't just pull her breast off and throw it at a city. It would be too painful and besides that, it's just plain impossible in real life."

"Really?" Radha said. A tiny smile crept across the corners of her mouth as she moved her right hand under her sari towards the left pocket of her blouse. She withdrew her hand and flung a white package towards him.

"See, it's not so hard after all," Radha said and laughed.

No one spoke.

The white lump of cloth shaped like a breast lay in Hari's lap. His hands trembled as he picked it up. It was a soft mass made of three pieces of white cotton stitched together and filled with layers of scrap cloth.

Savitri looked at him and began laughing. Suman and her mother, hitherto stiff and silent at the hijra's outrageous behaviour, smiled in relief. Hari giggled as he held the breast.

"So you don't have real breasts?" he said, staring at the flatness of her chest.

"What did you think?" Radha tugged at the empty pocket of her blouse. "I am a hijra, not a woman. Three years it has been and still they refuse to grow, what can I do? It's my fate."

"So they don't grow when you become a hijra?" Hari asked as he handed the breast back.

She ignored his question and slipped the wad of cloth back into her blouse and stood up. "Accha, I'll go my way. God keep you through your journey." She clapped her hands to make the sign of the hijra as she left their cubicle.

FOURTEEN

A STEWARD APPEARED in the corridor outside with Mukund's dinner tray. Mrs Sharma sniffed her disapproval at the smell of meat. Mukund, silent, huddled in his corner and, unable to contribute following his heroic effort to catch the thief, ate his chicken dinner. The aroma of food aroused hunger in the cubicle.

"Oh dear!" Hari's mother said. "We forgot to get your dinner at Warangal. Run, run after the steward and see if he has an extra meal. Lord, I cannot even feed my own son."

"Don't worry," Suman leaned over to stop Hari. "We have enough puris for the both of you. You eat with us. Forget the train food."

"Thanks, but I have some rice for myself. It's only for the child."

Out came the puri tin again and Suman pulled out plastic plates from under the berth. She handed Hari one of them, heaped high with lumps of potatoes and wads of puris. Her mother ate out of the lid. Hari's mother poured a little water over her curds and rice and put a handful into her mouth. She didn't chew, just sat there. The two Punjabi women and Hari watched her as they shovelled in the puris.

Finally Suman's mother took charge. "Eat, eat…you must eat. It is our fate as women to be abused. What can we do in this Kali Yuga? Three quarters of the world has gone evil, how can we not be affected?"

She stepped over to sit beside Hari's mother, in the empty seat next to the shut window. Even she could not resist glancing at the window for a moment before stroking Savitri's shoulder. As Hari lifted a piece of puri to his mouth, he could smell the train—its peculiar combination of rust, iron, and dirt that made his hands smell like blood and taste like salt.

Hari awoke with a start in the quiet cabin. The train was at Vijaywada station. It was the middle of the night but their cubicle fortress was hot. His clothes were damp with sweat. The windows were doubly fastened and the door was closed. The twin fans circulated the same dank air over and over.

Suman's mother slept across from him in the lowest berth. Suman was in the middle berth above her and across from Hari's mother. The upper two berths were empty. Hari got off his berth and opened the door. It grated and the dim light from the corridor cast a pallid circle inside their small cubicle. The old woman stirred and watched him sleepily.

"Soo-soo," Hari held up his index finger to indicate he was going to the toilet and stepped out.

The train lurched as it pushed off from Vijaywada junction, the last scheduled stop before Madras. The cool night breeze flowed from outside into the vestibule of the carriage. Hari slid to the floor and sat down.

Scraping noises came from the area between the toilets, and the hijra's sleepy face peeked out to peer at him. "Can't sleep?" she asked.

Hari shook his head.

"Is your amma sleeping?"

Hari nodded.

"Cried herself to sleep, I bet." Radha scratched at her scalp.

"How would you know?"

"I've done that myself, I know."

"But you are not a woman," Hari said. He felt tired and unlike other train journeys, this one had stretched him thin. "Were you always like this?"

She stopped scratching her scalp and looked at him. "What do you mean 'like this?'"

"You know, a hijra."

She cackled. "Aiii, chokra, they don't teach you nothing in your fancy eskool? No one is born a chakka; you have to be selected to become one."

"Selected? How?"

"It's a secret."

"Tell me," Hari said, craning his neck back and forth. "There's no one around."

"How much money do you have?"

Hari shook his head. "I am not going to give you money."

"Fine. No money, no story. You think my story is worthless, it comes phree?" She ran her betel-nut-stained crimson tongue over her lips and held out her hand. "Come on, fork it out and I'll tell you the story."

Hari squeezed his hand into his shorts pocket and drew out two fives. He looked up at her, then down at his money, and took one of the five-rupee notes and handed it to her.

She bared her teeth in a smile of triumph and stuffed the note in her bra. "So what did I tell you earlier in the cabin?"

"The mela."

"Yes, the Charitur Fair. Ever since I was little, I liked watching philims; the people are always dressed so smart and look so beautiful, especially in Hindi films. I wanted to go to Bombay: big city, bright lights, Bollywood. I wanted to see everything, make money. So when I was about your age…how old are you?"

"Twelve."

"Really?" she said. "Well maybe a year older than you, then. I think I was thirteen when I snuck away from home, took the bus to Kumbakonam, and boarded a train there to Bombay."

"You ran away?"

"I thought I was very brave and adventurous. Of course, once I reached Bombay, I found out that the rest of the country had arrived there with my dreams. It was impossible to get a studio job, so I did all kinds of things in Bombay. I lived there for more then ten years. When I was still very young, I scalped movie tickets, I washed pots, I carried water…all kinds of very hard work. And then I found a job assisting a makeup artist—"

"In Bollywood?"

"No. To make your grandmother look like a whore," she said. "Of course in Bollywood, where else?"

Hari pouted.

"Don't sulk like a girl," said the hijra, laughing. "So this makeup man said he would teach me everything I needed to know to work in the film industry. What did I know about men then? I thought here is someone who's nice enough to give me a job. Saala, he turned out to be a dirty man. You know what I mean?"

Hari recalled Vishu and nodded.

"He would try his make up on me or one of the other boys and he would show us how to do make up, but then he began to do nasty things. He would grope me; he would try to kiss me…"

Hari drew his legs up and hugged his knees.

"But what could I do? I was young, alone in the city, and he was the only one who could get me a job with a studio. So I let him do what he wanted."

"But you were still a boy then…"

"Of course I was still a boy. . .well, a man by then, you know." She winked at him.

"But how…"

"I am getting to it. Anyway, this went on for almost a year, and then he dumped me. There were other boys, you see. That's when amma came and took me. I was sitting alone, in the dark, crying, and this group of beautifully dressed women walked by. The oldest came up to me and asked me why I was crying. She spoke Tamil—you know she's just from near Puddukotta—and I was so happy to hear my own tongue in this foreign city that I just cried and told her everything, my entire story." Radha giggled nervously. "I remember she asked me if I was that way…you know…with men."

Hari bit his lip as he listened to her.

"I replied honestly…I liked wearing makeup and clothes but that I didn't enjoy that. She said good, good and took me into her family. There were six of them: Gayatri, Kamala, Vidya, Soumya, Nandini, and Chinnamma. It was Chinnamma whose house we went to. She was the one who had rescued the others and trained them. Just like she was trained by Periamma many years ago…none of us have ever seen Periamma…"

"So they were all hijras, like you?"

She nodded. "Of course, and I began to live with them. I started out doing their makeup. Then I began wearing saris like them, letting my hair grow long like Nandini. She was the most beautiful one there. Once she was dressed in a sari and I had done her makeup, no one could tell her from the real thing."

"So you became a hijra, just like that?"

"No, not just like that...always rushing, rushing, rushing to the end...a story cannot be rushed like that."

Hari looked abashed.

"So much to tell. The lives of six people in a Bombay slum and all he wants is his story. Did you know how we lived? How happy we were? How Chinnamma took care of us and raised us? How Nandini found a nice husband who took her away? No, no, you don't want to hear any of that. Fine, you take the story you want. Chinnamma decided that it was finally time for me to enter the biraderi and so she took me to the same temple where Periamma had taken her so many years ago and end of story."

"Listen, please, I am sorry." Hari put out his hands to calm her. "Just tell it as you like. I promise I won't interrupt..."

"Do you know what happened three years ago? Were you still a suckling back then or did you have some sense between your ears?" Radha said, the anger still in her voice. "Three years ago Chinnamma saved me. She brought me back to life. She took me, just the two of us, on a train, just like this, to Bhopal. Is it coming back to you? Do you know what I am talking about?"

Hari shook his head.

"The Bhopal gas tragedy."

"But I thought everyone died, I don't understand. Why are you alive?"

"Because I wasn't actually in Bhopal, you fool. We arrived in Bhopal the day before the gas leaked and Chinnamma immediately took me on a bus to a small village about two hours west. There we spent the night in an abandoned Devi temple. We had brought along some toddy, some fruits, and flowers. Chinnamma performed the pooja, offered the toddy to the goddess, and then she tied everything down here together, nice and tight." She pointed to her crotch.

"Did it hurt?" Hari said.

"Of course," Radha said. "So around midnight she gave me the toddy to drink and I lay there, in the sanctum of the temple, my head woozy with the drink and the pain. Hours passed and I began to lose consciousness as I drank more and more alcohol and then just before the first ray of the dawn sun hit the sky, Chinnamma took out this long knife and slick," she gestured a swift blade swiping through air.

Hari trembled at her narrative. He pulled his knees closer. After a few moments, he said, "That must have been very painful."

"No, no... no pain," Radha said. "It was a sacrifice to the Devi...so there was no pain, just the grace and blessings as I became a hijra. I remember lying there, the deity looking at me, and I almost fainted from the bliss of becoming a hijra. I knew then, even before we returned to Bhopal the next day, that the goddess had given me a new lease on life. I realized then that she had given me more than I ever wanted. It was only when we reached the nasty-smelling outskirts of Bhopal and later in the days ahead when we heard about the poison gas that I found out how the Devi had actually preserved my life."

As she spoke, her palms came together in salutation. Hari watched as she prostrated herself in the moving train, between the two toilets in that dirty passageway, the dark curtains of the umbilical rustling behind her, the cold winter wind whirling around them. Behind him, the door of the cubicle grated as it opened.

"Shush!" Hari whispered to her, flicking his fingers to motion her back as he clambered up to his feet and hurried into the corridor.

Mrs Sharma appeared at the door, her face wrought with wrinkles, which curved into a half smile as she saw him.

"Everything done?" she asked.

"Uh-huh," he nodded and stepped back into the dark warm cubicle. She shut the door behind him.

IV
Etrittal (opposition)

FIFTEEN

HARI STEPPED OFF the train onto the platform at Ennore station in the bright morning sunlight. The rough concrete felt hard under his thin plimsolls. He stretched and surveyed the quiet station. Small groups were congregated around the coach doors talking amongst themselves. Further up the train, army jawans milled around their coach, their rifles slung around their shoulders. A few among them smoked beedis and cigarettes.

His heart beat faster as he looked past the soldiers and noticed that the signal lamp beyond the engine shone bright green. The train had been signalled to leave, but the flurried beating in his chest eased as Hari realized that the pantograph above the engine was not up. They were not drawing power from the electrical wires that ran above the train.

Ennore was a small commuter station. So small, in fact, that all of the long train could not be accommodated here. Several end coaches trailed beyond the short platform. The only trains that stopped at Ennore were the yellow and brown suburban trains that shuttled workers to and from Madras. The station was open and without shade. Small concrete posts with fluorescent tube lights were scattered through its length. Half a dozen small watering columns—concrete mounds with taps protruding out in four directions—were the only service amenities. At each end of the station huge yellow signboards named the station in Tamil, English, and Hindi.

Hari walked up to the small building that served as the stationmaster's office. In the small corridor that connected the platform to the outside of the station, he ran into Mukund and the card dealer. "What's happening?" Hari asked.

"MGR is dead," Mukund said.

"The chief minister? How?"

"Heart attack last night," said the dealer and pointed to his radio. "Now there is a general strike. No one is here...the doors are padlocked, the windows barricaded. No signs, no information. Seems they left us here and ran off."

Mukund sucked on a beedi. He looked at the train as he blew out the smoke. The dealer seemed to be searching for something. His small transistor radio was turned off.

Hari pointed to it. "What else did they say?"

"Nothing," the dealer shook his head. "Just playing funeral dirges, loud moaning and groaning all morning long. There was one bit of news. They are telling people to stay home and not go out." He laughed. "Even the vice-president is stuck at the airport in Madras."

"If he can't get out of the airport, then there isn't much chance of us leaving."

"Look at this," Mukund said. "This is amazing. A man so loved by his people, his death has brought their world to a standstill."

"Mukund-mian don't get all philosophical and filmi on me now," the dealer said. "If the government had any sense, they would let us get home. Then we can pay homage to the dead man's memory. Dying and leaving us trapped on a train, most unkindly act to do."

"Arré don't blame them," Mukund said. "It's not the government's phault that we are stuck here. You heard what the guard said. The lights are green all the way from here to Madras Central, the tracks are aligned. All clear for our train. Nothing else is moving. So it is not the railway's fault. It's the people holding up the train. They are so affected by his death."

"Goondas and street thugs."

"No, no," Mukund insisted. "You are refusing to understand. Ordinary people...this is a demonstration of love and respect. This is true democracy. Look at them, they show they care through their courage. They are lost, like children without a mother. And what are we complaining about? A few hours delay...arré, what does it matter two hours here, two hours there. Do you think their suffering is going to pass as quickly?"

The dealer turned to Hari. "Look at him, he's also going crazy and revolutionary." He pointed to the front of the train. "That Christian kid Joseph has already left the train and is now one of the people standing in front of the train holding it up."

"Really? Why?" Hari asked.

"He's part of some MGR organization," Mukund replied.

"It's that film club he was talking about," the dealer added.

"So he has to join them. He belongs with them."

The dealer shook his head. "Saala, as soon as the tables turn and the train is stopped, there he is…standing shoulder to shoulder with mischief-makers." He wagged his finger at Hari. "Baba, you watch out for people like him—jumping ship at the first sign of trouble. They are rats, just looking out for themselves. They are dangerous, not good friends."

Mukund laughed and slapped the dealer on the back. "Don't listen to him. He is a cranky old woman this morning. Let's go up there and see what's happening."

They walked along the length of the platform. Mukund gave little soft sucks to his beedi from time to time and pursed his lips to blow the smoke out from one side. Hari thought he looked like a steam locomotive, dressed in black, puffing along smartly with rhythmic exhalations. Their little three-carriage train wound along the platform, Mukund in front, the dealer behind him, and Hari trailing, trying to keep up with their longer strides.

They stopped at the army carriage to chat with the jawans.

"So what is going on, Ji?" Mukund asked.

The oldest, a sergeant, answered, "It's a strike, Bhaiya."

"How long are we going to be here?"

The man shrugged his shoulders. The other men laughed at the question.

"Why don't you do something?" the dealer said. "If you went up there and arrested them, then we could continue on our trip."

"We cannot do anything. This is a civil matter and must be addressed by civilian police. Mil-tree policy." The sergeant shrugged his shoulders again. "But don't worry, we'll soon be on our way. I just sent a corporal to wake the Colonel-sahib in the first-class coach. He'll come down soon. He may talk to the people and ask them to let us continue."

Mukund laid his hand on the dealer's shoulder. "Come, let's go and see."

They left the soldiers and walked up to the engine.

Hari had never been up close to an engine that was shut down. It was an eerie feeling to walk past this gigantic, powerful engineering marvel and not hear it make any sound. Even engines idling on a siding made a low continuous hum, like a giant snoring in his sleep; but this engine was dead. High above him, the engine driver was visible, leaning out the cab window, smoking a cigarette, viewing the scene below. Hari gave him his brightest smile before looking further up the tracks to where a commotion had begun.

A group of young men had gathered in front of the train. Three of them lay across the rails less than a foot from the engine. Others stood around the tracks, shouting and raising slogans from time to time. Some held little bamboo sticks with black and red flags, the official colours of the dead chief minister's party. One man had tied two plastic bags, one black, the other orange, to a tree branch he was waving to signal his loyalty to the party and its dead leader.

Next to the men lying on the tracks, a small black transistor radio, smaller than the one the dealer carried, produced the scratchy dirge from All India Radio that served as the musical backdrop for this protest. Hari could hear MS Subbulakshmi's throaty voice singing a soulful Tamil devotional song.

"Hey, what's going on here?" Mukund asked in Hindi.

The man lying closest to the train sat up and waved him away. "Go away!" he said in a heavy Tamil-accented Hindi.

"What is he saying?" one of the men from the triad asked the man who had sat up. They spoke in Tamil.

"Some northerner, what does he know? Ignore him." Crossing his arms over his chest, he prepared to lie down again on the tracks. His neck came to rest on the rail. Uncomfortable in this posture, he put his hands under his head.

The dealer cursed them. "Saala," he said. "Why are you sleeping on the tracks? Is this any way of showing respect to the dead? You are just wasting everyone's time!"

Hari winced at the dealer's words. If the men had understood his speech in Hindi, they would surely be giving him a thrashing now, he thought. But the strikers must have recognized the insolence in the dealer's tone, because Hari heard one of them say in Tamil to the other two, "Let's get rid of these northerners."

Hari grabbed Mukund's arm. "We should leave now," he said. "They are coming to beat us."

From behind the engine, Joseph appeared with two men dressed in blue work suits with Ashok Leyland tags sewn on them in white. Hari recognized Vishu next to Joseph and stepped behind Mukund.

Mukund waved. "Hey, Joseph, what's happening?"

Joseph flinched at Mukund's use of Hindi. He hesitated, then nodding to the men around him, replied in Hindi, "What are you two doing here?"

The dealer said, "We just came to ask when you guys will let us leave."

Mukund squeezed the dealer's shoulder. "Sew your mouth shut for a bit, will you?" he muttered and then loudly said, "Don't worry about him, Joseph. He's just anxious."

"You'd better take him back to the train before these guys get angry and hurt him." Joseph pointed to the young men standing in front of the engine.

The young men looked uncertain now as Joseph spoke. He waved at them, and muttering, they lay down on the tracks again.

"Come," Mukund said, pulling the dealer away.

Hari wondered about the dealer's displeasure. Train delays were not unusual in India. Derailment, track switching, maintenance, special trains, power failures, Hari could list scores of reasons for them. And even he knew that political unrest always found its way to the tracks. There had been the derailments of British troop trains during the Raj, later the slaughter of refugees stuffed into trains crossing the new borders of independent but partitioned India. Newspapers carried articles about bombs buried under track beds by Sikh separatists in the north, Naxalite communists in the south, Bodo rebels in the east. Despite all this, the railways thrived. In their hearts, everyone knew that this strike too would pass. And they were just an hour north of Madras. They had to wait the strike out.

"Stop!" Vishu said.

Mukund, moving to grab the dealer, had exposed Hari.

"You there, the little boy," Vishu said in Tamil, pointing to Hari. "I know you. You are that little snot who snitched on me."

Mukund put his arm around Hari's shoulders and stared at the young man in the blue overalls.

"I didn't say anything," Hari said in Tamil.

"Don't lie to me, you little faggot, I'm here in Ennore and it's your fault."

"No, I swear, I did not say anything." Hari shook as he answered. He could feel Mukund's arms tightening around him.

"What's this about?" Joseph asked.

"Pah! Nothing," Vishu said. He spat to a side and turned to Hari. "Go and get lost with your friends. I'd better not catch you here again, otherwise…"

Hari shook his head in fearful assent and turned away. As they returned to their coach, Hari knew that Mukund and the dealer were staring at him. They had questions he did not wish to answer.

"He used to work for my grandfather," Hari said. "In Madras."

"What's he doing here, then?" the dealer asked.

Mukund leaned towards Hari, "And what did he say to you?"

Hari shrugged. "My uncle gave him a job at the Ashok Leyland plant." He pointed to the serrated roof of the large factory less than a mile from the station, beyond the slums. "He's angry that my grandfather made him leave Madras to come to Ennore."

"Well, good then," the dealer laughed. "Tell him to let the train go and he can come with us to Madras."

SIXTEEN

WHILE HARI AND HIS MOTHER were ensconced in the quiet cocoon of their ladies' cubicle in the still train, Madras was waking up to the reality of a dead chief minister. Hari's maternal grandparents listened to the radio broadcast in the early morning darkness of their kitchen.

"There is surely trouble brewing," Thatha said as he left to check the water. At the sump he realized the extent of his problem. Not a single drop of municipal water had arrived overnight. He sighed, switched on the pump and returned to the kitchen.

"I turned the radio off," Hari's grandmother said. "Who wants to listen to a funeral dirge in the morning? It's unholy."

Hari's thatha nodded as he sat down on the palakai and frothed his coffee. He was worried. His daughter Kalyani, visiting from Canada, was at the Shetty maternity home two streets down, about to give birth to his second grandchild. She was already several days overdue. Then there was the matter of Savitri and Hari arriving in Madras on the Tamil Nadu Express.

The kitchen clock chimed five. The train wouldn't arrive for another two hours. The telephone rang in the living room. Hari's grandmother, standing by the stove, waved at him to drink his coffee as she rushed to answer it. Thatha, never one to be left out, followed her.

"The contractions have become strong," she said, putting down the receiver. "The baby is due anytime."

He looked at the hamper, packed with the necessary items, both spiritual and temporal, that stood by the door, awaiting the child's birth.

"No," she said, "I'll go with Sivagami to the maternity home; you get ready for your trip. Sundaran will be here soon to take you to Madras Central. Bring Savitri and Hari home safely."

When he came out of his room fastening the buttons on his cotton shirt, Sivagami gave him a toothy smile.

"You watch," she said, hugging the hamper. "It'll be a handsome boy like our little Hari."

"Yes, and he'll be out sucking his mother's breasts if we don't hurry," Hari's grandmother said. She came out of the puja room and pushed the servant ahead of her, and the two departed on their short walk to the maternity clinic.

Hari's thatha stood in the courtyard and watched them hurry along, a bubble of happiness in the desolate street. Even MG Road, always humming with life, appeared silent.

He placed a call from the living room. Madras Central's telephone number for arrivals and departures produced a ring. He waited. There were no such things as answering machines in Madras then, and it often took ten or fifteen rings for someone to notice the phone and answer it. He counted the rings and waited. A busy signal would have left him happier; that meant someone was at the station fielding calls.

He consulted the wall clock again and rang Kollu-thatha, Hari's great-grandfather, who had worked as stationmaster at Madras Central. Kollu-thatha had retired several years ago, but he would know what to do, Hari's thatha hoped. Shanthi answered the phone and Hari's grandfather waited while the phone was conveyed to Appuswamy's wooden swing in the living room.

"Namaskaram," Hari's grandfather began.

"So what's the happy news?" Kollu-thatha asked. "Is it a boy?"

"We're still waiting to hear. We'll know very soon. The doctor expects the delivery within hours."

"Good, good. Better bring the child and mother home as soon as possible. Who knows what kind of nonsense will follow this news. You have heard about MGR's death?"

"Yes, yes, I have...rather a shock."

"What shock?" Kollu-thatha said. "The man has been living on borrowed time for so long, it's like a never-ending Tamil film. But I do wonder who'll replace him. I suppose we can now look forward to going back to a DMK state. Not that anything ever really changes."

"Sir, I called to ask you for a favour," Hari's grandfather interrupted Kollu-thatha's monologue.

"Say it, Hariharan," the elder relative said. "Don't beat around the bush."

"Savitri and her son Hari, your great-grandson, are on the Tamil Nadu Express…and there is no news of the train."

"Did you call Central?"

"No one is answering the phone."

"Oh," Kollu-thatha paused. "Well, let me try a few numbers."

"Thanks, Sir, I appreciate this very much."

"What's there to appreciate? She's like my daughter-in-law and he's my Kollu-peran."

Unnerved by the silence in the streets around him, Hari's grandfather paced the living room as he waited for the telephone call. A bell clanging in the courtyard attracted his attention. Sundaran was unchaining the front gate to bring his rickshaw in.

"Ayya, the streets are not safe," Sundaran said, his voice dropping to prevent the neighbours from overhearing. "These streets are quiet because educated people live here, but the main streets are blocked by poriki rascal students. Ayya, they have declared a strike. I told them I was going home. Only then did they let me drive. Everything is closed, Ayya."

"Well, we still have to try to get to the railway station…"

"But Ayya, the local trains are not running…"

Hari's grandfather snorted. He was about to give Sundaran a piece of his mind when the telephone rang. "Wait here," he said, rushing inside.

He returned after a few minutes, locked the door behind him and rang the tenants' bell upstairs. Having advised them to watch over the house, he waved Sundaran to the rickshaw and climbed into it.

"Central Station, saar?" Sundaran asked.

"No, first we are going to Appuswamy's house on the other side of Usman road."

As Sundaran pedalled the rickshaw through the residential streets, a few children watched them from behind their wrought-iron gates.

Thatha noted the shuttered shops and the barred windows of the apartments above them as they turned onto MG Road. Two young men, sticks with red and black flags stuck to their bicycles, hurried past them. In the distance Thatha saw a couple of auto rickshaws. All the shops and commercial buildings were shut. The street vendors had not set up their stalls. MG Road looked broader and cleaner. It reminded Thatha of the time in his youth when the area was quiet and gentrified.

Men had congregated in the square ahead. Sundaran observed the crowd anxiously; he had to go past them to turn onto the street where Kollu-thatha lived. The bicyclists, who had passed them, stopped and mingled with the gathered men. As Sundaran and Thatha drew near, they saw a young man in the centre pour a can of kerosene over himself. The circle around the youth watched him, some piously, others in shock. They all looked grief-stricken. Sundaran turned away from the scene but Thatha kept watching. The young man was barely out of his teens.

"How can I live without my hero?" the youth said, as the last drops of kerosene fell upon him. "Can fire burn without wood?"

The men shook their heads in reply. Soaking wet, the young man smiled as he lit a match and placed it on his heart. He turned into a flash of light as his clothes, skin, and hair caught fire.

"I'm coming to you, my father and my hero," he cried out, as the flames enveloped him. "May Lord Yama take my soul and restore yours to life."

Beneath the statue of Mahatma Gandhi, founder of the nation and in whose memory the road was named, the immolated man danced and chanted. Around him, the circle of men cried as they chanted MGR's name. Then he began writhing and screaming as the fire burned through his flesh. The crowd grew anxious as they watched him die. The bicyclists yelled out for a blanket to smother the flames. A man in the crowd protested this interference. Thatha tapped Sundaran to get the rickshaw going again. As they rode away from the group, the screams of the burning man faded. Soon they heard an explosion and black smoke rose in the sky, as a municipal bus burned in the distance. Sundaran turned away from MG Road into a side street. He drove Thatha through alleyways and residential roads and finally arrived at Kollu-thatha's residence. Shanthi stood in the courtyard watching the road, waiting for them.

"Come in, come in," she said, inviting him in with a relieved smile. "I'll make some coffee."

"No, no, we don't have time for coffee, Ma," Thatha said.

"Hariharan, you have all the time for coffee," Kollu-thatha said. He looked younger, dressed in the thin cotton shirt and black cotton pants from his work life. Hari's grandfather recalled the man who had come so many years ago to his house bearing a marriage proposal for Savitri.

"You stay here and watch over Shanthi," Kollu-thatha said, reaching for a cane. "I'll go to Madras Central and sort this out. Apparently the train is stopped at Ennore station and no one seems to know why. Sundaran will take me there and I'll make sure that Savitri and Hari get home safely."

"Let me come with you," Hari's grandfather said. "It'll be safer."

"For whom?" Kollu-thatha argued. "What are they going to do to me? I'm just a frail old man who trembles even without their threats. I've seen more politicians die than the number of years these fellows have lived on this earth. No, you stay here and look after Shanthi. We can't leave her here all alone."

Hari's grandfather reluctantly acquiesced and made a sign to Sundaran to take care of the elder relative as Kollu-thatha slowly boarded the rickshaw. Shanthi began sobbing as the rickshaw disappeared down the street.

"Don't worry, Ma. No harm will come to him."

"Forgive me, it's just that he hasn't gone out alone in so long…"

"Sundaran is with him. He'll take care of him."

Shanthi nodded, unconvinced, and headed back into the house. Thatha brought out a wicker chair to the shaded veranda and sat down to wait. There had been no newspaper delivery so he reread the previous day's newspaper. Shanthi served him a tumbler of coffee and stood uncertainly by the door, surveying the emptiness all around. The telephone rang within. The paper rustled as Thatha turned. He saw Shanthi disappear into the house.

"It's a trunk call," she said when she returned. "Girish is on the phone from Nagpur."

"The train is stuck in Ennore because of the strike; we can't do anything until it gets to Madras Central," Thatha said on the phone to Girish. He listened as Girish spoke on the line, then asked, "Did you want us to call him? No, okay. You ask him to check on them and make sure they are all right."

He hung up the phone and turned to Shanthi. "Girish just had a wonderful idea. He's going to call Tangarajan and have him check on the train in Ennore."

"Of course," Shanthi said. "The Leyland factory is less than a kilometre from the station. Good, things will be fine now." She smiled, relieved that she could turn her attention to more prosaic matters. "Shall I make some dosais for breakfast?"

SEVENTEEN

BACK IN THE TRAIN, hunger pains gnawed at Hari as the sun rose in the sky. There were no more puris in the tin. Savitri peered out into the corridor from time to time, hoping for a railway vendor to come by. Suman opened the steel shutters to let in the light, but left the glass pane down. She watched the small movements in the shantytown beyond the station.

"Shall I go to the pantry and see?" Hari asked.

Savitri frowned and shook her head. "They'll come," she said.

"It's already almost nine o'clock," Hari said. "It's been three hours and they still haven't come."

Savitri tugged her sari around her head tighter and just shrugged. Ever since the robbery, she had pulled the sari up like a shawl around her neck.

Mukund popped his head into the cubicle, a big grin on his face. "Breakfast is coming."

"I told you," Savitri turned to Hari.

"Really?" Suman said, looking towards Mukund.

Mukund nodded. "Some men are coming up with huge pots and walking along the train distributing food!"

"Thank God, at least we won't starve," Mrs Sharma said, twirling her prayer beads between her fingers. Then, when Mukund disappeared, she added, "I don't know about him. What kind of a ladies' cubicle is this with him coming in when he pleases?"

Savitri just bowed her head in reply. Hari got up to join Mukund, but she fixed him with a stare.

"Ma, he's just trying to help," Suman said.

"He should just leave us alone," her mother replied. "People will talk if a man his age keeps hanging around a ladies' cubicle."

"I think they are a little too busy with other things, to worry about us women," Suman said.

"I've said my piece," Mrs Sharma said and sighed. "What else can I do?"

"Savitri?" Tangarajan stood at the cubicle door.

"Athimbér. . ." Savitri addressed him by his kin title in a shocked whisper as she sat up in the berth. "What are you doing here? Were you on the train all this time?"

Tangarajan-athimbér smiled at her questions and yelled down the corridor, "Ranga, send someone with food down here."

He came into the cubicle, nodded politely to the two Punjabi women and sat next to Hari's mother. "Hari! How are you doing?"

"Did you bring the food?" Hari asked.

Tangarajan nodded. "It was your father's idea actually."

"Really?" Savitri looked surprised.

"Yes, the plant has suspended the day shift because of the strike," Tangarajan told her, reaching over to take the banana plates with jaggery rice from a blue-shirted worker. He passed them out to everyone. "Eat, eat," he said.

Hari stuck his fingers into the sweet chakra pongal. It was warm, full of ghee, and studded with fried cashews. His fingers were dirty, however, and made the first few bites taste salty. As he ate, he noticed that his mother had hesitated over the food in her hand.

"Have you eaten?" she asked Tangarajan.

"I ate at the factory," he said, and pointed to her food. "Eat, please."

With a reluctance that Hari found surprising, given their hunger, she pecked at the rich food. "Why chakra pongal?" she asked.

Tangarajan laughed. "You won't believe it. Ranga, our cook at the factory, cooked the pongal because it's the general manager's birthday today. He made huge vats of it to feed the six hundred workers and staff. Then we got news that the factory was to be shut down because of

MGR's death."

Suman said, "But your factory is private, no?"

Tangarajan explained. "No matter, it's a hartal as you say in the north. Full state shutdown." He turned to Savitri. "Anyway, the general manager did not even show up. So here I was stuck with all this food and no workers."

"That's when your father called," Tangarajan turned to Hari. "He said that the train was stuck at Ennore. So I thought why not grab the kitchen staff and bring the food out here? I could make sure that you two are well and do a good deed alongside."

Mrs Sharma nodded deeply at this statement. "Yes, it is very honourable to feed the hungry. You will accrue great merit for this action." She lifted her plate up as she spoke.

As Hari ate and listened, he watched his Tangarajan-uncle with renewed interest. He recalled that morning many years ago when he had first met Tangarajan at the railway yard in Nagpur. How long ago that seemed now. Tangarajan lived in Ennore and made his appearance in Madras during festivals. Since Hari spent only his summers in Madras, their meetings had been rare.

Hari's mother did not meet Tangarajan-athimbér's eyes as she ate, keeping her head bowed. Would she tell him about the robbery, Hari wondered. He was about to ask her when loud noises from the corridor interrupted their breakfast. Joseph, at the head of a posse of young men, pushed his way into the cubicle. An unhappy and shaken Ranga stood behind them.

"What is the meaning of all this?" Tangarajan asked.

"Are you the person behind this mockery?" Joseph tossed a banana leaf plate with its heap of jaggery rice. It splattered on the red floor and Ranga gasped in the corridor.

"How dare you!" Tangarajan stood up.

"How dare I?" Joseph said. "How dare you go around distributing sweets on such a black day? MGR is dead and you are handing out pongal!"

"Listen," Tangarajan put up his hand. "Let's talk about this outside. You are scaring the women and the child."

Joseph stared angrily at them, but relented, and the men walked out onto the platform. Ranga bent low as he came into the cubicle. Apologizing for the insult, he squatted and cleaned up the mess.

Heated conversation could be heard outside, as Tangarajan explained why the pongal was being distributed.

"I don't care," Hari heard Joseph's angry voice say. "Let it rot. But no one should eat a dish like this today."

"It's just food." Was that the dealer's voice? Hari wanted to be closer to see. He ate up the last bit of rice, crushed his banana leaf, and stood up.

"Where are you going?" Savitri asked.

"Just to get rid of this," Hari raised the banana leaf.

"Open the window and throw it."

"I still have to wash my hands."

Without waiting for an answer, he stepped around Ranga and walked out into the vestibule.

Radha sat crouched between the two toilets, furtively eating her ration of pongal. She nodded towards the yelling match outside. It was the dealer of cards screaming at Joseph.

"Who do you think you are to decide what we can or cannot eat? First you keep us holed up here for hours, now you won't even let us eat? Do you want us all to die?"

"Why should we live, if MGR does not live?" A young man beside Joseph said.

The dealer threw up his hands at this. Joseph himself put up an arm to silence the man.

"We are not saying you can't eat. Just don't eat this." He pointed to the vat of jaggery rice beside them.

"There is nothing else to eat! If not this, what shall we eat? Mud and rocks?"

Hari saw that Tangarajan-athimbér had withdrawn to a side as the argument progressed. Nothing new was said, but each iteration escalated the tone and soon the passengers and strikers were yelling at each other. Tangarajan and his blue-shirted kitchen staff stepped further back, relegated to the role of bystanders.

"Baba, you better go to the army jawans and get some help," the hijra said to Hari, in between morsels of her breakfast. "There is going to be trouble otherwise."

Hari ran down the corridor, through the coach, and out onto the platform. Behind him, he could hear sounds of fighting as words were backed up by pushing and shoving. As he ran alongside the train, Hari saw Mukund sauntering down the platform towards him, a cigarette in his mouth.

"Did you get something to eat?" Mukund asked.

"Mukund, we have to get help," Hari panted. "There's fighting back there."

"What do you mean?"

"Joseph wants to stop the pongal distribution," Hari pointed to the coach filled with military personnel near the engine. "They are fighting with the passengers and my uncle. We have to get the army...to stop them."

"You wait here, I'll get them," Mukund said and ran towards the army coaches.

A Muslim woman in burkha walking down the platform flinched as his cigarette butt flew in the air past her. Hari slipped into the nearest coach and returned through the train corridors. Nearing their coach, he again heard the commotion on the platform. The passengers had locked the carriage doors from within. Even the ladies' door was shut. Hari wondered how his mother had let the door be closed upon him. In his anger he almost rapped on the aluminium shutters, but decided against it.

The confrontation with his mother would leave him trapped within, he figured. Instead, he squatted in the vestibule next to Radha and observed the fight through the window in the coach door. She had shut it to prevent anyone from coming in.

Tangarajan-athimbér was standing with Ranga, who was brandishing a ladle like a weapon. They watched powerlessly as the passengers and strikers battled it out.

"Joseph and that loud man started the fight," Radha explained, gesturing towards the dealer. "But see that one, that striker in the blue shirt..."

Hari nodded as she pointed Vishu out to him.

"He brought a tree branch over the loud man's head," Radha said, "So he's finished."

The dealer was sitting down, a shirt pressed against his head. There was blood on the shirt.

A passenger swung his thermos flask at Joseph. It hit Joseph on the back. As the passenger drew it back to lash out again, Joseph turned and grabbed the flask, pulling the passenger in, and socked a punch at his face.

Then Hari heard whistles and heavy shoes trampling on the concrete. He peered through the window as the jawans ran into the crowd, their rifles held across their chests like pikes. The crowd parted and Mukund stood in the centre with two of the soldiers. They were the sergeant and a younger officer.

"Now, what is all this commotion?" the officer asked as the platform fell silent.

Radha shuffled closer to take a look at the army officer. In the silence that followed his question, they could see the two camps that had fought over the train's fate. Beyond them, Tangarajan stood with his worker escort. The sergeant whispered into the officer's ear. Hari turned to Radha as the officer ignored the pleas of Joseph and the card dealer and went up to Tangarajan.

"That's my uncle," he said.

Radha peered at the two men conversing on the platform. "Sure, and the officer is my brother."

"No, I am serious. He works at the Leyland factory here in Ennore. My father telephoned him when he found out that we were stuck here. So he came over and brought the entire train breakfast."

"Really? He seems a little young."

"He studied in Manchester. That's in England. He's very smart."

Radha nodded at the statement and watched Hari. Hari, nonplussed, stared out the door. The officer brought his uncle, Joseph, and the card dealer together. As the four men talked, a medic bandaged the dealer's wound. Mukund stood next to the sergeant. When the medic had finished, the officer led his men up the platform back towards their carriage. Mukund went up to the officer and spoke to him in a low voice. The officer motioned to the sergeant and left. Mukund returned to his place next to the sergeant.

Radha laughed. "Saala, look at him. He thinks he is a big hero and everything."

"He did bring the jawans, you know. I asked him to."

"And that's why he is so afraid." She spat on the floor. "He wants to stay close to the officer otherwise the strikers will probably break his bones and scar his lovely face."

"You don't like him, do you?"

"And you like him too much."

Hari turned to her. "What do you mean by that?"

Radha peered at him. "Aren't you a decent convent-educated boy?"

"If you only knew what happens behind those high walls."

"Don't you get coy with me, boy, you have no idea about anything," she said. "I'll tell you the truth about your filmi hero."

Hari leaned against the formica-lined wall of the toilet in the vestibule, his knees bent.

"I know how you look at him, the one in the black clothes, whose pants are so tight that his balls are scrunched up…"

Hari cringed at the tawdry reference and Radha stiffened.

"See, I told you, you can't hear talk like this. You are just a chokra after all. But you know I am telling the truth. You have been making eyes at him during this entire trip. You can't keep from staring at him if he is around. Don't think that I don't notice. I may be an ignorant chakka, but God has given me eyes to see."

"And a mouth to match," Hari said.

She looked at him, bemused, like a parent. "All right little master, don't pout. You want to hear something about that tight-pants…"

Hari nodded.

"Yesterday, in the afternoon, when the train was still running, I caught him sneaking into the toilet with that young woman in your coach…you know, for some nooki," she motioned, with a wink, forming a ring with one hand and pushing a finger from the other hand into it.

"Mukund? With Suman? Are you sure?" Hari's voice rose in uncertain cadence. It did not make any sense. Mukund he could imagine slipping into dank toilets for a quickie in the style of a film personality but he just hadn't thought that a woman like Suman would do something like that. Then he remembered Anamika and grew silent.

"Arré…I just told you, no? I saw with these very eyes," she gestured. "Besides, I waited around to see what happened in the end. The slut slipped out first and I knew from her guilty look as she rushed off. Then last night I saw her in your cubicle, Baba. After she left the toilet, she left the door open a bit so I saw that little prick smoothing his shirt."

Radha clasped Hari's arm and drew close. "He was styling his hair…maybe the bitch likes to grab hair when she rides a man, huh?"

Hari did not pull away from her. His mind was transfixed by the thought of a sexual coupling in a train toilet. It seemed dingy and dirty, but also attractive and adventurous. His eyes barely registered the animated face of the woman-man as she cackled on the dirty floor of the railway carriage. Images of Suman grabbing Mukund's hair and rubbing against his nakedness caused his body to tremble with nervous excitement. Hari grew conscious of the fact that the hijra was holding his hand and that he was wearing little but thin cotton shorts over his enlivening crotch.

With a hoarse noise, halfway between a cry and a moan, Hari jerked her hand off, and ran past her. Radha's raucous laughter followed him. Two large bamboo baskets lined with jute sacks blocked his path. He shrunk to scrape through. Stumbling past the people chatting, he thrust his hands deep in his pockets to distract attention from the rise between his legs. The coach was dark, since the engine had long gone silent.

Finally, the toilets on the other side of the coach! The door of one was unlatched; he slid inside and locked it. A slight stench of urine accosted him, but otherwise it seemed clean. It was one of the few western-style toilets interspersed through the train. No one Hari knew, other than Mani-mama and Sarah-aunty, sat on such toilets. Everyone else preferred to squat on their haunches on the Indian-style toilets. So despite the long train journey and the inordinate delay of the strike, this particular toilet hadn't been used. The stench, which Hari had been steeling himself against, proved to be benign here.

He eased his shorts around his penis and let them fall on the floor. In the tiny mirror of the sparse toilet, Hari watched himself squirming as the swelling increased. In his experience, after a few minutes of painful throbbing, it settled back down. Hari was still unsure why his penis did what it did, so he rubbed the dry pink of the prickly head to calm it. A droplet of blood appeared on it. This had never happened before. Hari grew afraid that his penis would burst and bleed him to death. Instinctively, he spat on his palm to coat the head with saliva.

His eyes glazed over as he tried to film Mukund and Suman in his head, the fumbling and the grating, the unzipping of the fly. He smelt the musk of the pubis and felt the friction of flesh against flesh. Lacking a vocabulary for sex, Hari drew fear and confusion from his experience with Anamika; and the longing and desire from fumbling with Mohan in the dark movie theatre. He knew nakedness and near nakedness from the lean, sinewy, burnt-chocolate-brown backs of construction workers, the sadhus in Benaras, and street children on Marina beach, but the nudity of sex was beyond him. Unaware of the rhythm and persistent activity of sex, Hari imagined Mukund's body moving little as he caressed the still dressed Suman. But then, Hari had no use for Suman in his lusty imagination, for she was only a means. It was Mukund he was interested in. His eyes ran over Mukund's body, stripping him of his clothes, blending him with all the naked bodies in his imagination.

Soon Hari felt a strong urge. His body went stiff. His hands fell off and he watched as his penis throbbed of its own accord. He wanted to move and point it towards the toilet bowl so he wouldn't pee all over the floor of the toilet and yet he could not move. It was unlike anything he had ever felt. Something surged from within him and he was powerless to control it. In three painful spurts, he squirted out blobs of white mucosal gloop. Even as he ejaculated, Hari brought his hands to cover himself and ended up spewing semen all over the palm of his right hand.

Once it was on his hand, hot, wet, and clammy, he breathed out a sigh of relief. This was it—semen! This was sperm. His sperm! This is what comes out—not urine, he thought. In a flash, Hari realized that Mohan was right about how babies were made, and even Anamika's overture during their doctor game seemed less threatening.

Deep inside his pubis, body parts groaned and creaked from their first test run. He could sense the dull pain along the back of his testicles in tubes that he never knew existed, and which he had felt for the first time, and the rush of semen past them. He could feel his erection finally subsiding.

There was now other business to attend to. Holding the dollops of semen steady in his right hand, Hari reached to push in the spring-loaded tap in the sink with his left hand. Nothing came out from the tap. He pushed again, harder, and felt the spring squeeze in. Nothing.

The water tanks were empty.

Hari stared at the clammy jelly trickling down his fingers. He observed the spots of rust and streaks of dirt on his palm. As he raised it to his nose, instead of the usual smell of commingled soap, lemon, and salt from the musk of his thin pubic hair, he smelt rust and iron, bloodlike in its strength. Hari leaned against the tap spring with all of his strength hoping for a trickle of water.

When none came, he squatted and looked underneath the steel sink. Someone had slathered the underside with hideous ochre yellow paint in streaks. Hari wiped his hands on the pipe. When he lifted his hands back to his nose, he retched at the smell of the rust and dust from the railway carriages. Most of the gloop was off, stuck under the sink, but a few bits remained on his fingers.

He nibbled against a finger, tentatively scraping a small blob off. He ran his tongue against the mucosal jelly, feeling its texture and taste in his fast drying mouth. Quite insipid, he decided but upon swallowing it, Hari felt his throat constrict and become scratchy.

All thoughts of Mukund and Suman, and their tryst in the other toilet had fled his mind. The lust that provoked the masturbatory session was spent in the worry to conceal the evidence. Hari pulled up his shorts, and sliding his still dirty hand into a pocket, he ran out into the platform.

At the single operational tap on the platform, he stood in the line, waiting for his turn. His tongue moved constantly in his mouth to find more saliva. His hands fidgeted, rubbing against the cloth of his shorts, trying to spread the jelly stain to conceal the evidence.

EIGHTEEN

HARI WASHED HIS HANDS and scrubbed his face, ignoring the people who jostled him to get access to the water. It was almost noon and when Hari left the tap, his face and hands dripping water that dried rapidly in the sun, he could see that the mood on the platform remained sour. The confrontation with the strikers over breakfast had left both sides angry. Small groups of army jawans strolled along the platform, as if on a promenade.

Tangarajan-uncle beckoned him. Hari waved back. As he walked towards him, he wondered what his foreign-educated uncle thought about the strike. Mani-mama would have called the strike an example of typical Indian backwardness. But Mani-mama liked to rile people, especially his father, Hari's thatha.

"Your mother's worried," Tangarajan said. "She sent me to look for you."

Hari shrugged. "I was just taking a walk on the platform. What did the army officer say?"

"Not much to say," Tangarajan motioned to the front of the train. "He sent the strikers back. Seems he's got a good head on his shoulders. They wanted him to promise not to interfere."

"Did he?"

"He just said that the strike was a civilian matter. Unless it was an emergency, he had no power here."

"An Indira Gandhi-style emergency? That won't happen, will it?"

"No," Tangarajan laughed. "I don't think Rajiv Gandhi believes in wielding the stick like his mother."

"So the colonel won't help."

"No, Hari. He won't help, yet. But you have to learn to read between the lines. When the colonel decides it is time to leave, the train will leave."

Hari looked at his uncle as they walked along the platform. What did he know? "Do you remember that time long ago when I met you at the railway yard in Nagpur?"

"Yes, you were just a little boy then. You've grown up quite a bit since then."

"You promised me that you would let me ride a train engine."

Tangarajan stopped and studied Hari for a moment. "Yes, I did, didn't I? Have you never been inside an engine yet?"

Hari shook his head.

"Really? And you still want to try?"

Hari nodded.

"All right, let's go up and ask. But this is an electric engine. Not a steam one."

"I know that."

Tangarajan whistled a happy tune as they walked past the carriages to the front of the train. As they drew near, Ranga, who was chatting with the driver, pointed to Tangarajan and said, "This is who decided to serve the company breakfast to the train."

The engine driver nodded and brought his hands together in salutation.

"What new troubles are you brewing, Ranga?" Tangarajan said.

"Ayya, I would never do anything…" Ranga's plaintive protest stopped as Tangarajan smiled and raised his hand.

"So, are they giving you problems?" Tangarajan asked the driver, gesturing to the tracks below where the strikers lay in front of the engine.

"No, no. Once they got the train to stop, they haven't bothered me. After all, what can I do while they lie on the tracks?"

"True enough, what's your name?"

"Cherian, saar."

"Cherian," Hari said. "You are from Kerala, aren't you?"

Cherian smiled at Hari's question.

"Joseph," Hari pointed out the young man among the strikers, "he is from Kerala too."

"Ranga! Did you serve them breakfast?" Tangarajan said, watching the strikers. Indeed, several of them were eating jaggery rice as they squatted on the tracks or stood in their clumps.

"Ayya, even they get hungry," Ranga replied.

Tangarajan laughed. "Cherian, look at that. They fought us earlier to stop distributing breakfast and now they have no problems eating that same food."

"It is very good, sir," the driver said. "Especially when you are hungry."

"Hmm, Cherian, do me a favour." Tangarajan waved towards Hari. "This is my nephew. Show him the inside of your engine cab, will you? Who knows, he may end up designing the next generation of these engines, huh?"

"As you say, Ayya." Cherian climbed the rungs and opened the cab door. Once in the engine, he stooped and helped Hari up.

It was a WAM-4 electric engine, with a silver-coloured roof. A thin yellow strip of paint, like a cummerbund, separated the top half of the engine, painted rust red, from the navy blue bottom. Four portholes covered in dark tinted glass peered out from each side of the engine. When he climbed within, Hari was surprised by the coarseness of the interior. Gone were the clean lines and the sleek finish of the outside. Here, teal-green paint had been slapped over the walls and the ceiling, so that it had dried in rivulets. The windows and consoles had been attached to the frame by black tar that had oozed and bubbled.

Under the grille-covered windows on either side of the cab were wooden seats covered with green rexine sheets. Standing between these seats, Hari peered out through the glass windows at the front of the cab. The strikers, who were lying on the tracks, were not visible from this vantage point. The signal glowed a bright green, and the two silver rails stretched out to the horizon, chaperoned by concrete poles and catenated wires.

"This is where the engine driver sits," Cherian said. "I'll tell you more about these dials later, but come this way now." Cherian led him to the back of the engine. The portholes weakly lit the narrow corridor and

Hari smelled heavy oil fumes.

"The power in the line above is 25,000 volts; it comes through the pantograph on top, then is brought down to about 3000 volts through these transformers here before it is fed into the motors that run the train."

"You have your own transformers here?" Hari asked. "My father built the transformers on the Itarsi-Bhusaval section of the tracks."

"Well, those are step-up transformers, which raise the voltage; these ones in the engine bring it down."

"Why raise it and lower it?"

"It's a lot easier to move current when the voltage is high. . ."

"How do you get the pantograph up?"

"Come, let's go back into the engine cab, I'll show you."

Cherian led Hari back into the cab. There he pointed to a rubber-covered lever. Hari's attention wandered to the gauges, their needles limp at zero.

Hari tapped the glass covering the dials and asked, "If we raise the pantograph, the dials will go up?"

"Some of them will," Cherian replied and pointed to the speedometer. "Others like this one will not do anything right now."

"Can I push up the pantograph and see what happens?"

Cherian looked out through the windows of the cab. Tangarajan and Ranga were talking on the platform. Below him, on the tracks, the strikers lay chatting with each other. One got up to pee off the edge of the platform.

"Please?"

Cherian sighed and nodded.

"Can I do it?"

"All right, but I am going to stand right next to you and help you with it. It's a bit cranky sometimes. Come on over."

Hari pushed against the rubber insulation of the lever. It did not budge. Cherian covered Hari's hand with his own palm. Instead of pushing up like Hari had done, Cherian jiggled the knob before moving it up in a fluid stroke. The engine cab reverberated with the hum of electricity.

"Hey!"

The shout came from the tracks. Cherian opened a side window and leaned out. Hari climbed up on the driver's seat and saw Joseph and

Vishu running towards the engine. At Vishu's approach, Hari moved to the platform side of the engine, away from where the strikers were approaching, and stood at the cab door. People crowded back into the train. A few men stood by the carriage doors along the train, looking towards him.

"What's happening?" Hari asked.

"The lights and fans have come back on," Tangarajan said, pointing to the pantograph raised above the engine.

Ranga said, "Nothing good can come of this, saar."

"Quit yapping. This might just be the break we need."

Mukund and the army sergeant sprinted up to the engine. Hari waved to them from the driver's cabin.

"Are they letting us go?" Mukund asked.

"No," Hari said. "The driver was just showing me how the engine works."

"That is dangerous," the sergeant said.

"Come now, he is just a child," Tangarajan said. "Might as well let him have his fun while we wait here. There is not much else to do."

"It is not the boy I am worried about," the sergeant said. "Look there, at the people getting back on the train. Do you think they are going to be happy if they find out that the lights and fans came back because a boy was playing?"

Mukund laughed. "It will be like Lord Krishna's lila—except there are no comely gopis to play games with."

"Maybe this Hari's lila will lead the train out of this godforsaken station," Tangarajan replied.

The sergeant's eyes squinted thoughtfully as he studied the young manager's face. He looked at the engine cab, walked up in front to observe the strikers, who lay visibly afraid and confused on the tracks. The engine headlight burned a bright white despite the noonday sun. The sergeant returned to the trio on the platform. "This is a dangerous game you are playing, and with a child. Nothing good can come of it."

Hari spoke up, "But Uncle, this is so much fun. The dials are all turning and my whole body is shaking from the engine."

"What are the strikers saying to the driver?" Tangarajan asked him.

Hari drew back into the dark cabin, close to Cherian, and listened to the engine driver's conversation with Joseph and Vishu, who were on the other side of the engine, on the tracks below.

"Nothing," Hari said, leaning back towards his uncle. "They thought we were going to start the train, but Cherian told them that we need power from the line to recharge the coach batteries. He says the people will need the fans to work for the afternoon."

Tangarajan directed an I-told-you-so look towards the sergeant. Then, a playful smile on his face, he faced the engine cab again and said, "Hari, why don't you give two hoots on the horn. Let's see how loud it is!"

"Really, can I?" Hari said.

"Sir!" The sergeant said. "Are you trying to alarm the strikers?"

"If I were you, I'd get your jawans here quickly," Tangarajan said and turned to Mukund. "And you, you are in the same coach as Hari and his mother? Run back and tell her that he is safe up here with me. Otherwise she will worry."

Mukund nodded and raced down the platform. The sergeant licked his lips and sighed. Then he turned and walked briskly back to the coaches containing the army jawans. Behind him, two short blasts and a single long hoot sounded from the engine horn. The platform was now deserted and only a few plucky men stood next to the doors, grasping the handles. For the moment, they watched the scene up front where two men stood next to the engine cab, in front of the signal post with its green lamp.

The sergeant's mind was troubled as he walked back to the train. The colonel was at the end of his tether with the strikers. The navy ship to ferry the troops was scheduled to depart Madras Port for the Jaffna peninsula in Sri Lanka in eight hours. Perhaps it wouldn't leave, given the strike, but the colonel was impatient to get to the docks. The sooner the men arrived in Sri Lanka, the better for the beleaguered troops there. The sergeant had served in Punjab during the thick of the insurgency. The only thing worse for a soldier than being in a battle was not making it to one in time.

Back at the engine, Cherian whirled away from the cab window where he had been talking to the strikers when Hari sounded the horn. "What are you doing?" he said.

Hari stepped away from the horn. "I just wanted to see what the horn sounded like."

"Who is in there with you?" Vishu shouted from the tracks.

They could hear him climbing up the rungs. The handle shook as Vishu tried to open the door from the outside. Cherian ran and fastened the door shut. Vishu stood on the rungs, hanging from the railing outside. Hari could hear Joseph screaming curses at the driver. The strikers, who were squatting in groups and eating, flung their food down and scrambled towards the engine. The three men lying on the tracks watched the engine nervously. One tried to sit up on the concrete sleeper, but the other two pulled him back down.

"There is just a little boy who wanted to know how the engine works, Ayya," Cherian said. "Forgive him. He mistakenly hit the horn, saar."

"You rascal!" Vishu said, thumping the steel door. "Do you take us for fools? We'll just swallow that load of shit about you giving a child a joyride while we're striking? Let me in!"

"Please don't let him in," Hari said.

Cherian discreetly waved Hari away, keeping his hand below Vishu's sight, and spoke out of the cab door. "Ayya, I cannot let you into the engine cab. Railway policy."

"Don't you Ayya me!" Vishu shouted. "Let me into the cab now!"

"Yeah! If you are letting children in, you better let us in as well!" Joseph yelled from the tracks. "First that Leyland man with his chakra pongal and now you getting all the people riled up in the carriages, you will not leave!"

"I'm coming in, whether you like it or not," Vishu said. "We should have removed you from the engine when we stopped the train." Raising himself on one foot, Vishu peeked into the cab and caught sight of Hari. "You rascal! I told you not to come here. I'm going to give you a proper thrashing."

Vishu pummelled the driver through the open window. Cherian tried to fend off the blows with his palms, screaming at the young man to stop. Hari watched Vishu, his features wild and animated like a rabid street dog's, struggle with the driver. Perhaps if he shut the engine down, Hari thought, everything would return to normal. He tugged the lever in front of him to wrench the pantograph down from the live wire.

Instead, the train lurched forward. The uproar among the strikers drowned out the engine as it revved up, the transformers running and motors turning. Cherian abandoned his post at the window to brake the runaway train. Vishu fell off the railing from which he had hung on to Joseph. He lay sprawled on the gravel, his leg broken.

The three strikers on the tracks made a futile effort to scramble up and out of the way. The engine rolled over them; it faltered and came to a stop atop the broken bodies. Blood pooled on the tracks and concrete sleepers for a brief moment before dispersing in the gravel. In the shocked silence that followed, Hari and the driver heard a roar from the carriages. It could have been a roar of delight from the passengers because the train had moved. Or a roar of annoyance because it had stopped again.

Joseph stood up, shaken by his fall but unhurt. He screamed. His arms flailing at his sides, he yelled and shrieked at the brutal steel monster in front of him. He kicked at the wheels, spat obscenities at the engine, the railways, and the driver. Then he collapsed, sobbing on the gravel.

With shrill whistles and the trample of heavy boots, the sergeant led his column of troops to the engine. There he found Tangarajan white-faced with shock. Ranga squatted on the platform, wailing like a widow. The troops ran past the three men and crossed the tracks to where the strikers stood on the far side of the engine. The sergeant could not see the bodies under the engine, below the edge of the platform. However, he heard Cherian's call for help. Hari lay unconscious in the engine cab.

Tangarajan ran up the steps of the cab to his nephew; a jawan brought the news of the casualties to the sergeant.

"Go, get Colonel Sahib here and rouse the company," the sergeant commanded. "We will need at least two more columns here."

The sergeant climbed up into the engine. The air inside smelt of burnt wire and grease fumes. Tangarajan huddled over the boy stretched out on the floor as Cherian wiped a wet rag across the boy's face.

"You have to pull the engine back," the sergeant said in a hushed voice to Cherian.

Cherian nodded and sat at the controls. His hands were shaking, so he worked the controls slowly. He brought the dials back to order and after giving a short hoot, he wrenched the engine back over the mutilated bodies on the track. Then he put the brakes on, ran to the door overlooking the platform, and retched violently.

The sergeant patted the driver on the back. "Why did you start the train when you knew they were lying down?"

"I didn't," Cherian said. "It was an accident. I was at the window talking to the strikers. The boy pulled the lever…"

A small crowd of men crept up the platform behind the column of infantrymen, drawn towards the engine by the unusual commotion.

"Havaldar!" the sergeant commanded from the engine door. "Form a cordon around the engine. No, go and make a cordon starting from the mail carriage behind the engine. Let no one through. And send a medic to the engine."

Onlookers from the slums gathered in the distance to watch the scene. Soldiers hauled out stretchers and wrapped the broken bodies of the three strikers in bed sheets and plastic. Murmurs arose from the passengers behind the cordon as they saw troops transporting the bodies into the mail carriage.

The crowd pressed against the troops, pelting them with questions. The corporal in charge moved along the ranks of his jawans wondering if the crowd would become unruly and break through. Then, suddenly, the crowd fell silent. The corporal turned and saw the sergeant and the man from the Leyland factory lead a young boy down from the engine. He looked limp and weak.

"Hari!" Mukund shouted.

Hari turned and gazed into the crowd of peering faces, his face ashen with shock and fear. He did not recognize anyone behind the khaki wall. His head fell again and the two men beside him led him to a bench under a tree. There he sat. The colonel joined them and they conversed in low voices.

Mukund fought through the crowd to run back to the ladies' cubicle. Hari's mother stood at the carriage door watching the clot of men far away. Above their heads, the signal lamp now shone a deep red. There was still no sign of Hari. It had been over an hour since he'd left. Mukund's message that he was with Tangarajan had brought her some solace. But this jerking and clanging of the coaches as the train first moved forward and then back…what was going on up front?

She spied Mukund as he broke through a clutch of men and ran towards her. She waved to him in relief and then caught herself. It was indecent for a married woman like her to wave to a young man like that. Abashed, she withdrew into the vestibule and cast a quick glance at Radha, who watched her from the floor. There was no emotion on the hijra's face as Savitri drew back into her cubicle.

"What's happening?" Mrs Sharma asked, counting her rosary beads.

Savitri said, "That young man, Mukund, is coming. Maybe he will have some news."

"Hari is fine," Mukund said, barging into the cubicle. "He's just up near the engine."

"What is happening up front?" Mrs Sharma asked.

"Some kind of accident," Mukund said. "The jawans are putting bodies into the mail van."

"Hai, hai!" Suman covered her mouth with her hands in shock.

A small crowd of people had converged at the ladies' cubicle upon Mukund's arrival. Stories have an aroma that rivals food, Radha thought, as she pushed her way into the mass of people by the door.

"Are you for real?" Mrs Sharma said. "Such horror!"

"Ma," Suman said. "It's probably the strikers. Remember how they said the strikers were sleeping on the tracks in front of the train?"

"Béti, if that were true, then why would the train start in the first place? No sane person will start a train and roll over people lying in front of the tracks."

"I don't know about sane people, but I know what I saw," Mukund said. "The train did start, and some strikers are now dead."

Radha nodded her head in agreement. "Maaji, this won't be the first time that a train has rolled over people, and I can tell you, it won't be the last either."

"Yes, but it's my son up there," Savitri said. She turned to Mukund, "How could you just leave Hari there, up front, now that the strikers are sure to be upset and angry?"

"No, no," Mukund said. "The army jawans are there. They formed a ring around the engine. He is very safe. Arré, right before I left, I saw the colonel sahib and the army sergeant interviewing him. He was with his uncle, the one who brought the food."

Radha sighed as she heard him speak.

"Interview?" Savitri exclaimed. "What has he done? Tell me, you are not telling me everything!"

Mukund cringed at her outburst. Finally he said, "Nothing, I really didn't see anything. Only, Hari came out of the engine with his uncle after the train came to a stop."

"Hari was in the engine! Hai Ram!"

The people around her took a collective breath. In the silence that followed Savitri could feel all eyes upon her. She pulled her sari closer around her, covering the welt on her neck. Then she said, "I have to go. I must go to my boy."

"Perhaps I should come with you," Suman told her and stood up.

"No," her mother said.

"Ma!"

"I said no. Stay here."

Radha spoke up. "No, sister, you take care of your mother. It would not be good to leave her here and run off." She turned to Savitri, "I'll walk with you up to the engine and we can take the hero with us. He'll fight off the crowds for us."

She laughed, but no one laughed with her.

When the trio arrived at the cordon, the crowd had thinned. There was little to see or hear from the platform. The slum dwellers had stood their ground, watching the strikers sitting stunned on the gravel and the soldiers clearing the tracks. The colonel, his sergeant, Tangarajan, and Hari were speaking in low voices. The corporal overseeing the cordon watched the woman, her sari wrapped around her head, hurry towards him. The hijra pushed people away to make way for her. As she came closer, the corporal walked up to her.

"That's my son," Savitri said, pointing to Hari, "sitting there with his uncle and your officers."

The corporal nodded and signalled the jawans to let her through. Mukund made to follow her, but Radha grabbed his arm. "Not so fast, hero. We wait here."

Tangarajan turned to Savitri as she arrived. "It's okay. He's unharmed and fine."

She nodded and sat next to Hari on the bench. Hari shrank away as she reached out to touch him. She withdrew her arm. Her son was not able even to look at her. His hands between his thighs, his head bowed low, Hari sat motionless on the bench.

"You are the mother of the child?" the colonel said.

Savitri nodded.

The colonel pursed his lips, sucked in his breath, and looked over the crowds, his eyes settling briefly on the sergeant beside him. Then he said, "Well, Madam, it seems that your son was responsible for turning on the engine. The driver here—" he pointed to Cherian standing beside them "—was trying to keep the strikers from entering the engine when Hari pulled some lever and caused the train to roll over the strikers lying on the tracks."

Savitri started at the colonel's statement. She watched the bent figure of her son, not knowing what to do next. The colonel's voice caused her to turn to him again.

"Of course, it was just an accident. But there will be a police report."

"Is that necessary?" Tangarajan asked.

"Three people are dead! Of course, we have to file a report."

"But he is just a child. Dragging him into all this…"

"If you had only heeded my words, Sir," the sergeant said.

"It's too late for that sort of talk," the colonel silenced the sergeant with a wave. "Driver, is the engine still working?"

"Yes, Sir." Cherian's voice was flat.

"Good, okay, then the sergeant will ride with you in the engine. Go start it, give a couple of hoots on the horn when you are ready." The colonel turned to Savitri. "We'll head back to the carriage you were travelling in, Madam, and head to Madras. No point staying on this platform."

"What about the red light sir?" the sergeant asked.

"The red light?" The colonel looked at the signal lamp and then asked the driver, "What does that mean?"

"Oh that, no, we can go. When the engine ran forward—" His voice cracked.

Tangarajan spoke up. "It ran over the automatic signalling wires. Yes, yes. So Madras Central thinks we've already left the station."

"Very well, Sergeant," the colonel said. "Withdraw the troops and tell the strikers that they must stay here. Only those who have a ticket can ride on the train. Better yet, send the troops throughout the train to make sure. Only those with tickets should be on the train!"

A quarter of an hour later, the train resumed its journey to Madras. Vishu sat on a bench on the platform, a crude splint over his broken leg. His only consolation was that Joseph, with his ticket, was able to ride on the train onwards to Madras. The party leadership had to be informed of the incident in Ennore. Unknown to the strikers, one person without a ticket was taking a ride on the train. The colonel, contravening his own orders, invited the ticketless Tangarajan to join him in the ladies' cubicle where the two chatted all the way to Madras Central.

V
Patukappu (protection)

NINETEEN

THE STATIONMASTER OF BASIN Bridge Junction rang to say that
he had seen the Tamil Nadu Express moving towards Madras. At this
news, Divisional Manager Iyer and Kollu-thatha hurried from the
administrative offices of the Southern Railways to Madras Central
Station. The stationmaster had included in his telephone report the
sighting of army jawans at each carriage door. DM Iyer slowed his pace
out of consideration for the elder relative, but Kollu-thatha muttered
under his breath as he caught DM lagging and strode faster towards the
station.

Under the large sandstone arches of Madras Railway Station, its
stationmaster met the two men with a posse of railway policemen.

"Swamy, where is the 2622 coming in?" DM Iyer asked.

"Platform Three, Sir," the stationmaster said, and then by way of
explanation, "Sir, the other platforms still have the rakes of trains that
haven't moved."

"Well, Three it is, then. Has there been any trouble at the station?"

"No, Sir. The order came from the Chief Minister's residence early in
the morning about the strike, but just ten minutes ago, they called to
say that we could resume operations. Apparently, the President called
from New Delhi because the Vice-President is stuck at Madras Airport.
So they are letting flights and express trains run. Local services are still
cancelled."

"Bastards are probably afraid that Rajiv Gandhi will declare

President's rule and take over power like his mother Indira," Kollu-thatha said.

They walked down from the overpass to Platform Three. People had gathered on the platform: relatives awaiting arriving families, coolies tying up their red turbans in anticipation of the loads they would lift, vendors hoping for hungry passengers. There was astonishment and relief on the faces as the announcements came on the line, in English, Tamil, and Hindi. Finally, at 2:20 pm, nearly seven hours behind schedule, the Tamil Nadu Express was arriving. DM Iyer led Kollu-thatha through the gap that the railway police cleared for them, and they moved down the platform to where SL-9, the sleeper coach from Nagpur, would berth. The engine, its lamp still on, turned away from the main tracks and drew towards the platform. As he passed them, the engine driver signalled trouble, two short hoots followed by a longer blast on his horn. Kollu-thatha raised his eyebrows.

"I'll send someone up front," the stationmaster said.

"No," Kollu-thatha said. "You go up to the engine. Stay there with the driver and find out what happened."

The stationmaster turned from the elderly gent who gave orders so easily to the divisional manager for help. DM Iyer nodded his assent. As the stationmaster unhappily walked up the train, Kollu-thatha grabbed his shirt sleeve. "And remember. Keep anything you find to yourself. Don't let anyone else talk to the engine driver till you bring him to us. Understand?"

"Swamy is a good man," DM Iyer said behind the disappearing stationmaster.

"He may well be. But I doubt that good will be good enough today." Kollu-thatha shook his head as the train carriages rolled past them, an army soldier at each door. "Even we may not measure up to what may have happened today, DM."

"I'm not sure I follow what you are saying, Sir."

"I don't know what I am saying either. It's just a feeling, watching the jawans go by on rail carriages." Kollu-thatha sighed. "When did Swamy say the all-clear came for rail traffic to resume?"

"About ten minutes ago."

"And this train left Ennore over an hour ago…how?"

DM Iyer looked at his old boss, who sounded so full of foreboding. The presence of the jawans at the train doors did imply some sort of trouble, but DM Iyer assumed that they had forced the train to leave Ennore. After all, he knew about the requisition papers from military headquarters. These jawans were in a hurry to get to the Indian Peace Keeping Force in Sri Lanka. But Kollu-thatha seemed afraid for other reasons. He is an old man, DM Iyer thought, who started service with the railways before independence. Maybe that's it. Maybe he's remembering the refugee trains that crossed Punjab in the days following Partition. They had left Pakistan with Hindus and Sikhs and arrived in India filled with corpses. The trains with Muslims leaving India were sent under soldier escort up to the border. DM Iyer gave voice to his thought: "The ghost trains of the Partition?"

Kollu-thatha waved his hands in irritation. "Don't act like a stupid young man. I never served in the Northern Railways." Then he remarked more kindly, "I've known you too long, DM, I know how you think. But don't stop. Before this day ends, we may yet use that brain of yours. Come now, let's get in," and with that, he grasped the door handle of the sleeper coach from Nagpur and stepped in. The army jawan at the door, amazed at the sight of an old man climbing with such strength and sureness, gave way. DM Iyer, however, found his way barred by the jawan, who, having failed to stop an octogenarian, was determined not to let others in.

"Sir, please let people get off the train."

"Move out of my way or I'll have you arrested for blocking a railway official."

"Sir, it's just that with all those policemen coming in, there will be no space. The passengers want to leave…"

"Fine," DM Iyer pointed to the head constable, "the police can stay here and keep watch outside the carriage. I have to go in, though. You, there, come in with me."

He snorted with impatience as he caught sight of the hijra standing between the two toilets.

"Ayya, it's my fault," the hijra said, her hands joined together in salutation. "If I had only kept my big mouth shut, perhaps the little boy would have remained safe with his mother."

DM Iyer looked at the eunuch, his distaste masked by apprehension. He made a sign for the head constable to stand guard over her and walked into the ladies' cubicle. Immediately he forgot his encounter with the hijra in his surprise at seeing his son there.

"Tangarajan!" DM Iyer said. "What are you doing here?"

"Appa!" Tangarajan rose from his seat. "I am so glad you have come. We need your help."

"Wait," the colonel said. "Let's first allow these people to leave. Maaji, give the captain my warmest wishes for a complete recovery. God is with us."

"Thanks, Béta," Mrs Sharma said, then turned to Savitri. "Béti, remember what I said about the Kali-yuga. You should not blame yourself for what happened."

"Maaji, you and Suman have been so good to me," Savitri said, her head bowed. "You have fed my son and taken care of us through the darkest of hours. God will keep you and your children in the best of health and wealth. I gave Suman our address in Madras. You must come and visit."

Suman and her mother nodded. Mukund helped them carry their bags and soon the two women and their luggage were cleared from the ladies' cubicle. Hari sat hunched in the corner by the window. Kollu-thatha sat beside him, his arm around the boy's shoulders. The colonel motioned to the door. DM Iyer shut it. Then, without interruption, the two men listened as the colonel explained the situation, Tangarajan filling in.

In the silence that followed, there came the sounds of metal clanging as workmen walked alongside the train banging open the release valves of the braking cylinders under the carriages. DM Iyer looked to Kollu-thatha for help. This was a terrible crime and, in his estimation, impossible to hide. But Hari was only a child. The Indian judicial system worked at a glacial pace; the boy would be thirty before the verdict arrived one way or the other.

Kollu-thatha cleared his throat. "What will you have us do?"

"I think it best if I take the boy with me to police headquarters and explain the situation to them," the colonel said. "Of course the boy's mother and uncle will have to come along, together with the engine driver, so that they can lodge a complaint. We also have the bodies to deliver. They need to go to the morgue soon."

Kollu-thatha hung his head down, staring at the red linoleum floor of the cubicle as his hands mechanically tapped Hari's shoulders. DM Iyer stared open-mouthed at the colonel. His proposal was correct, but it sounded harsh and unfeeling. He could think of nothing to say.

Tangarajan prodded his father. "There is the question of jurisdiction."

"Huh?" DM Iyer looked blankly at his son.

"The incident took place at Ennore railway station," Tangarajan said. "It is not a matter for the Madras police to handle. He should be reported to the railway police."

"Oh, yes, the First Information Report will be made with the railway police, but we will probably turn the case over to Madras anyway," DM Iyer spoke mechanically. "I mean, I don't think Ennore police will mind. The forensic examinations, the morgue facilities, and so on are much easier to deal with here in Madras."

Kollu-thatha cleared his throat. "I think what your son means, DM, is that there is no need to trouble the colonel by having him take the boy to police headquarters. He could turn the boy over to the station police here. They could deal with the processing. That way, the colonel can take his troops to where they are going, which is—?" Kollu-thatha turned from DM Iyer to the colonel with his question.

"Jaffna."

"Ah, the Indian Peace Keeping Force…well, well, you have enough things to worry about without having this on your plate, no?"

The colonel turned to Tangarajan. "Are you sure about the railway police?"

"Yes, the railway police has jurisdiction over all crimes committed on railway property." DM Iyer stood up and opened the door. "We'd better admit the head constable in. He can take your statements. Come in, come in. What's your name?"

"Murukan, Sir."

"Well, Murukan, do you have any FIR forms with you?"

"FIR forms, sir?"

"Well, apparently the boy there has committed a crime and these two gentlemen here will relate the crime to you. I want you to take the report and then go to the engine. Stationmaster Swamy is with the driver—"

"His name is Cherian," the colonel put in.

"The driver's name is Cherian," DM Iyer repeated. "You will interview him as well and prepare your report. Take the boy and his mother to the holding cell in the main building." Turning to the colonel, DM Iyer said, "I hope that this satisfies you."

"Yes, I suppose this will work for us as well." The colonel's voice softened. His eyes darted to the downcast Hari as he said, "You don't think that they will actually take the boy to jail? I mean he is so young."

"That's out of our hands now, isn't it?" DM Iyer said. Then he addressed Kollu-thatha, "Come, Sir, we'd better leave these men to their business. Murukan, remember to bring their belongings to the station, otherwise they might get stolen."

"Of course, Sir."

"Appa," Tangarajan said. "Where shall I come and see you at the end of this?"

"Me, oh, I'll be in my office. Just come. We'll go home. Your mother will be so happy to see you."

Outside, on the platform, Kollu-thatha asked, "Where to, Iyer?"

"Shall we walk up to the front of the engine?"

"You are leading the way so far."

"Oh, I don't think so," DM Iyer shook his head. "You have your son-in-law to thank."

"He is your son after all."

"Ah! There is Swamy. I am beginning to understand what you said earlier. I can only hope he is as good as we will need him to be."

"Is he your man?"

DM Iyer shrugged and called out, "Swamy! Come, we need to talk, let's go to your office."

"Sir! It's a calamity! I need to alert the police. The train rolled over strikers—"

"Be quiet!" DM Iyer hissed. "Do you want a riot here? Let's go to your office and talk about it."

"Sir, but the criminals…"

"I've already dealt with it. The constable is right now taking the information. They will be waiting for us in the station. Now enough of this. Take me to your office. Now!"

The stationmaster, cowed by the vehemence in his boss's voice, turned and led the two men over the overpass to the main building. Kollu-thatha smiled behind the shuffling stationmaster.

At the stationmaster's office, DM Iyer locked the door behind them. It was dusty and warm; the piles of papers on the large teak desk looked orderly, although the files themselves looked messy with papers peeking out in all directions. Kollu-thatha observed the framed pictures on the wall. The images of Gandhi and Annadurai, familiar to him from his time in this office, were now joined by pictures of Indira Gandhi, her son Rajiv, and the just-deceased Chief Minister, MGR. As in all his portraits he wore his characteristic felt Kashmiri cap, the thick sunglasses that hid his eyes from the public, and a muslin shawl with gold borders. It was a calculated image that identified the Chief Minister. Universally recognized, he beamed down at the people from office walls, political billboards, and the television. He may have been struck by bullets, he may have lisped after a stroke, but the smiling figurehead in the photograph conveyed only charm and permanence. His image had no business in a railway office, but such was the state of affairs. Kollu-thatha felt a great sense of relief at having retired years earlier.

"Swamy," DM Iyer said, "I want you to make absolutely no mention of this."

"But Sir," Swamy replied, "I have to make a note in the station log and take disciplinary action."

"No. You will do nothing of that sort. Think, Swamy. When the party cadres and ministers find out what happened in Ennore, what do you think they are going to do?"

Swamy considered the divisional manager's words.

DM Iyer continued, "That train left well before the all-clear came from the Chief Minister's residence."

"But we had nothing to do with it," Swamy said. "It wasn't our fault. That's why we need to document this and make sure that they know who committed the crime."

"Yes, but you are the Madras stationmaster. It is not your business to be taking reports on actions that occurred outside your station," DM Iyer said. He drew closer to the Swamy. "Heads will roll, Swamy. I want you to stay out of this. Let me handle it. The whole thing started in Ennore and ended in Madras. You are just an innocent bystander. Remember that."

"Sir, what should I do, then?"

"Turn into Gandhiji's monkeys. See no evil, hear no evil, and speak no evil. Make sure that there are no records here in Madras."

"Sir, the bodies…"

"Find a priest; pay him from the discretionary account. Take the bodies to the loco shed and cremate them in the furnace there."

Swamy's jaw dropped. "Sir! This is very irregular."

"Remember the monkeys, Swamy," DM Iyer wagged his finger. "They are your best hope. Let the stain of this evil daub only me."

"Don't forget me, DM," Kollu-thatha said. "Tar and feather me in your crimes too, then you and I can go to Benaras together and dip in the Ganges one more time. God! Is today the reason why I am still here on this earth?"

Kollu-thatha sank into the armchair in front of the desk where he had worked decades earlier, buried his head in his arms, and wept.

Joseph ran out of the train, sliding past the policemen through the crowds on the platform, and fled the station. Outside on the broad Periyar EVR Highway, he stood and watched the emptiness of Madras without the traffic. A rickshaw stood to one side of the station; the driver smoked a beedi beside it and watched the passengers pouring out of the station. Joseph strode towards him, his light suitcase swinging by his side.

"Take me to Tottam," Joseph said, trying to climb in.

"Ayya," Sundaran blocked the young man's movement. "This rickshaw is already booked…" Then as the word "Tottam" registered in his mind, he looked uneasily at the young man. "The Chief Minister's residence?"

"Is there any other Tottam today?" Joseph said.

"Ayya, maybe you don't know. MGR Saar is no more."

"I know that," Joseph snapped. "Just take me there."

"Ayya, the streets are full of people," Sundaran said. "There is no way for me or anyone to drive you to Tottam. The radio says that thousands of people are blocking the roads."

"I have to get there."

Sundaran considered the young man's reply. The vehement insistence in his voice bothered him. What could this young man want that he needed to get to the Chief Minister's residence? But then again, perhaps it was best not to get involved in such things, Sundaran reminded himself. He joined his hands together and said, "Forgive me, Ayya, but this is not the rickshaw that can take you there."

Joseph spat and turned away, cursing him. Sundaran, shocked at the young man's behaviour, cast away his beedi and moved to follow him. But he reconsidered and wiped his face with the rag around his neck.

He watched the young man reach the road and flag another rickshaw.

Joseph had to cajole the driver and offer to pay extra to have him drive close to the Chief Minister's residence. They rode for several minutes in silence, the driver afraid and unhappy, Joseph fuming and lost in thought. Several blocks away from the Chief Minister's house, the rickshaw stopped. The streets were jammed with people. There was no space to move.

A white Ambassador with dark windows—a government car—was also stuck, unable to move forward or backward. The door opened and a woman came out. She still retained much of the beauty from her youth although the slim build of her film heroine career was vanishing, leaving her matronly in middle age. A ripple of jubilation passed through the crowd as they recognized Jayalalitha, the party secretary of the AIDMK party and mistress of the dead Chief Minister.

Joseph smiled at the sight. He jumped off the rickshaw and ran into the crowd to get closer to the dignitary. The rickshaw driver was about to yell demanding his fare, but thought the better of it. Nervous at the size of the crowd, he turned and rode his rickshaw away.

As Joseph drew near the former film star, he blushed at the thought of having loved her as a teenager. But that was before he had discovered that she was the beloved of his hero MGR. Since then, he had thought of her as Amma, his mother. It was this word that he heard over and over again as the crowd drew near her, surrounded her, and cried with her. Jayalalitha, wrapped in the plainest of white saris, the red bindi of her forehead wiped clean, her eyes swollen and red, wept with the people on the street. Silver-haired, wrinkled old women beat their chests in anguish while young men cried on each other's shoulders, propping those amongst them who would have otherwise collapsed on the warm asphalt.

"Amma," Joseph said.

Jayalalitha turned to him, and he was stuck speechless by the cinema legend standing so close to him. "Little brother, we have all lost so much today," she said.

Joseph nodded and without any help, tears rolled down his cheeks. "Amma, such a terrible crime has occurred today."

"Yes, a terrible crime. The gods have sinned against the people by taking away the light of our lives." She turned from him and repeated her words to the crowd, her voice gathering strength and conviction.

The ring of people closest to her nodded their heads in agreement.

"Amma, I meant a crime against the AIDMK party."

"Yes, of course. We are but children without him. No parent should be taken away from his children thus, but thumbi, even little brothers like you have elder sisters like me who will take care of you when our father and lord is gone."

The people roared their approval. Joseph bowed his head deeply at this recognition and grace. He missed the tumult among the larger crowd in the street. Those near the Tottam could neither see the white Ambassador nor the white-clad figure. Nervous enquiries ensued, rumours circulated. A wail could be heard.

Joseph inched closer to the party secretary, buoyed by her words. "Amma, not everyone needs to hear this, but you must."

Jayalalitha bent her ear to the young man who had given her such a public relations coup. Her face darkened with wrath as she listened. The crowd around her grew silent as they read her face, its expressions intimate to them from years of magnification on the cinema screen.

"Come with me, we must go to the Tottam now," Jayalalitha said, pointing grandly to the Chief Minister's residence. The crowd roared its approval and parted to allow their darling actress through. Some of the young men followed her, crying loudly and calling her name. News travelled ahead of them that Jayalalitha, the Chief Minister's beloved and AIDMK party secretary was making her way through the crowds and seeking entry into the Tottam.

The wrought iron gates of the Chief Minister's home opened and a delegation of white-clad party workers headed out to meet her, taking a few police officers with them. The crowd let them through only to close ranks behind them. The delegation met Jayalalitha, Joseph, and her posse amidst a sea of humanity, far from the waves of crying mourners lapping against the white shores of the Chief Minister's mansion.

"Where do you think you are going?" the leader of the delegation asked.

Alerted by the aggression in the tone, Jayalalitha answered in a demure, soft voice. "I've come to pay my respects to my leader."

"In Hindu tradition, a man's family must be by his side when he dies. It is the time for the family to grieve and prepare for his departure."

"He was father to us all, we are all his family," she spread her arms out like the figure of the Madonna at Mt Carmel Church. Her pious grief and her words drove the people near her into a frenzy. They wept, cried, and ululated.

"Have you no shame, foisting yourself on his family so. Think of his wife!" The delegation leader's voice was low and tense as he leaned closer. Joseph, standing next to Jayalalitha, could barely make out the words. It was the education minister, he knew. Paddi had given him a scholarship for his studies in recognition of his service to the All World MGR Fan Club.

"I must go in and talk to the party leadership. We have a crisis. This young man—" Jayalalitha said, changing tack, but found herself interrupted.

"He's not even dead for a day and she is already thinking of power," Paddi announced.

The crowd gasped. The young men around the minister roared in anger. Joseph shrank away from her.

"How dare you?" Jayalalitha said. Dropping all pretence of decency, she now yelled at him, inviting the crowd to her side. "Don't think I don't know what is happening in those rooms. In one chamber you have Brahmin priests chanting while in the next you divide MGR's legacy. Watch me, if you desecrate MGR, I'll burn Madras like Kannaki destroyed Madurai!"

"You're getting it confused," Paddi said. "Kannaki was Kovalan's wife. And this ignorant harlot wishes to become mistress of the house, I think not."

"MGR stood for Dravida culture and in death you sully his corpse with the Hindu rituals of the Aryan invaders! Have you no shame?"

"MGR was a family man, a man of decency. What business does an ex-starlet like you have at a decent man's funeral? Keep your unclean presence off the door. Get rid of her," Paddi spat on the ground close to her and turned to march off. His own men pushed a way for him to start a triumphant return, but closer to the gates, despite being the education minister, despite the police escort, he had a tough time getting through. During his trip back to Tottam, Paddi did not once look back to see what his henchmen did with Jayalalitha.

"Keep your hands off me," she yelled.

"If you just walk back to your car, we won't have to filthy ourselves," a young man said.

"My little brother, where are you?" Jayalalitha said. "Come help your sister out."

Joseph held out his hand but she ignored it. Instead she put her hand on his shoulder like a blind woman and let him lead her out to the waiting Ambassador. Tears flowed freely across her cheeks but her eyes were flinty with anger and she grated her teeth. Joseph could feel the tension coursing through her body from her hand on his shoulder. This was power play beyond his imagination. He thought fleetingly of abandoning her and taking his case to the residence. Perhaps it was the education minister whom he needed to sway. But it was too late.

They had seen him with her, and if Jayalalitha was being eclipsed by the party leaders, then a minion like him had already become invisible. He cursed himself for not thinking his actions through. Of course, battle lines would be drawn after the death of the leader. Camps would be arrayed against each other. And he had stumbled into the loser's camp. Who would rise to challenge Jayalalitha for the role of party leader? Joseph wondered this as they were pushed and shoved through the crowd towards her car. The education minister was only acting on orders. Would it be Janaki, MGR's widow, also a film star? Her reputation in films was nowhere near as stellar as Jayalalitha's. But she had the respectability of a widow, and the mantle of leadership fell easier when kept within a family.

"Little brother, what are you thinking?" Jayalalitha said, rousing Joseph as they approached the car. "Will you open the door for me?"

"Akka, please forgive me. I was so affected by your ill-treatment that I was thinking of how to avenge you."

She smiled. "Come with me and tell me what you have thought."

Joseph shut the door as she took her seat in the back, then he ran around the car to sit next to the driver. The education minister's henchmen now helped the car make its way through the crowds, hundreds peering through the windows at the humiliated figure of the party secretary, who had been refused entry to see the dead leader.

The car finally reached the open and they drove off.

DM Iyer took the call when the phone rang in the stationmaster's office. When he had finished with it, he said, "Swamy, I think you should show Appuswamy the new control room."

"Now?"

"Yes, now." And he forced out a laugh, "And be careful of the old fox. He may look fragile, but he is cunning. He used to have your job when you were still running around in diapers."

"Well done, now he is going to treat me like a relic," Kollu-thatha said and stood up. "How long should our trip take?" he asked.

"Oh, about half an hour should do. I don't want to tax you."

"Very well. Swamy, take me to the railway canteen and let's see if the food is still edible."

On their way out, they ran into the head constable, Murukan, rushing up the stairs, a tin file folder under his arm. He saluted them and stopped in confusion.

"Sir," he said. "They said that you wanted to see me."

"Me? No…who said?" Swamy replied.

"Sir, on the telephone, he said to bring the files on the Ennore accident to the stationmaster's office immediately."

"Well, why are you dawdling here?" Kollu-thatha said. "Follow your instructions and go to the stationmaster's office."

"But the stationmaster is…"

"No, Murukan, just go," Swamy told him. "The divisional manager is waiting for you in my office. He has taken over the case. And listen carefully to what he has to say. This is a very sensitive case. Just follow his instructions to the letter and we may all yet live through this."

Then he led Kollu-thatha down the stairs to the canteen on Platform One.

"Come in, come in," DM Iyer waved Murukan to the chair across the large teak desk. "So, what do you have for me?"

"Sir, here is the report with the eyewitness testimonies. The engine driver's and the boy's accounts match, Sir. We just need to get confirmation from this Joseph; apparently he was the leader of the strikers."

"Hmm. He's probably in Ennore, isn't he?"

"No sir, one of the jawans saw him on the train, coming into Madras, Sir."

"What!" DM Iyer stood up. "And he did not come forward to give his testimony?"

"No, Sir." Murukan remembered his training and jumped to his feet. "I checked with the station. He must have left the train right after it arrived."

"Sloppy, very sloppy work," DM Iyer mused. "Has he contacted Madras police?"

"We haven't heard anything from them yet. Shall I call them?"

"No...we don't want them to think that something untoward has happened." DM Iyer paced the room. Returning to the desk, he tapped the tin folder. "Is the passenger list in this file?"

Murukan shook his head. "Not yet, Sir, the reservations clerk is printing it out right now. He said that it would be ready in another ten minutes, Sir."

"And the woman and child?"

"Sir, they are in the station, in a waiting room. I took the liberty of ordering lunch from the railway canteen for them."

DM Iyer smiled. "Is it customary for your inmates to receive such good treatment?"

"Sir, your son is with them, so I thought..." The policeman's voice trailed off.

"You did well, Murukan, much better than I expected; there may even be a promotion here."

Murukan puffed up at this commendation.

"Now listen carefully. Are these all the records? You don't have any carbon copies in the station, do you?"

"No sir, I brought everything."

"You are smart, aren't you? What do you think I am going to say next?"

"That this case was never registered at our station. I haven't told the men why the three people are in the station. I just said that we are keeping them safe until their relatives arrive to pick them up."

"Good, good. I think we understand each other well, Murukan."

"Thank you, Sir." The head constable stepped back.

"But if there is an inquiry," DM Iyer said, "they will wonder what kept you in the train all this time. I mean someone or the other will tell them that you were in the train taking statements all morning. What will you do then?"

"Don't worry, Sir," Murukan answered him and gestured towards the police station below them. "When we brought the woman and boy out of the cubicle, that hijra you had me watch was still on the train. I took her into custody. I'll make up a case against her for travelling without a ticket in the vestibule between the coaches."

"Hmm," DM Iyer responded. He looked at the police constable for a while before saying, "That should do well. But don't hold her too long."

"No, Sir, she wants to go to Kumbakonam. I'll put her on the express tomorrow."

"Make sure she can't be traced."

"Oh, the address on file is from some chawl in Bombay. No worries, Sir."

DM Iyer held out his hand. "It is good to see smart men still working hard for the railways."

"Thank you, Sir," Murukan said, before adding, "Sir, I will need the tin folder back, just to be safe."

DM Iyer laughed. He turned the folder around and emptied its contents onto Swamy's desk. Then he took one of the railway files from Swamy's desk and stuffed it into the empty folder. Handing the folder back to Murukan, he said, "Just make sure that the file comes back in a week or so, Swamy shouldn't miss it."

TWENTY

THE DRIVER DROVE Kollu-thatha, Tangarajan, and the two travellers to Kollu-thatha's house in DM Iyer's railway-issue white Ambassador car. There Kollu-thatha and Tangarajan got off. Hari's thatha, who had spent all morning fretting in that large house, asked a thousand questions but Kollu-thatha sent him off with the promise that he and Tangarajan would come later in the evening to visit. The driver then dropped Thatha, Savitri, and Hari off at their home in T-Nagar. Sivagami awaited them at the doorstep.

"Finally, you have come!" she said. "Come in, come in. You must be so hungry."

"How's Kalyani doing?" Thatha asked.

"You have another grandson. He's big and a big crier too. Nice loud screams just like our Hari here. But once he took to his mother's teats, not a whimper. Dr Shetty says he will discharge them in three days." Her smile vanished as she turned from Hari's thatha to Savitri. "Come, come with me." She grabbed Hari's mother, rushed her through the living room into a smaller bedroom and shut the door behind her.

"What was that all about?" Hari's thatha said. Just then, they heard the bell at the gate. Sundaran, who had followed their car from the station, had arrived.

"You won't believe it," Sundaran said as he hauled the luggage into the living room. "They've begun fighting over who is going to succeed MGR as Chief Minister."

"It doesn't surprise me," Hari's thatha said. "What's the word on the street?"

"People are saying that Paddi, the education minister, humiliated Jayalalitha in the streets in front of Tottam today. They wouldn't let her come in and see MGR's body or to pay her last respects."

"Chi, chi, that is just uncouth," Thatha said. He turned to Hari to see what effect this conversation had on his grandson. But Hari sat quietly on the swing. He seemed to be in another world.

Sundaran put down the last suitcase and wiped his brow. "They say that MGR's wife wouldn't allow it."

"In life the man chooses mistress over wife, but in death, it is the wife who lords over her husband's body. Ahh, revenge must be sweet for her, eh, Sundaran?"

"Kanna, what's wrong with you?" Sundaran said, turning to Hari. "Why so glum and quiet? Usually you are running around the household."

"Leave the boy be, Sundaran," Thatha said. "He's had quite a day so far. Go, Hari, and lie down in the puja room."

Hari nodded and went out.

"Where's Hari?" Sivagami inquired when she arrived.

"Taking a nap," Thatha said.

Sivagami turned to her brother. "Sundaran, go and take your rickshaw out."

"What, and ferry ghosts around the town today?" He laughed.

"At least go out and make sure that no one takes the rickshaw as a donation to the Party," she invited. "Maybe they've already chopped it up for the funeral pyre."

Sundaran scowled at his sister and left. Sivagami drew closer to Hari's thatha and narrated to him the theft of Savitri's wedding necklace in the train and the happenings at Ennore station. When Sivagami finished, Thatha stumbled to the swing and sat on it. He rocked back and forth in silence.

"Ayya, say something," Sivagami said. "You are frightening me."

"I am frightening you, Sivagami, this is rich indeed," Thatha sighed. "First you tell me tales of horror and then accuse me of scaring you...send Sundaran to fetch Savitri's mother from the Shetty clinic."

"Ayya, but she is with Kalyani..."

"Kalyani can manage, there are enough nurses there!" He was angry.

"I'll go and send her here," she said.

Thatha nodded. When she had locked the door behind her, he rose and took a few steps towards Savitri's room, but then hesitated and turned and walked into the puja room to his grandson.

Hari lay on a palmyra mat in front of the wall of deities. From his foetal crouch, he studied the images of gods and goddesses in front of him. Closest to him were the small gold sculptures: the elephant god Ganesha, Lord Rama standing next to his wife Sita with the monkey god Hanuman at their feet. Behind them was a photograph of the large black rock carving of Lord Venkateshwara, housed in the sprawling temple complex at Tirupathi. Around his image were arrayed Saraswati, the goddess of learning, Lakshmi, the goddess of wealth, Meenakshi, Murukan, Ayappan, and Krishna. Hari's eyes moved from one image to another as he smelt the lingering camphor, ash, and sandalwood. He tried formulating a petition, an apology to the gods; instead he could only recollect the legends of these gods that his paathi had told him so many years ago. He had killed her too, Hari thought. His throat burned with shame, the memories of fish bones pricked him again and again, robbing him of his voice and his ability to breathe.

"Hari," Thatha said.

"Thatha," Hari's voice cracked as he turned on the floor to lie on his back and look at his grandfather.

"Shh, sit up. Be careful now, you don't want your feet pointing to the gods," Thatha said as he sat next to his grandson. "Is it true? What happened on the train?"

Hari nodded, his eyes averted from his grandfather's.

"Who else knows?"

"Everyone, Thatha! Tangarajan uncle was there, and then in Madras, Kollu-thatha and the other thatha, Tangarajan-uncle's father were there too." Hari started crying.

"DM Iyer was there?"

Hari nodded. "They took me into a police station. Thatha, I don't want to go to jail."

"Nonsense! No one is going to send you to jail, come here." Thatha cradled Hari. "Just you watch. Your Kollu-thatha and DM Iyer will take care of everything. Did they take your fingerprints at the station?"

"No."

"Did they take photographs of you?"

"No, why?"

"That's what I thought. You'll be fine," Thatha said, and he rocked his grandchild in his arms. They sat, a tableau of domesticity and continuity in front of the myriad god-eyes watching them. Hari felt safe, like the earth coddled by the sky around her.

"Thatha," Hari spoke quietly. "Sivagami will never forgive me."

"Sivagami?" Thatha smiled. "What does she have to do with anything?"

"Vishu was there." Hari felt his grandfather's body tense.

"Sivagami did not say anything about him."

"Mother doesn't know about it."

"He's not...one of the..." Thatha's voice faltered.

Hari shook his head, "No, but the army medic said that his leg broke."

"Do you mean the train ran over his leg?"

"No, he fell from the engine in the commotion and his leg bone was fractured. Tangarajan-uncle sent Ranga with him to the hospital."

"Bless us, broken bones can be reset, Kanna. It will only be a few weeks of recovery. I'm sure Sivagami won't mind. I had imagined quite worse."

"I don't have to imagine. I have seen it."

"Shush, child. Don't think of it," Thatha said. "It was just an accident, a nightmare from which you are now awake. It is gone."

"Appa," Savitri stood at the doorway, her sari clutched around her neck, hiding the shame of the welt where her necklace should have been.

"Come, my child, come sit next to us," Thatha said and patted the palmyra mat.

Savitri shuffled next to her father and sat down. She looked to the images of the gods and goddesses in front of her and began crying. "What is to become of us?"

"Shoo, quiet now," Thatha admonished her in a low, gentle voice. "Why do you worry about these things? Do you not have a father and a husband? You have not one but two families that love you. Will we not help you overcome this?"

Savitri sobbed; then she turned to look at her father and she saw her son nestled in his arms.

"It's because of this rascal, this demon-rakshaha that I bore in my

own womb. He has brought nothing but misfortune upon us!" She
rained blows upon her son and screamed at him. She slapped Hari, hit
his legs, and clenching her fists, she beat him on his chest and arms.
"Die, die. Why didn't you jump in front of the train, at least then I
could mourn you? Your actions are poison to us. Why don't you die?"

"Nirritu! What has possessed you?" Thatha held up his hands over
the boy to protect him from the assault. "Control yourself. Have you
lost your mind, beating a child like this in front of the gods?"

Savitri crumpled with a wail. As she fell prostrate in front of her
mother's shrine, she beat her arms against the floor, shattering her
glass bangles.

Back at the headquarters of the Southern Railways, the divisional head
stared down the engine driver, who was sweating despite the air
conditioning.

"Well…," DM Iyer said.

"Saar," the driver started, "I was at the window, when…"

"At the window? Then how did the engine begin to roll?"

"Well, Saar, there was this boy—"

"You let a boy into the engine?" DM Iyer yelled. The veins in his bald
head stood out. "At a time like this, you let a child into the engine. Did
you leave your brains back in Vijaywada?"

The engine driver cringed. "Saar, the train was stopped, nothing was
happening, so I thought, what's the harm…"

"What is the harm, idiot," muttered the divisional head. He scanned
the papers on the desk. "Listen, Cherian. There will be an inquiry. Not
now, but when the situation calms down. In a few weeks, people will
start asking questions. Someone will remember the train accident, and
that men were killed. They'll come to me and ask me what I did. What
will I tell then?"

Cherian stood there in the cold office. Images of Nehru and Gandhi
stared down at him from behind the gigantic desk at which DM Iyer
sat. Cherian squirmed.

DM Iyer said, "Look. It is one thing if there was a mechanical failure
or even if you mistakenly got the train rolling. These things happen.
But to let a boy start the train when you are in the engine, how am I
supposed to deal with that?"

"Saar, his name…"

"What?"

"Saar, I know his name," Cherian said. "The boy's name is Hari."

The divisional head leaned back in his leather chair and considered the driver standing before him. Moments passed in silence and the driver began to relax. He had offered something of value.

Suddenly, DM Iyer leaned forward and screamed. "Hari! That's all you have to say? What will you have me do with that name? Go and drag every child in Madras with the name Hari and parade them in front of you? Do you want to turn me into that demon Kansa and send out witches to hunt down this child?"

Cherian cringed at this outburst.

"Or perhaps you would like me to turn into King Herod and murder every child in Madras?"

Cherian joined his hands together and shook his head as he cried.

DM Iyer noted Cherian's fear with satisfaction. "No, no. Here is what you are going to say. There never was any child in the engine cab. You were pushed into the cab by one of the protestors…what did you say his name was?"

"Vishu, Saar, but—"

"No buts," DM Iyer held up his hand. "This Vishu pushed you and you fell against the starting lever. The train started and rolled over the strikers. You did your best to protect the train and its passengers once you realized the tragedy."

Cherian looked blankly at his boss.

"Do you understand me?" DM Iyer thundered.

Cherian nodded, but he was confused.

"You will be suspended without pay for six months and transferred to South East Railways," DM Iyer said, scribbling furiously on the papers lying him.

"Ayya," Cherian fell on his knees at the desk and supplicated. "Six months…but my wife and child. How can they survive without my pay for that long?"

DM Iyer looked up from his papers and not unkindly asked, "Who is your union man?"

"Saar, Ponna Kuttuvan in the engine shed."

"Send him to me. I'll make sure that he has money to take care of you."

Cherian smiled for the first time.

"Now go," DM Iyer instructed. Cherian looked back and bowed several times, his hands held together in salutation as he left the stationmaster's office. Once the doors closed, DM Iyer dialled Kollu-thatha's home.

"Shanthi, how are you? It's DM Iyer here for your grandfather. Can I speak with him?"

That afternoon DM Iyer, Kollu-thatha, Tangarajan, and Shanthi came to visit Hari's grandfather. Hari slept in the puja room, while Savitri lay on the bed in her old room. Shanthi helped Hari's grandmother in the kitchen with coffee and snacks. In the living room, the four men planned and plotted.

"Sundaran says that there is a split in the Party," Thatha said.

"I haven't heard anything over the radio," Kollu-thatha responded.

"Not the radio or the newspaper this time," Tangarajan informed them. "It's the little people who know the news. They're in the thick of the politics. If Sundaran says there is a split, you can be sure that we'll hear about it in a couple of days."

"It's true," DM Iyer said. "And it may buy us some time. One of the strikers made it to Madras on the train and took his story to Jayalalitha. Somebody from her office called Swamy at Madras Central."

"What did he say?" Kollu-thatha asked.

"Oh," DM Iyer gestured with his arms. "Swamy just said that the matter was under investigation but that he couldn't give details to a private citizen."

"That's not very smart, Appa," Tangarajan said.

"No, no. It's fine, really," DM Iyer said. "You see, Swamy also got a phone call from Tottam. The party leaders are on the phone calling everyone. They say that Janaki, MGR's wife, is the anointed successor and they are trying to sideline Jayalalitha."

"Hmm," Kollu-thatha said. "Our striker seems to have picked the wrong side to report to…"

"Exactly," DM Iyer nodded. "So they won't hear him as long as he is with Jayalalitha. And since the wife hates the mistress, we might just be saved."

"No, Appa, I don't think so," Tangarajan said. "I think Jayalalitha is going to win this battle. She is the propaganda secretary and has a huge following among the people. The young men from the fan clubs would rather follow her. After all, who saw Janaki after her marriage to MGR?"

"But she is his wife," Kollu-thatha said. "His legacy will go to her. It's the way these things have always played out. Besides, she will be easier to control, the party leaders will probably try to ally with her so they can have legitimacy and seize control for themselves."

"Like what the Congress did when Indira Gandhi was assassinated," Hari's thatha added. "They chose her son Rajiv as their leader."

"And look where that has gotten them," Kollu-thatha said.

"No," Tangarajan stood up and paced the room. "I totally disagree with you. This is not old-style top-down politics. This is going to be a bottom-up kind of deal. The people will dictate who will be leader. Not the ministers, but the people in the manrams. They will not accept Janaki. They will only follow Jayalalitha. She is their star. She is the one who is coupled to MGR in their minds."

"Be that as it may be," Kollu-thatha said. "It will still be a few months before anything real happens. I mean there has to be an election again, and who knows, maybe this time the AIDMK might actually lose power without MGR to lead them."

"By then, it will be too late," DM Iyer noted with a smile. "There will be no evidence left to find Hari, much less prosecute him."

"And what of the army officer," Kollu-thatha said. "Those jawans that hauled the dead bodies into the train, the hundreds of passengers who doubtless talked amongst themselves?"

"Hundreds of people talking only generate thousands of tales," DM Iyer said. "Rumours and fancies. I still say that we are fine."

"What of the driver, Cherian?" Tangarajan asked.

"What of him?"

"Well, if someone follows up with Joseph and questions Cherian, then what?"

"I've dealt with Cherian," DM Iyer said. "They'll have to find him first and even if they do, he has a story for them, sans garçon."

Tangarajan smiled at his father's self-satisfied air. He said, "Still, I think we should send Hari out of Tamil Nadu. There is no reason to keep him in the lion's lair."

"He's as safe here as he will be in Nagpur," Thatha said.

In the silence that followed Thatha's firm tone, Kollu-thatha sighed. "That's another way of saying he is no safer here than he is in Nagpur."

"What is it?" Hari's grandmother entered the living room. The coffee tray shook in her arms. "What have you found out? Why is he not safe here?"

"Don't interrupt in the middle, Ma," Thatha reprimanded gently. "And you'd better put the tray down before you spill all the coffee. What is up with this shivering fright?"

Tangarajan took the tray from her arms. She smiled her thanks to him with a brief nod and turned to her husband. "It's not fright," she told him. "I just wish Sivagami were here. She is so useful to have around." Hari's grandmother gestured to Shanthi, who brought out murruku and ladoos. "Please enjoy the ladoos, we ordered them for Kalyani's boy."

"They are very good," DM Iyer said, his mouth full.

"So what do you think, about Hari?" Shanthi asked.

"We are not really sure," Tangarajan said. "To worry or not to worry, and if so, how much to worry."

"What if you send me to America, to Mani-mama and Sarah-aunty?" Hari said. He stood half hidden in the doorway of the puja room.

Thatha beckoned him in. "How long have you been listening to us talk?"

Hari went to sit next to his grandfather on the swing.

"Send him to America?" DM Iyer asked. "Kalyani is here anyway from Canada and Mani is in New York. Perhaps it isn't a bad idea. Can it be done?"

"That would put him beyond the reach of Indian law," Kollu-thatha nodded. "We won't have to worry about if and when this Joseph causes trouble."

"Or what happens with the AIDMK party politics," Tangarajan said.

"Or even if the army colonel comes back," DM Iyer said.

"Hmm, it's not easy emigrating to America," Thatha commented.

"Are you out of your minds?" Hari's grandmother couldn't contain herself. "Send Hari off to America. What about Savitri and her husband? You are talking about separating a child from his parents."

"Perhaps if we send the parents along. . ." DM Iyer said.

"I wonder if Girish would be interested in moving to Canada," Thatha said. "It would be easier."

Kollu-thatha nodded slowly. "India is changing. Tamil Nadu is just the beginning. I remember when educated Brahmins like us wielded real power. Now even the bureaucracy kowtows to these mass-minded politicians."

"Democracy is finally wresting power away from you technocrats," Tangarajan said. "One way or another."

"Keep your democracy away from us," DM Iyer retorted. "It's demon-o-cracy and foolishness more than anything else."

Kollu-thatha raised his hand to silence father and son. "It matters not what happens. DM, you and I are old, vestiges of a different time. With luck neither of us will be around when we have lost all semblance of power and prestige. Tangarajan here has made his peace with the new order and if Hari remains here, he will no doubt see even more ground slipping from under his feet."

"He's my grandson," Thatha said. "I'll be damned if I give him up to the riffraff that passes for our leaders now."

"It won't come to that." Kollu-thatha's voice was reassuring, as if he could look into the future. "We may not be as strong as we once were, but we are not yet without influence. DM has already muddled an investigation that has not yet begun. We can hope foolishly that the police will never investigate, but too many people are involved." He looked around the room. "I will talk to Girish. We may have bought Hari some time, perhaps a year, maybe a bit more. I'll sell my house in T-Nagar if I need to, but we should think about sending them away. In the long run, it is the safest bet."

"'They're here," Sivagami said, bursting into the room. Behind her, Kalyani entered, leaning against Dr Shetty, cradling the newborn baby in her arms.

A minor commotion broke out at her arrival. Hari's grandmother and Shanthi fussed over Kalyani while Sivagami passed the baby to Thatha. Hari watched the baby with its wrinkly skin and enormous head as it slept in his grandfather's arms.

Thatha said, "Dr Shetty, what is the meaning of all this?"

Dr Shetty, his mouth full with the ladoo that Sivagami had given him, shrugged, and pointed to Kalyani.

"When I heard the news I told him to bring me home," Kalyani said, faltering as she looked at Sivagami. "Besides, what am I supposed to do in that clinic now?"

"There is a lot a new mother needs to learn," Dr Shetty said in a reproachful voice.

"And Sivagami, my mother, and my sister can help me through it, can you not?" Kalyani said, turning to her mother for support.

"Hmm…Shetty, what is done is done," Thatha said. "These young people are beyond us. Can you spare a nurse and make sure that she is here during the day to help with the baby?"

"Already done, Sir," Dr Shetty said. "That was my condition for discharge. She'll be arriving tomorrow morning."

"With the bill, no doubt," Thatha said.

The men around him laughed. Dr Shetty demurred. Muttering excuses about work at the clinic, he decamped after wishing Kalyani and the baby well.

"Where is Savitri?" Kalyani asked.

"She's lying down, taking a nap," Thatha said, rocking his new grandson in his arms.

"I'll go see her." Kalyani walked up to her father, collected her son from his arms, and took him into Savitri's room.

Sivagami moved to follow her, when Hari's grandmother called out. "Sivagami, you come with me to the kitchen. Shanthi, you come too. We'd better start working on dinner. There is just too much to do."

Kalyani's arrival with the infant gave the men a respite. Kollu-thatha and DM Iyer talked with Tangarajan about his job and his prospects at the Leyland factory. Thatha listened to their conversation and added his two bits when he thought appropriate. Hari walked up to the doorway and watched Kalyani and his mother chat in low voices. Savitri rocked her nephew in her lap as she talked to her sister. Hari wondered at how large the baby's head was on that small body and how he slept through all the excitement and conversations around him.

Behind him, Sivagami laid out five palakais in a row on the floor, for the four men and Hari. Then she brought out the dinner plates, while Shanthi brought tumblers and a brass pot of water.

"Come, come, let's sit and eat," Thatha invited the men.

Sivagami bellowed to Savitri and Kalyani to come for dinner.

"You sit on the swing with the baby, we'll manage," Savitri said to Kalyani, as the two sisters came into the room. Hari's mother went into the kitchen to fetch the sambhar and rice. Shanthi brought out the bean curry with coconut flakes, and Hari's grandmother brought the rasam and dhal.

"So tell me, ma," Kollu-thatha asked Kalyani as she swung gently, rocking the infant in her lap. "How long do you think it will take Girish and his family to emigrate to Canada?"

"To Canada?" Kalyani looked at Savitri. "I'm not sure. Probably around two years to sponsor them. It is a slower process because they are not directly related to us."

"What do you mean not directly related?" Hari's grandmother said. "She is your elder sister."

"No, Amma," Kalyani shook her head. "It doesn't matter what I think. It has to do with what the Canadian government says. See, this little baby in my arms, I can automatically bring him to Canada, but my sister, Savitri, is an adult. She doesn't need to be with me."

"What a strange thing to say about families," Hari's grandmother said. "Of course, she needs you. Well, you need her. She is the elder."

"Be quiet," Thatha said irritably to his wife. "Always muddling the issue. Let's focus on what we can do for Hari."

"Two years," Tangarajan turned to his father and said. "Do you think we can hold off an investigation that long?"

DM Iyer nodded, his mouth full of food.

"Good," Kollu-thatha said. "Let's make a trunk call to Nagpur and talk to Girish after dinner."

TWENTY-ONE

THE DAY AFTER Christmas, Girish flew down on an Indian Airlines flight from Nagpur. Tangarajan brought him home from the airport.

"So, you finally got your wish to ride a train engine," Girish said as he hugged Hari.

"Appa, I will never ride a train again, I promise."

"Shush. Don't say such things. Go, go to your paathi in the kitchen. I need to speak to your thatha." Girish knelt to touch the feet of his father-in-law.

"May all the grace given to me pass to you and keep your family strong," Thatha said, placing his palms on Girish's head.

"Are things that bad?"

"Who knows?" Thatha replied and pointed to the bedroom where Savitri spent her waking hours. "But we can wait to talk. Go and first see Savitri. She's waiting for you."

As Girish left, Thatha turned his attention to Shanthi's husband. "Come, Tangarajan. You are reduced to being a chauffeur for our family now, eh?"

"I must atone for my part in this," Tangarajan said. "After all, I should have known better than to encourage Hari in that engine—"

"What is done is done," Thatha interrupted. "But since you feel guilty, do me a favour. Is that taxi still out there?"

"Yes, I think so."

"Good, then take this cheque to the State Bank office in Anna Salai and cash it."

Tangarajan read the cheque and said, "All of it?"

"Yes, of course. What kind of question is that? Take that briefcase to hold the cash."

"Do we really need this much?"

"No, we might need more."

"For what?"

"Precautions," Thatha said, looking out into the neighbourhood from his verandah. The streets were quieter than usual, but the bustle of commerce had already begun. Eulogies broadcast over the radio filled the streets, and in the shops, television sets displayed images of the late Chief Minister lying in state at Fort St George. The queue of mourners was already miles long even though they wouldn't be permitted inside for another day. In the house, the television in the living room was switched off, and the radio in the kitchen remained silent.

"Savitri?" Girish said.

At the sound of her husband's voice, Savitri sat up on the bed and drew her knees up to her chest. Her hair was tousled, her cheeks were streaked with dried tears, her sari was askew. Around her neck, the faded ring of red was evidence of her missing wedding necklace.

"How did this happen to us?" Girish asked, sitting on the bed. He reached out to put a hand on her knees. She drew away from his touch. He sighed and let his arm fall on the bed.

"I always said that standing at the doors of these trains would ruin my family," Savitri said.

"That has nothing to do with anything."

"I'm not the one who took him around to meet low-class engine drivers and signalmen—"

"Stop sopping up the spilt milk, Savitri," Girish said.

"If we don't learn from what happened, we are bound to repeat it," Savitri retorted, recollecting a lesson from college.

Girish smiled; they had already started repeating aphorisms. He spoke in a quiet voice, "Savitri, I'm sorry I wasn't there when all this happened."

She stared at him in silence. The defiance in her gaze dissolved as tears gathered. "I was so afraid," she said. "First the thief stole my wedding necklace, and then the next day, that army colonel was talking about sending my boy to the gallows."

"Shush," Girish came closer and put his arms around her. "It'll be all right."

"No," she shook herself free. "You can't just say all right and make it happen anymore. For hours, I was neither wife nor mother. You will never know what that feels like. All the symbols of my marriage gone..."

Girish just nodded where he sat on the bed. As she grew silent, he wondered if he had been a good husband to Savitri, a good father to Hari. Had he not toiled in the summer heat to support them? Perhaps he could have done more. It was true that he had let Savitri raise their son; she was more suited to being the mother than he the father. But that would have to change.

"We can't continue as before," Savitri said.

Girish looked up at her and smiled; their thoughts were one.

She continued, "Kollu-thatha thinks we should emigrate to Canada."

"Canada! Why?"

"Somewhere away from India," she said. "It'll be safer for us."

Girish snorted. "He's going senile."

"There you go again. Think about it. It's not such a bad idea."

"Maybe. I'll talk to him today. But first, let me re-tie the thaali around your neck."

Savitri wiped the tears off her face. She shook her head. "I still have to bathe."

That afternoon, Hari witnessed his parents renewing their vows. He stood next to Kalyani cradling her baby boy in the puja room. His father tied a cotton thread dipped in an emulsion of turmeric around his mother's neck. Savitri cried as she prostrated to her husband in front of the images of the gods and her parents to receive their blessings. With Girish's parents gone from this world, they turned to Kollu-thatha as the elder from his family to bless their renewed union.

"May you have lots of children," the old man said. "May they live long and flourish."

Hari's mother started at this blessing, Girish looked at Kollu-thatha as if he had gone mad.

That night phone calls came from Toronto and New York. They would continue for the next two weeks. Kalyani held her infant son next the bakelite phone so he could send a wail across the trans-atlantic line to his father before being handed to the nurse for the night. Then Kalyani spoke into the mouthpiece, conferring with her husband about sponsorship forms and immigration paperwork. Mani-mama called, worried about the strike situation and learned about the family crisis. He offered help to pay for the sponsorship costs for Savitri and her family. Sarah-aunty spoke at length to Savitri, and from what Hari could glean she seemed to listen to his mother more than offer anything.

The following morning, Hari received a rather rude shock as he picked the dead leaves off the rose bushes in the front garden. The compound gate squeaked open and Sundaran stood there, helping Vishu in. Vishu hobbled on a crutch, his leg encased in thick white plaster, grimacing at each step.

Hari ducked to hide as he caught Sundaran's eye. Vishu stopped and looked at the house. From among the leaves and thorns, Hari could see the scorn and derision in Vishu's gaze. Then he heard Sundaran try to hurry Vishu along the side of the house, to Sivagami's quarters.

Hari lay low among the bushes, wondering what would happen next. Did he have enough time to run into the house? But since the accident, everyone in the house had looked at him queerly, treating him with care and deference like one would an old man with brittle bones, whilst keeping their distance as though he carried a plague. Did he even want to return into the dark cold of his grandfather's house?

A low cough made Hari look up. Sundaran twirled a rag in his hands as he stood on the flagstone walkway, peering into the rose garden. Hari stood up from behind the bushes, a sheepish look on his face.

"Enough hiding, no?" Sundaran beckoned him. "Come, I'll take you for a ride."

Hari crumpled the dried yellow leaves in his hands and followed Sundaran to his rickshaw.

"Where are we going?" he asked, climbing aboard.

"Marina Beach," Sundaran said. "I want to show you something."

"But it's so far away. Thatha never lets you drive us there in the summer."

Sundaran laughed and pedalled. "But it's just you today. You are so light; we'll be there in no time."

Hari sat back in the rickshaw and watched the city around him as they drove past the silk shops at Panagal Park. The larger emporia remained closed, their steel shutters pulled down and fastened shut. Sundaran turned the rickshaw north on GM Chetty Road and then veered east on Peter's Road. Hari knew the way well. Peter's Road became Besant Road, which brought them to the southern tip of Marina Beach. As they rode the streets, Hari saw the vendors at the pavements with their neat piles of eggplants, coriander, and chillies, and tomatoes and white onions laid out on the brown jute rags. People shuffled on the footpaths but their clothes were drab, the colours muted compared to those of the produce. The men wore mostly white; black flags hung off the telephone poles on the street. It seemed like the world around him was in mourning, and Hari couldn't help but feel responsible for the loss of joy.

Sundaran chained the rickshaw to a lamppost on Mylapore Bazaar Road, which ran parallel to the sea. Below them, the waves crashed and foamed against Marina Beach. The breeze was cool but the sand under their feet felt warm from the morning sun.

"It's very different from the summer when Thatha and I used to come here," Hari said.

Sundaran nodded. "Much cooler now."

"That's where I used to buy ice-cream," Hari said, pointing to the boarded-up shack. "Looks like they've closed for the winter."

"No, little master," Sundaran said, shaking his head. "They'll open again, once the funeral is over."

"Funeral?"

"Come, I'll show you," Sundaran said, walking northwards, next to the crashing waves. More people crowded this part of the beach. Khaki-shirted policemen wandered about twirling their laathi sticks. Sundaran pointed to the workmen constructing a platform. Trucks awaited, loaded with wood, cement, and bricks.

"It's for MGR's funeral," he said. "They are going to cremate his body here on the beach day after tomorrow."

They walked up to the palisade being built around the cremation pyre and watched the construction with the other loiterers. The workers, under the watchful eyes of the police, party cadres, and the public, piled up sandalwood in neat rows for the pyre. Hari remembered his visit to Benaras and the fires that burned day and night on Manikarnika Ghat to cremate the bodies. Almost a year ago, he had seen the Chandalas tending the fires push half-burnt corpses into the Ganges, even before the pyres had died out, to clear space for more corpses. On this beach, however, the pace was almost glacial as the priest sprinkled holy water over each log of sandalwood brought down from the trucks.

"What's Vishu going to do now?" Hari asked.

Sundaran shrugged his shoulders and pulled away from the wooden fence around the platform that housed the funeral pyre. As they walked back south, away from the crowds, he said, "He's an angry man. I almost wish your grandfather had not sent him to school. It's given him a taste for wealth and power."

"But everyone should go to school, get educated," Hari said.

"Maybe." Sundaran appeared unconvinced. "But look what's happened here. Your grandfather spent good money on educating Vishu, and what does the rascal do, he uses that very education to put down Brahmins like your family. He pisses in the pot that feeds him."

"Now he has more reason to be angry with my family."

"Why?" Sundaran stopped.

Hari tapped his right leg. "I broke his leg."

"You did nothing of the sort." Sundaran spat on the sand. "He's a grown man. If he falls from a train that is his own fault."

"That's what you think," Hari said. "But now he has the upper hand. You know that Thatha is trying to hush up the whole thing. Vishu can get me arrested any time, so he will use this power against Thatha."

"You're watching too many of those Hindi films, little master," Sundaran cackled. "He's not a bad boy, our Vishu. His head may be a bit turned by that film club of his and the politics in Tamil Nadu, but he is no villain from the films. Besides, even if he wanted to do something, do you think Sivagami would allow it?"

Hari could only smile. Sivagami was perhaps a more potent force than his thatha. And with this thought, Hari realized that Tangarajan-uncle was right. The mantle of power in his grandfather's house had slipped off the men in his family.

Hari grinned at Sundaran and ran towards the water. He sprinted to the crashing waves and flung himself into the cold waters of the bay.

The noise of rushing water and breaking waves filled his ears, the sea sapped warmth from his skin, his clothes floated on his body and for a buoyant moment, Hari felt completely free.

But the waves cast him back on the wet sands, and as he sat, shivering in the wind, Hari could hear Sundaran scolding him for his impulsiveness. Hari hugged himself as the water evaporated off his skin and laughed at the shocked rickshaw driver.

Epilogue
Paruttal (ripening)

KOLLU-THATHA PASSED away in the winter of 1989. His will split the inheritance evenly between Shanthi and Girish so that when Hari's family left India for Canada in May 1990, Girish brought along a tidy sum from the sale of the house in T-Nagar.

Jayalalitha won the factional fighting in the wake of MGR's death, but as Kollu-thatha had predicted, without the charismatic film hero to lead them, the party suffered defeat in the elections. Jayalalitha had to be content with the role of leader of the opposition.

The families of the three men who died in Ennore launched appeals for an inquiry both with Southern Railways and the state government. For two years they failed to interest anyone in the new DMK government and their requests languished on DM Iyer's desk. Finally in October 1989, the families filed suit in Madras High Court to force an official inquiry. DM Iyer retired in November of that year and was felicitated by the government for his distinguished career.

Following a judicial order, an inquiry was instituted into the railway accident of Ennore in early 1990. Railway police inspector Murukan was appointed as liaison officer. Despite his best efforts, no files relating to the event were found in the offices of Southern Railways. The retired judge, who led the inquiry, was inundated with scores of eyewitness reports that varied both in content and style. The passengers spoke of an army officer in charge. But both the colonel and the sergeant, victims of a claymore mine attack in Sri Lanka, had long made the journey in to the lists of the victorious dead of the Indian Peace Keeping Force. Without any official records or corroboration, the judge was forced to draw his inquiry to a close in the spring of 1992. In his final report, he noted with some irony that there was so little evidence to support the inquiry that a cover-up could not even be alleged.

But by then Hari and his family had already left India. Just as the sun cleared the horizon on a warm May morning in 1990, a British Airways Boeing 747 jet took off from the Anna International Terminal of Madras Airport. Seated between his parents, Hari felt his stomach being pulled down. He gripped the arm rests tight as the plane's wheels lifted off the ground. In that moment, Hari felt alone, as if an umbilical had been severed.

Acknowledgements

Many individuals and institutions provided valuable assistance, support and encouragement in helping me birth this novel. RL Nesvet shared her plays and generously read several drafts, constantly demanding more from my characters, especially Radha. Thanks are due to Martin Weiner, Mohamed Hagelamin, Ben King, and my colleagues at the University of Toronto and Humber College writing courses for reading drafts and discussing them with me.

A special note of thanks is due to MG Vassanji at the Humber School for Writers for reading and critiquing the manuscript, for teaching me to sharpen the focus of my writing and for trying to teach me how one tells a story. To my other teacher, Gail Anderson-Dargatz, I owe an immense debt of gratitude for helping me find my voice and for sharing so many of her own experiences. Thanks are also due to Guy Vanderhaeghe and Ray Robertson who welcomed me into writers' worlds and taught me to appreciate good writing.

Of course, this novel would be nowhere without Nurjehan Aziz, who believed in the book, and Margaret Hart, who put her persuasive voice behind the book and championed it on more than one continent. Thank You.

Funding for my work on this novel at various stages came from the Ontario Arts Council and the Toronto Arts Council and I am very grateful to these institutions for supporting writers and the arts in Canada.